William Page Wood Hatherley

A memoir of the Right Hon. William Page Wood

With selections from his correspondence

William Page Wood Hatherley

A memoir of the Right Hon. William Page Wood
With selections from his correspondence

ISBN/EAN: 9783337275884

Printed in Europe, USA, Canada, Australia, Japan

Cover: Foto ©Raphael Reischuk / pixelio.de

More available books at **www.hansebooks.com**

A MEMOIR

OF THE

RIGHT HON. WILLIAM PAGE WOOD

BARON HATHERLEY

WITH SELECTIONS from his CORRESPONDENCE

EDITED BY HIS NEPHEW

W. R. W. STEPHENS, M.A.

PREBENDARY OF CHICHESTER AND RECTOR OF WOOLBEDING, SUSSEX
EDITOR OF 'THE LIFE AND LETTERS OF DEAN HOOK' ETC.

IN TWO VOLUMES

VOL. I.

LONDON

RICHARD BENTLEY & SON, NEW BURLINGTON STREET

Publishers in Ordinary to Her Majesty the Queen

1883

PREFACE.

In the year 1863 Mr. Foss, author of the well-known work entitled the 'Judges of England, with Sketches of their Lives,' requested Vice-Chancellor Wood to supply him with some notes of his life. The Autobiographical Sketch which forms the introduction to these volumes was written in compliance with this request, and from it Mr. Foss compiled the notice which concludes the last volume of his work published in 1864. The Autobiography breaks off, as will be seen, rather abruptly; and, although it is a careful and accurate record of facts, it does not pretend in any sense to be a finished composition. The original manuscript is very roughly and hurriedly written, and I have found considerable difficulty in de-

ciphering some passages, and more especially proper names. For kind assistance in this labour, and
also for supplying me with some useful information
for other parts of the Memoir, I have to thank my
uncle's old and much valued friend, Mr. Gordon
Whitbread, who for many years acted as his
private secretary.[1]

Some explanations and illustrations of the
Autobiography have been added; for the most part
in footnotes; but occasionally, when they seemed
to be too long for footnotes, or to be more closely
connected with the narrative, they have been
incorporated in the text, only enclosed in brackets,
and signed ED. for ' EDITOR.'

I have to express my sincere thanks to the
present Lord Chancellor, the Earl of Selborne, for
his kindness in giving me some information respecting the measures of Law Reform introduced
by Lord Hatherley, and also for some observations
upon his character which will be found at the end
of the second volume.

The life which it has been my lot to depict,

[1] On the day after these words were written I heard with much
sorrow that Mr. Whitbread had died on the previous evening; but I
leave the passage unaltered.

although an exceedingly active one, was not full of startling incidents. Yet it may be read with interest and profit by any who have a mind to trace the career of one who by great ability, persevering industry, and singular purity of goodness, steadily found his way to one of the highest official positions in the country, although he never made it the object of ambitious pursuit. His letters will be found replete with wise and instructive observations upon religious, philosophical, political, and social questions. The example of his long and consistent advocacy of the most advanced Liberal measures in politics, combined with his steadfast fidelity to the teaching and practice of the Church of England, will be deemed by many to be especially valuable in the present day, when the best guarantee for the preservation of the Church as a national establishment consists in her proving that she can be the common home of men of all political parties.

The letters published in these volumes have been selected, with a few exceptions, from the correspondence of Lord Hatherley with his life-long friend, Walter Farquhar Hook, beginning in

the year 1818 and ending in 1875. There was
no other person with whom he so habitually corresponded, and there can be no more faithful revelation of any one's thoughts and sentiments than
the letters which are written constantly and un-
reservedly to an intimate friend. It would have
been possible to add a few letters to and from
eminent persons, written during Lord Hatherley's
tenure of office as Lord Chancellor; but they
would have been comparatively devoid of interest,
unless supplemented by others which it would not
have been desirable to publish. And here I will
take the opportunity of saying that neither in
this Memoir, nor in the 'Life of Dean Hook,'
published five years ago, have I suppressed anything which is of the smallest interest or importance as tending to illustrate the character of
the person who has been the subject of the biography. I have endeavoured neither to magnify
virtues, nor to conceal or extenuate blemishes
and defects. How far I may have succeeded in
this effort, it is not for me to judge ; but, at any
rate, my aim has been to produce a faithful and
honest portrait. And, in executing this design,

I do not believe that it is necessary to introduce anything which can cause serious annoyance or pain to any human being. If a biography cannot be kept clear of these vices, it had better, as it seems to me, not be published at all.

I make these remarks because I believe memoirs of great and good men to be fruitful sources of instruction as well as of entertainment, if executed upon sound principles ; but at the present day the interests of biography seem to be at stake. If the publication of inaccurate reminiscences, and the reckless abuses of editorial power with which the world has lately been favoured, were to become the prevailing fashion, good biography would before long become an impossibility. And this for two reasons. On the one hand, the taste of the reading public would become so vitiated that they would pronounce all biographies to be vapid, incomplete, or insincere, which were not seasoned with the piquant sauce of idle gossip and mischievous scandal. On the other hand, men whose lives were worth recording would become more reserved in all their communications, or they would destroy all the most interesting material for their own history, lest it should fall into the hands of inaccurate, indiscreet, or unscrupulous editors. In the case of one illustrious person a large destruction of letters has already been the result of the publications to which allusion has been made.

WOOLBEDING RECTORY:
January 29, 1883.

P.S.—The Bill for Legalising Marriage with a Deceased Wife's Sister was introduced for the first time into Parliament in 1842, not in 1849 as stated in vol. ii. p. 26 ; but the persistent and organised agitation in favour of that measure dates from the latter year.

I regret that a letter on the Philosophy of Bentham, which I had intended to reprint from the ' Life of Dean Hook,' vol. i. p. 245, has been inadvertently omitted.

CONTENTS

OF

THE FIRST VOLUME.

———◆◆◆———

MEMOIR.

CHAPTER I.

CHAPTER II.

Errata.

Page 73, line 13 from foot, *for* 1844 *read* 1843.

  ,, 141,   ,,   8   ,,   ,,   ,,   Bird's ,,   Reid's.

AUTOBIOGRAPHY.

I WAS born on November 29, A.D. 1801, in Falcon Square, in the parish of St. Giles, Cripplegate, in the City of London. My parents were Matthew Wood (then carrying on business as a hop merchant, in partnership with Mr. Wigan, in Falcon Square), and Maria, daughter of Mr. John Page, of Woodbridge. in the county of Suffolk, surgeon.[1] They had six children, of whom the youngest, Henry Wright Wood, died in his infancy. Of the others four are still living;[2] including myself, my eldest brother Sir John Page Wood, Bart., rector of St. Peter's Cornhill, and vicar of Cressing in Essex;[3] and my

[1] Crabbe, the poet, was apprenticed, when a youth, to Mr. Page. An old scrap-book which belonged to my mother contains a copy of a play-bill, rudely printed, announcing that 'This present evening will be performed an English burletta,' called Midas.' A list of the *dramatis personæ* follows, the actors being my grandmother, and her brothers and sisters. My mother used to tell me that Crabbe printed the play-bill and supported the part of Apollo, which is left blank in the list of actors. The play-bill is not dated.—ED.

[2] All now deceased.—ED.

[3] Sir John's fifth son, Henry Evelyn, has achieved at the early age of forty-four a very high military reputation; but not higher than was confidently expected and predicted by his uncle, who watched

two sisters, Maria Elizabeth, the wife of Edwin
Maddy, Esq. D.C.L., and Catharine, the wife of
Charles Stephens, Esq., banker, of Earley Court, near
Reading. I was the fourth child, and my brother
Western, late M.P. for the City of London, who
died in 1863, was the fifth. My father's family had
once been a family of some note in the counties
of Cornwall and Devon, under the names of
Attwood and Wood. Our branch of it had early
settled at Tiverton, and one of my father's direct
ancestors acted as Squire at the funeral of Catherine,
Countess of Devon, sister of Edward IV. But in
the eighteenth century the family had become so
much reduced that my grandfather, who was a
serge manufacturer, was incapable of making any
provision for a family of ten children. My father,
who was the eldest, received the rudiments of
education at Blundell's Free Grammar School in the
town of Tiverton, but at a very early age he was
employed in assisting his father to collect the serge
from the cottages where it was manufactured. On
one occasion before he was fourteen years of age
he went to Exeter by himself, owing to the sudden
illness of his father, on the usual day for the sale
of manufactured goods, and, after calling upon
several merchants, disposed of his wares to the

his career with extraordinary interest from the beginning, when he
distinguished himself, at the age of sixteen, in the naval brigade before
Sebastopol.—ED.

house of Messrs. Baring & Co. The event was strongly impressed upon his memory by the circumstance that, in returning home after dark, he had a bad fall from his pony. He was taken up in a state of insensibility with a wound in his cheek, of which he bore the scar to the end of his life.

At the age of fourteen he was apprenticed to Mr. Newton, his first cousin, who then carried on an extensive wholesale and retail business as a druggist, tea and hop dealer, in Fore Street, Exeter. Here my father gave great satisfaction to his employer and his customers, and at the age of nineteen he was engaged as a traveller by Mr. Waymouth, the head of a very old firm of wholesale druggists in Exeter. It is singular that at this time Mr. Gibbs, the father of Sir Vicary Gibbs,[1] resided next door to Mr. Waymouth's house of business, whilst Dr. Woolcott (better known as Peter Pindar), and Mr. Baring, the father of Lord Ashburton, were frequent visitors at Mr. Waymouth's residence at Topsham.

Before he had attained the age of twenty-two my father had attracted notice by his ability and integrity as a traveller, and was invited by Messrs.

---

[1] Sir Vicary Gibbs became Lord Chief Justice of the Common Pleas in 1814, and held that office for nearly five years. His professional learning and ability were of the highest order; but he was unfortunately not less distinguished for acerbity of temper.—Ed.

Crawley & Adcock, of Bishopsgate Street, London, to accept a situation in that capacity under their firm, and he accordingly went to London early in 1790. About two years afterwards a partnership was formed by one of the Messrs. Adcock and Messrs. John and Thomas Price, into which my father was admitted, and they carried on their business as druggists in Devonshire Square. This partnership was not of long continuance, and upon its dissolution my father set up business on his own account in Cross Street, Clerkenwell.

In 1796, being twenty-eight years old, he married, and soon afterwards entered into partnership with the late Mr. Wigan and his son, and went to reside at the house of business in Falcon Square, Cripplegate.

At the time of my birth my father was a Common Councilman for the ward of Cripplegate. A few years afterwards, in 1807, during his absence on a tour in Ireland, he was elected Alderman for the ward : and about that time went to reside at Highbury Place, Islington.

We, the children of the family, passed much of our time at the house of our grandmother at Woodbridge in Suffolk. My grandfather Mr. Page and all his children except my mother, and my uncle William Wood Page, were now dead. My uncle had been educated for the medical profession at Edinburgh ; but on the death of his father and of his only brother, he resided with his mother, and had become a landowner and magistrate in the county. After him I had been named, and to him I attribute in a great measure a very early taste for literature. In him and in my father I had examples of scrupulous honour and integrity; while to my grandmother and mother I owed the yet deeper obligation of early religious training.

In 1808 I went as a day scholar to the Free School at Woodbridge, founded by Mr. Thomas Seckford, Master of the Court of Requests in the reign of Queen Elizabeth, which was then kept by the Rev. Alan Barker. Curiously enough, I lately had the satisfaction, as Vice-Chancellor, of settling a scheme for a great extension and improvement of this school. The Master of the Rolls and the Chief Justice of the Common Pleas for the time being are trustees of a large and improving property in Clerkenwell, forming the endowment of certain almshouses and other charitable foundations of Seckford at Woodbridge; and the present Master of the Rolls [1] suggested the propriety of a scheme for the general improvement of the charity, including a considerable development of the school, which scheme was brought before me judicially as Vice-Chancellor.

I attended this school for about a year and had

[1] Sir John Romilly.—ED.

acquired the rudiments of Latin when in 1809 I was placed as a boarder at Dr. Lindsay's school at Bow near London, where my elder brother had been for some time a pupil. Dr. Lindsay himself was a highly respected Presbyterian minister ; but although my father had been originally brought up as a Dissenter, all his children were baptised as members of the Church of England, to which my mother belonged, and were trained pursuant to its doctrines, and I and my brother, while we were at Dr. Lindsay's, attended service at Bow Church, as did the majority of the boys belonging to the school.

Dr. Lindsay's school consisted of about seventy or eighty boys, so that the rough training of life began here. There were several foreigners amongst them, including a Dutch boy, a Swede, and a Spaniard ; and hence I imbibed a great desire to become acquainted with modern languages—a desire, however, which was not gratified till seven years afterwards. There were also several Highland boys in the school, who, strange as it may now seem, could scarcely on their arrival speak one word of English. I remained at Dr. Lindsay's till 1812, and in September of that year was removed to Winchester, where my elder brother had preceded me by about two years.

At Dr. Lindsay's school I had acquired the rudiments of Greek and sufficient knowledge of

Latin to translate Cæsar and the easier parts of Virgil. I had also maintained the taste for poetry which I had derived from my uncle Mr. Page, and had pursued a course of romance and novel-reading so eagerly, that by the time I went to Winchester my enthusiasm for that species of literature had much abated. It must be remembered that Miss Porter and Mrs. Radcliff were then our chief authors in that department. Miss Austen's charming tales were beyond the appreciation of a boy.

In 1809, the year in which I went to Dr. Lindsay's school, my father served the office of Sheriff with Alderman Atkins. In this capacity he was called upon to discharge the duty of arresting Sir Francis Burdett on a Speaker's warrant. He implored the Government in vain to abstain from calling in the military on this occasion; but he was more successful in remonstrating against their employment on the release of Sir Francis, and preserved the public peace inviolate, notwithstanding the disappointment of the myriads who were assembled to witness a procession from which the intended hero unexpectedly absented himself.[1]

[1] The circumstances which led to the arrest and imprisonment of Sir Francis Burdett are probably known to few persons in the present day, and a brief notice of them may, therefore, not be out of place here, as elucidating Lord Hatherley's references to the event. In January 1810 a motion had been carried in the House of Commons that the House should resolve itself into a committee to inquire into the policy and conduct of the disastrous military expedition to Walcheren.

In 1812, the year in which I went to Winchester, my father was a candidate for the representa-

The Ministry, who had been defeated in their opposition to this motion, were extremely anxious to hinder publicity being given to the results of the inquiry; knowing that an amount of military blundering and incapacity must be disclosed which would excite the indignation of their own countrymen and might stimulate the efforts of Bonaparte against England. It was therefore resolved to enforce the standing order for the exclusion of all strangers from the gallery during the inquiry.

A debating society in London discussed this resolution, and unanimously resolved that 'it ought to be censured as an insidious and ill-timed attack upon the liberty of the press, tending to aggravate the discontent of the people, and to render their representatives objects of jealous suspicion.' The walls of London were presently covered with printed copies of the resolution. This was complained of in the House as a gross violation of the privileges of the House. The printer of the handbills was summoned to the bar of the House, expressed his contrition, and revealed the name of the author, the president of the debating club, Mr. John Gale Jones.

On the morrow, February 21, Mr. Jones was brought to the bar, and by a unanimous vote of the House committed to Newgate. On March 12 Sir Francis Burdett moved that John Gale Jones be discharged, and in so doing he questioned the legality of the commitment. He was outvoted by 153 to 14; but he printed his speech a few days afterwards, prefaced by a letter to his constituents, and published this in Cobbett's *Weekly Register*. Both speech and letter contained vehement expressions which were considered by many calculated to inflame the passions of the people against the authority of Parliament. The matter was brought before the House, and on April 5, a resolution was carried, by a majority of 38, that Sir Francis should be committed to the Tower, under the warrant of the Speaker, as guilty of a libel on the House. Sir Francis shut himself up in his house in Piccadilly, barred his doors and windows, declared that he would yield to nothing but force, and wrote a letter to the Speaker in which he maintained that the warrant was illegal. A huge mob collected in Piccadilly, who shouted ' Burdett for ever ! ' compelled all passengers to take off their hats and join in the cry, and smashed the windows of Lord Chatham, Lord Castlereagh, and other unpopular

tion of the City of London in Parliament, but the
old Tory members were returned by a majority
of 1,000.

public men. I have in my possession some manuscript notes of my
grandfather Sir Matthew Wood's life, written in a hand unknown to
me, but evidently by a contemporary, and apparently by one who held
some office at the time of the Burdett riot. I quote his account of
my grandfather's part in these transactions: He was at his house
at Highbury when he received the Speaker's warrant. He immediately came to town, sent off for his colleague Mr. Sheriff Atkins,
called on Mr. Gurney, a barrister, now Baron Gurney, an old acquaintance, and took his advice on the case. Having called also on the
Speaker to consult him, he took a room at the Gloucester Coffeehouse,
and with great activity kept the peace until Sunday evening, when the
magistrates insisted on clearing the street. He protested strongly
against this measure ; but one of them mounted a horse of one of the
dragoons, and with the dragoons they cleared the streets. But the
moment it became dark the people put out the lights, took down some
building materials from some houses under repair, and laid them across
the street to prevent the cavalry from acting. They then got into the
courts and alleys, and fired on the soldiers or threw stones at them.
Mr. Wood went several times during the night to Sir Francis Burdett,
and asked him if he would surrender; but he replied he would not be
taken except by force.

On Monday morning the military broke in and he was taken to
the Tower. The livery of London met at the Guildhall and voted an
address to Sir Francis, which they requested the sheriffs to convey to
him. Mr. Sheriff Atkins refused; but Mr. Wood went with the state
coach to the Tower and was received by Lord Moira (the Constable
of the Tower).

Sir Francis Burdett remained in the Tower till June 1811, when
the prorogation of Parliament necessitated his release. The excitement of the people and their devotion to the man whom they deemed
the champion of their rights had not abated, and a vast multitude
assembled on the morning of his release to escort him in triumph from
the Tower to Piccadilly. To avoid all risk of a riot, however, Sir
Francis very prudently resolved to quit the Tower privately and proceed by water to Westminster. Meanwhile the mob waited in
anxious suspense for the appearance of their favourite. A soldier on

When I entered Winchester, Dr. Gabell was head-master and Mr. Williams[1] the second master, while Dr. Huntingford, Bishop of Hereford, was warden of the college. I and my brother were not on the foundation, but were members of commoners, and, as such, pupils of the head-master. The number of commoners was then limited to 130, and that of the college or foundation boys to 70. We remained at Winchester till May 1818, and I always recognise the inestimable value of the instruction which I there received. Dr. Gabell especially was pre-eminent as a teacher, though defective in his management as a master, owing to his bad habit of mistrusting the boys and leaving nothing to their sense of honour. Dr. Williams, on the other hand, was admirably qualified to win the affection of his pupils by his gentlemanly and confiding treatment of them, though his teaching was

the walls of the Tower roared through a speaking-trumpet, 'He is gone by water!' but the people would not believe this announcement, even when repeated by several other officials, until at last the two sheriffs, Mr. Atkins and Mr. Wood, entered the Tower, and on their return convinced the multitude that Sir Francis had actually departed, and induced them to disperse quietly. The commotion caused by the arrest of Sir Francis was the most formidable disturbance which had occurred in London since the celebrated No Popery Riots of 1780. On the day of his imprisonment about 40,000 troops were collected in or near the metropolis, the southern counties were in a state of extreme alarm, and the foreign newspapers informed the world that a Revolution had taken place in London.—ED.

[1] Afterwards Dr. Williams. He became head-master of Winchester and the Warden of New College, Oxford.—ED.

not so searching and effective. Dr. Gabell allowed nothing to be slurred over ; not the slightest Greek particle was to lose its effect, not a syllable in reading was to be dropped by carelessly allowing the voice to sink ; and the method which he adopted (though it would be tedious to state it here in detail) was such as to render escape from detection impossible on the part of the ignorant and careless who were not prepared with their lessons. No boys reached the Universities so thoroughly grounded in Latin and Greek, or so thoroughly masters of their books which they affected to know, as the pupils of Dr. Gabell. It is great praise to him to say that he enabled every boy to gauge himself and to measure his own ignorance.

The whole administration, however, of a public school, should rest on confidence in the gentle-manly spirit of the boys. The discipline of the school depends at Winchester upon the head boys called prefects. These boys should never be required to act as spies, and should themselves be treated with such trust as to make them ashamed to abuse it. In consequence of a failure on Dr. Gabell's part in these respects, a want of confidence had sprung up between him and the head boys ; and the conduct of one of the tutors which assumed too much, as the boys thought, the character of espionage, led in May 1818 to a rebellion. At this time, having worked my way up from the lower form, and having gained the prize in each form, I was the second prefect in commoners. I deeply regretted afterwards the pain I must have occasioned to a really kind (though I still think mistaken) master, but at the time I heartily joined in the insurrection. It lasted about twenty-four hours, during which time the boys were masters of the old collegiate buildings, where they had barricaded themselves and withstood a summons by a magistrate attended by the constabulary. The military were then sent for—a very foolish step, for there had lately been a quarrel between the boys and the men of the regiment about the use of a bathing place. Dr. Gabell, however, bethought him of an ingenious scheme. He said the boys had better all go home. They marched out of college with this intent, and met the military in the churchyard, who were ordered to charge them, when it must be confessed the boys ignominiously fled, having happily no weapons but bludgeons at hand, and the military being fully armed. Two who were fortunate enough to be made prisoners dined afterwards at mess. The rest of the boys were easily captured afterwards, whilst they were packing up, by the locking of the outer gates. The head boys were called up *seriatim* before the master and second master, and the first and third prefects were expelled. I was then called up, and I asked what had become of the other two, as a paper had been signed by the first three forms that all would share a common fate. My inquiry was not answered, but I was sent into another room to reflect in order to submission. From the window of this room, however, I saw and conversed with the other two prefects and learned their expulsion, and immediately on my return I stated that I must follow their example. I left the school taking with me my younger brother,[1] who had signed the paper as well as myself.

The reason why I received such lenient treatment was, that up to that time I had been very regular in my conduct and was somewhat of a favourite with the head-master ; and it was supposed that as I was younger than many of the prefects, being only sixteen years old, I had been misled by them. This, however, was not the fact. I had no special, personal grievance, but I had conceived the most intense disgust at the constant want of confidence and the suspicions exhibited by the head-master, of the extent of whose regard for myself, as subsequently expressed in a letter to my father, I was not then aware.[2]

[1] Mr. Western Wood. Their elder brother John had, I believe, left Winchester before the rebellion.—ED.

[2] I have not discovered this letter ; but the following letter from the Bishop of London (Howley) to my grandfather, written in December 1816 just after he became Lord Mayor, contains a striking testimony from Dr. Gabell :—

The masters (most erroneously) afterwards attributed my conduct to my 'Radical propensities,' derived, as was supposed, from reading the 'Morning Chronicle.' It is indeed most amusing to look back upon the horror which was then felt at the supposed fearful Radicalism of 'Alderman Wood,' who had now become the single Liberal representative of the City of London in Parliament, the other three being staunch supporters of the existing Government.

My younger brother was sent back to Winchester, and I myself was sent shortly afterwards for two years to Geneva. My father was induced by the suggestion of my uncle, Mr. Page, to adopt this course, in preference to sending me to a private tutor, as being more calculated to enlarge my mind.

On looking back to my career at Winchester I have always acknowledged the immense advantage of a public school education. The school discipline of fagging was to a young and rather sensitive boy very severe, but it was just that which was wanting to brace one up to face the realities of life ; and in spite of some cruelty

'My Lord,—I transmit to your lordship a letter from Dr. Gabell which he sent under cover to me, and I cannot resist transcribing a paragraph from his letter to me, as I know it will give your lordship and the Lady Mayoress great pleasure.

'"He (the Lord Mayor) has a son here of extraordinary ability, industry, ability, good temper, and good conduct." Your lordship has of course heard this from Dr. Gabell, but you will not be displeased at finding that he says the same thing to an indifferent person.'—Ed.

amongst the head boys, and of the disadvantage of their not being all treated by the head-master on the principle of honour, the tone of the school as a whole was that of highly honourable young lads. There might have been something better if there had been more confidence, and something higher in the best sense. The religious element, indeed, which happily is now more highly developed in almost all schools, was perhaps more than commonly kept back by the want of confidence between the master and the boys. Still it will always be to the credit of Winchester that Arnold was brought up there, and that (at a later period than that which I am now discussing) he sent his sons thither.

But the highest advantage of a public school remains yet to be noticed. It is there that the friendships of life are formed, and in this respect I was singularly blessed. In the very year of my arrival at Winchester (1812) I formed a friendship with Walter Farquhar Hook which has lasted through life. From 1812 till the present time scarcely a month has intervened without correspondence between us. Hook was three years older than myself, but he had devoted himself so much to English literature that he fell below me in the school. In this respect we became mutually useful to each other. Hook was passionately fond of reading Shakspeare and Milton when I first knew him, and a small order of knighthood, called after them the

Order of Saints Shakspeare and Milton, was founded
by him, of which he and I were styled the Knights
Grand Masters.[1]   The other Elizabethan classics,

[1] The following list of the Knights of this 'most poetical Order'
was written by W. F. Hook in pencil in the blank leaf of vol. iv. of the
pocket edition of Shakspeare which he had at school in 1810.   See
Life of Dr. Hook, vol. i. p. 341, or page 601 in the small edition.

'A list of the Knights of the most poetical Order of SS. Shakspeare and Milton:—

W. F. Hook } Founders and
W. P. Wood } Knights Grand Masters.
Henry Minchin, William Heathcote } Knights
Edward Austen, Philip Hewett   } Grand Crosses.

'By His Majesty's command.

W. F. Hook } Secretaries of State.
W. P. Wood }

'God Save King Shakspeare!'

Since Lord Hatherley's death this pocket edition of Shakspeare has
come into my possession, and on the blank leaf of vol. ii. the following lines in pencil in W. F. Hook's hand are faintly traceable:—

I.

'To arms, ye brave mortals, to arms;
To Honour the road lies before ye,
And the name of King Shakspeare has charms
To rouse ye to action of glory.

II.

'Away, ye brave mortals, away,
'Tis Nature that bids ye to save her;
And who would not Nature obey,
And fight for his Shakspeare for ever?

'By His Majesty's command the above is to be the national air in
the Shakspearian court.

W. F. Hook } Secretaries to His Majesty.
W. P. Wood }

'God Save King Shakspeare!'—ED.

however, were gradually drawn within the circle of the studies, or rather the recreation, of our leisure hours. Beaumont and Fletcher, Massinger and the 'Fairy Queen,' were made to contribute to our amusement ; and though of course much more was read than we digested, still the benefit derived from these studies has been lasting. We even read through Hoole's 'Tasso and Ariosto,' a work of some labour owing to the extreme dulness of the translation. Dr. Gabell himself encouraged English reading. He would frequently repeat Pope's 'Imitations of Horace' to the boys at their lessons, and expected them to read the 'Spectator,' Johnson's 'Lives of the Poets,' and some of the English historians. The time, however, was short for this ; but, being rather quick over my work, I was able to help my older friend forward in Greek and Latin in return for the improvement I derived from his maturer judgment and larger powers of thought in English and classical reading.

But a far greater blessing was derived from his friendship. When I was just fifteen, a confirmation was held by the Warden in the college chapel upon rather short notice. I was much excited by this, and it was owing to the invaluable counsel of my friend that I was encouraged to prepare myself for that rite and the more solemn one which succeeded it. This was an epoch of life never to be forgotten.

It is not right to say more on this subject here than that from this moment, though with many stumblings and falls, I was enabled to pursue a course of life animated by a principle then for the first time appreciated and understood.

Hitherto I have spoken of school life only; but during that period from 1809 to 1818 much education had been going on under home influences; for it has been well observed that everything said or done before a child forms part of his education, and I may be excused, therefore, for stating briefly some of the leading events which, as a boy, I was led to contemplate.

My father by virtue of his office was bound from time to time to attend the sessions for the trial of prisoners at the Old Bailey, and he frequently took his sons with him, riding in on horseback with them from Highbury. I soon became very much interested in these trials; perhaps they gave me an early inclination for that profession to which my father, when I was about fourteen, told me that I was destined. I was, however, very early shocked at the course of Old Bailey procedure. Capital offences were at that time almost the rule, and minor offences the exception. Stealing above the value of forty shillings from a dwelling house was capital; and I heard a jury acquit a man of the capital charge who had stolen a two pound note, on the suggestion by his counsel of the depreciation of that currency, and notwithstanding the judge's direction to the contrary. The criminals who had been capitally convicted (except those convicted for murder) were brought up in a batch at the close of the session and condemned wholesale. I once saw thirty or forty so condemned, some of whom were making grimaces at the judge, whilst others who expected to be left for execution were deeply distressed. The scenes were sometimes most painful; and the chaplain or ordinary, whose conversation I sometimes overheard when dining at the Old Bailey, but too nearly resembled him who is depicted in Jonathan Wild. On one occasion I heard a poor young fellow of seventeen tried for forgery, who was afterwards executed with five other criminals, not one of whom had committed any crime attended with violence, and not one of whom had attained the age of twenty-four. The last trial I ever heard at the Old Bailey was later in life when Sir John Copley,[1] Attorney-General, led the prosecution against Fauntleroy, who might, had he committed his offence a few years later, been, like his aged and distinguished prosecutor, still numbered among the living.

[My uncle witnessed a few years later in 1818 a curious incident in the history of our criminal law which he has not recorded here, although he

---

[1] Afterwards Lord Lyndhurst.—ED.

frequently related it to friends. The case was this: A man named Thornton had been tried for the murder of a young woman; the legal evidence was insufficient to procure a conviction, but the moral evidence was very strong, and in fact the relations of the murdered girl had not the smallest doubt of his guilt, and Ashford, her brother, appealed against the verdict of the jury. By the suggestion of a solicitor the defendant availed himself of the antiquated but unrepealed law of wager of battle, whereby a person accused of murder could offer to maintain his innocence by single combat with the next of kin to the murdered person. Thornton therefore pleaded on the appeal 'Not guilty, and I am ready to defend the same by my body.' The right to this wager of battle was argued before Lord Ellenborough and others. The case naturally excited very great interest. My uncle was exceedingly anxious to hear the argument, and knowing that the court would be densely crowded, and being rather short of stature, he asked Mr. Wilde, who afterwards became Lord Chancellor Truro, but who had then just been called to the Bar, and was engaged as a junior counsel in the case, if he could help him to get into a place in court where he could see and hear. Mr. Wilde said that the only method he could suggest was that his young friend should walk behind him into court carrying his bag of books.

This my uncle did, and so the two future Lord Chancellors went in together, one acting the part of clerk to the other.

The argument was decided in favour of Thornton's right of challenge, but the combat did not take place. Thornton was a big, powerful fellow; and Ashford, who was a puny man, withdrew from the encounter. Thornton emigrated to America and was never heard of again. The 'wager of battle' law was repealed by Act of Parliament in the following year.—ED.]

I remember being very much struck with my father's expressions of indignation at the mode in which Bellingham's trial was hurried on in 1812. I was at school at Dr. Lindsay's at the time of the assassination of Mr. Perceval and could not be present at the trial, but I recollect that my father's indignation was aroused by the refusal of any postponement, though it was physically impossible (at that time) to produce from Liverpool the evidence to prove the alleged insanity of the prisoner before the day fixed for the trial. No one, indeed, was more shocked than my father at the crime. He had been in very friendly communication with Mr. Perceval about the removal of the Post Office (as originally suggested by my father) from Lombard Street to the present site, and he had been struck by Mr. Perceval's friendly courtesy; but that which at all times of his life interested him more deeply than any other subject was the due administration of criminal justice.

In the year 1815,[1] whilst Lord Mayor Elect, he had been also elected member for the City of London in place of Alderman Harvey Combe, who had long been the sole representative of Liberal politics in the City. In 1816 he had distinguished himself as mayor by a general improvement of the police; amongst other things he totally prohibited the appearance of women of the town in the public streets of the City —a point in which we are sadly behind all Continental towns. He felt convinced that many a young shopman and apprentice fell into sin who would not have sought out vice, but was too weak to resist it when temptation stood in his path.

My father's mayoralty was, however, most distinguished by his quelling, with the aid of special constables only, the fearful Spa Fields riots,[2] before the military had arrived. Sir John Shaw and himself had personally seized the ringleaders (though they had armed themselves by plundering Beck-

[1] This is an error. My grandfather was first elected M.P. for the City in 1817.—ED.

[2] It was a period of great distress and discontent amongst the operative class. Wild, revolutionary projects were concocted by a small band of demagogic agitators, of whom the most notable were Hunt, Thistlewood, and Watson. They held a mob meeting in Spa Fields on December 2, 1816, when inflammatory speeches were made. The mob then marched in a turbulent state through Clerkenwell and Smithfield to Snow Hill and thence to the Exchange, where they were checked as related above.—ED.

with's gun-shop) and conveyed them and their flags into the Royal Exchange, which was then closed, while the magistrates went out to disperse the rest of the mob.

In the same year he rescued three unfortunate Irishmen from death. Three policemen, named Pelham, Brook, and Vaughan, had laid a plot against these poor men, in order to obtain the 'blood money,' as it was termed, of a Mint prosecution. One of the policemen hired them at the Seven Dials to come and do some work for him, and took them to a room to rub quicksilver on thin brass plates. He then went out and brought in the other two policemen, who pounced upon the Irishmen, and on searching the room all the implements of coining were found, which had been placed there by these villains. The poor Irishmen were tried at the Old Bailey, convicted and condemned, and ordered for execution.

My father was present, and was so much struck by the story of the Irishmen that he suspected there had been some foul play. They could not speak a word of English; but, with the aid of an Irish priest as interpreter, he examined the prisoners, became convinced of their innocence, and ended by detecting the whole plot, and convicting the conspirators. The Irishmen were of course pardoned, and only a few years ago I learned that one of them was acting as head-gardener to Sir George Staunton.

In November 1816 my father was elected mayor
for the second time, the first instance of the kind
since the days of Whittington. He sat in Parliament as member for the City till his death in 1843,
a period of twenty-eight years. His politics were
consistent through life ; he was vehemently opposed
to the Corn Laws and to the Test and Corporation
Acts. He was not less earnest in supporting
Roman Catholic Emancipation and Parliamentary
Reform. These views were not the result of a
desire for popularity. In supporting Roman
Catholic Emancipation he made one of his few
speeches in the House just before a general
election, being well aware, as he said, that it was
at the risk of losing his seat. For the first and
only time he thus found himself at the bottom of
the poll, and nearly lost the election.

These circumstances are all mentioned as forming no insignificant part of my education. I not
only frequented the Old Bailey, but also sat very
often under the gallery of the House of Commons,
during my boyhood. I heard Canning, Brougham,
Tierney, Wilberforce, Plunkett, Mackintosh, and
Burdett. I heard also Lord Castlereagh not infre-
quently indulging in those flowers of false rhetoric
which have been immortalised by Moore in the
'Fudge Family.' During all this time I imbibed my
father's hatred of injustice, and his political opinions,
in supporting which I encountered much ridicule

at school; but there is scarcely any political principle then advocated by my father which has not been since embodied in an Act of Parliament by our Legislature.

In company with my father I visited Cobbett when he was imprisoned in Newgate for a libel; and I also accompanied him when he left the hustings in Covent Garden to inform Lord Cochrane, in the King's Bench prison, that he had been re-elected member for Westminster.

During the two years that my father resided at the Mansion House, I greatly enjoyed the advantage of a good English library there, and still more the advantage of a very valuable general library founded by Dr. Williams in Red Cross Street, Cripplegate, in the time of Oliver Cromwell. It is the chief public library of the Dissenters. On my father's introduction, when I was between fifteen and sixteen years of age, I was most kindly received by Mr. Morgan, the librarian, and spent many a morning there without the appearance, strange to say, of a single other visitor. At the Mansion House I read through the whole of Clarendon (the Rebellion and his Life) and rose from the perusal with an intense aversion to Charles I.

At the Red Cross Street library I sat under the shadow of an original portrait of Milton (who is buried, as all know, in Cripplegate church) and revelled in a large assortment of English works.

In poetry I chiefly remember, as being new to me, Fairfax's translation of 'Tasso,' immeasurably superior to Hoole's. But there was one work which then made an impression upon me for life— Bishop Berkeley's 'Dialogues;' and subsequently his 'Principles of Human Knowledge.' It was the first opening to me of the metaphysical field, and has been my guide in many a metaphysical and theological inquiry.[1] I still hold the same opinion as to the merits of Berkeley, and have been astonished at its ever being supposed that Reid had confuted him.

My love for Shakspeare was greatly enhanced by my father thinking it a part of his children's education to take them to see good plays acted. This began so early with me that at nine years old I saw Cooke in Sir Pertinax Macsycophant. At the age of ten I saw John Kemble and Mrs. Siddons in 'Henry VIII.,' and a year later John Kemble and Young in 'Julius Cæsar.' My father took a particular interest in the elder Kean, who had come from a Devonshire stage, and he took me to the fourth performance of Shylock, the first of Richard, and the first of Sir Giles Overreach.

---

[1] The very admirable account of Berkeley and his philosophy in Dr. Hook's *Dictionary of Biography* was written by my uncle. See also his letter on the same in Dr. Hook's *Life*, vol. i. p. 256, or 170 small edition.—ED.

The society, also, which I met in England, especially during my father's residence at the Mansion House, was favourable to the development of my mind. I frequently saw Lord Erskine, and Curran, besides judges, bishops, and others of more or less note. My greatest enthusiasm was excited when the Duke of Wellington dined at the Mansion House to receive the silver shield presented by the merchants of London. I frequently also saw and had the honour of being noticed by the Dukes of Kent and Sussex, my father being one of the trustees to whom the former nobly made over his income for the payment of his creditors, reserving only a small allowance for himself.[1]

In the winter of 1817, after the expiration of his mayoralty, my father went with his family to Paris, and there I and my younger brother joined him in our Christmas holidays, travelling alone from London to Paris. We spent upwards of a month there. My father was cordially received by the French Liberal party. The Duke of Orleans (Louis Philippe) invited him and the ladies of his family to dinner, and they became acquainted with the Duke de Broglie, Generals Lafayette and Foix, with Casimir Perier, Lafitte, Benjamin Constant, and with Denon, the traveller in Egypt.

All these I had an opportunity of seeing, and heard them converse, though I could only listen,

---

[1] See more respecting this transaction below, page 71.

being unable to reply in French. I also saw the King, Louis XVIII., his family and ministers, at the Chapel Royal.

Just at the time when I arrived at home from Winchester, after the rebellion in May 1818, my uncle, Mr. Page, happened to be residing at Geneva, and the well-known Dumont, the friend of Sir Samuel Romilly, was in England, and strongly supported my uncle's recommendation of a two years' course of education for me at Geneva in preference to a private tutor, as a preparation for the University.

On my taking leave of home my father called me aside and brought seriously before me his own position as a man of business, exposed to the hazards of trade, and told me that my education was all that I could rely upon as my portion—a lesson remembered through life with deep gratitude ; neither did I during my father's lifetime ever receive anything beyond my education at my father's expense.

At the end of May I travelled alone to Geneva, and there found arrangements made by my uncle for my being placed *en pension* in the family of M. Duvillard, Professor of Belles Lettres in the Geneva University, called the Auditoire. Two Frenchmen—one of them belonging to the old noblesse, and the other being the son of a wealthy manufacturer of Marseilles—and one Englishman,

were at that time the only other boarders in M.
Duvillard's house. Subsequently during my two
years' residence an old Winchester schoolfellow
and friend, and one other Englishman joined us.
M. Duvillard's son had a few young boys as
pupils under the same roof, amongst whom, during
part of the time, was Jerome Patterson, the eldest
son of the elder Jerome Bonaparte ; his mother,
Mrs. Patterson, residing at that time at Geneva.

Within a few weeks after my arrival I had acquired a sufficient knowledge of French to pass
the examination necessary for entering the Auditoire ; but so imperfect was my knowledge of the
language as yet, that I translated the Greek
authors, in whose works I was examined, into
Latin in preference to French. At this time
Decandolle lectured on botany, Pictet on natural
philosophy, Prevost on moral philosophy, and
Lhuilier on mathematics. The lectures were delivered from eight till twelve, each lecture occupying an hour. They had to be taken down by the
pupils, who were examined the next morning in
the lectures of the preceding day, and at the end
of the year there was a general examination on
the whole course. Besides attending these lectures
I took private lessons in mathematics, and M.
Duvillard kept up some reading with his pupils
in the Latin classics. The Genevese were not
strong in Greek, but many of them were good

Latin scholars. I also took lessons in Italian, and had the very great advantage of attending two courses of lectures by the eloquent and learned Rossi, who arrived as a refugee from Bologna whilst I was pursuing my studies at Geneva. He afterwards became a peer of France, and finally was murdered when he was first minister of Pope Pius IX.—an act most disastrous to the Liberal cause in Italy, for there never was a more sincere patriot, and there have been but few wiser statesmen. The lectures of Decandolle and Rossi were of a first-rate order. The former lectured one year on botany, and the next on zoology ; the latter on the history of Roman law, expounding clearly the views of Niebuhr, which had recently been made public, and adding much lively and suggestive illustration of his own from modern sources. These lectures of Rossi's were delivered to classes who paid for them, Rossi not being then a professor of the Auditoire. He was afterwards elected Professor of Civil Law, the first Roman Catholic so elected since the Reformation. The lectures of Prevost were sound and interesting, and those of Pictet remarkable for clearness and for his adroit manipulation in experiments.

Geneva then presented great additional advantages to the young pupils who flocked thither from all countries in the society which it afforded. Young men of rank, and many of great ability,

from France, Russia, Poland, and every part of
Germany, were to be found there, as well as from
England and Scotland. All, however young, were
received at the evening parties of the Genevese,
which parties were by law compelled to terminate
at midnight. Great opportunities were thus given
of acquiring the refinements of society, and facility
in speaking any language which might be desired,
without much risk of unduly wasting time. Dumont,
Sismondi, De la Rive, and many other eminent men
were to be met in the society of Geneva at this time.
Amongst other young German princes the late
Prince of Leiningen, half brother to Her Majesty,
was then studying at Geneva, and the Duke of
Kent had written to him and to his tutor, Mr.
Wagner, expressing his desire that the Prince
should become intimate with me, and we were
accordingly much thrown together.[1]

[1] Copies of two letters forming part of the correspondence on this
subject have come into my possession. The first is from Mr. Wagner,
the Prince's tutor, to the Duchess of Kent, and is dated Geneva,
December 10, 1819. The following is a translation of the letter :—

'We have had the good fortune to become acquainted with Mr.
Wood, the young gentleman named to us by His Royal Highness the
Duke of Kent. Of all his countrymen here he is a most distinguished
example, and I consider that his becoming intimate with my young
charge would be a most important benefit to him ; but, unfortunately,
the strict rules of the *pension* to which Mr. Wood belongs prevent the
possibility of our meeting nearly as often as I could wish. To conduct
the most prudent, gentlemanly, and creditable Mr. Wood unites an
unequalled application to his studies. He attends, at the same time with
my young charge, the lectures of Professor Decandolle, and he has
uniformly been distinguished for having profited by these instructions

I went through the first year's examination, which is conducted in public, and was complimented by the Rector on its result. The next year I was about to be examined for the degree of Bachelor of Arts, when I had occasion to leave about a fortnight before the examination, owing to my father's wish that I should accompany Queen Caroline to England, she having taken Geneva on her route from Italy.

I have never ceased to regard my training at Geneva as one of the most satisfactory portions of my education. It enabled me to acquire sufficient

more than any other person, be he whom he may, that has attended them. In short, he is a perfect pattern for a young man to copy, and I earnestly entreat your Royal Highness to use your good offices with Mr. Wood's father so as to give every possible effect to my anxious wish that he may be a great deal with my pupil.'

Soon after the receipt of this letter the Duke of Kent wrote to my grandfather to the following effect :—

'Sidmouth : December 25, 1819.

'My dear Sir,—The Duchess, feeling for every parent who has a child abroad as she does for her own, conceives it would be acceptable to you to learn what has been written to her respecting your son at Geneva by that valuable man, Mr. Wagner, who has the charge of hers. I therefore annex, at the foot of this, the paragraph of Mr. Wagner's letter that relates to him, and I have great satisfaction in adding that the Duchess wishes you would write to the master of the *pension* to which your son belongs to afford every facility in his power to their meeting frequently, as the Duchess is satisfied that the example of manliness and application set by your son in his studies will be a great stimulus to hers. . . . Pray remember me to Mrs. Wood and your daughters in the kindest manner ; and believe me to be at all times, with friendship and esteem, my dear sir, yours faithfully,
—ED.   'EDWARD.'

mathematics for my Cambridge career, and at the same time to master the French and Italian languages, whilst it greatly enlarged my knowledge of and interest in the general departments of science, and promoted a healthy appreciation of the advantages of intercourse, not only with men of high intellectual power, but also with ladies of natural and simple tastes and kind sympathies, at an age when in England a youth is rarely permitted to enjoy such opportunities.

I returned to England in May 1820, in the suite of Queen Caroline. I met my father and Lady Ann Hamilton at Montbard, and we all arrived at St. Omer without passing through Paris. The day after we reached St. Omer Mr. Brougham arrived, accompanied by Lord Hutchinson, and I was sent to them by the Queen to beg that they would immediately wait upon her, as she wished to proceed to Calais and embark for England without delay. She rejected with indignation the proposition that she should accept 50,000*l.* a year and give up the title of Queen, and she set off that day for Calais, and slept on board the English steamer in the harbour.

[The proposition here alluded to was conveyed by Lord Hutchinson, and was submitted to the Queen at her desire in the form of a letter addressed to Mr. Brougham. This letter has been preserved amongst my grandfather's papers, and is

thus endorsed in his handwriting :—'Lord Hutchinson's original proposition to the Queen of England
at St. Omer, June 4, 1820. This paper was addressed to Mr. Brougham after his arrival at St.
Omer, and delivered to the Queen, who came out
of the room in great agitation and gave it to me
(Alderman Wood'). The letter is as follows :—

'Sir,—In obedience to the commands of the
Queen I have to inform you that I am not in
possession of any proposition or propositions,
detailed in a specific form of words, which I could
lay before Her Majesty. But I can detail to you
for her information the substance of many conver-
sations held with Lord Liverpool. His Majesty's
ministers propose that 50,000*l.* per annum should
be settled on the Queen for life, subject to such
conditions as the King may impose. I have also
reason to know that the conditions likely to be
imposed by His Majesty are that the Queen is not
to assume the style and title of Queen of England,
or any title attached to the Royal Family of England. A further condition is that she is not to
reside in any part of the United Kingdom or even
to visit England. The consequence of such a visit
will be an immediate message to Parliament, and an
entire end to all compromise and negotiation. I
think it right to send to you an extract of a letter
from Lord Liverpool to me. His words are :—" It
is material that Her Majesty should know con-

fidentially that if she shall be so ill-advised as to come over to this country, there must be an end to all negotiation and compromise ; the decision, I may say, is taken to proceed against her as soon as she sets her foot on the British shore." I cannot conclude this letter without my humble, though serious and sincere, supplication that Her Majesty will take these propositions into her most calm consideration, and not act with any hurry or precipitation. On so important a subject I hope that my advice will not be misinterpreted. I can have no possible interest which would induce me to give fallacious counsel to the Queen ; but, let the result be what it may, I shall console myself with the reflection that I have performed a painful duty imposed upon me, to the best of my judgment and conscience. . . . Having done so, I fear neither obloquy nor misrepresentation. . . . I have the honour, &c.'—ED.]

When the Queen was on board the steamer at Calais she wrote a letter to King Louis XVIII. saying that she had relieved him as early as possible of her presence, though she thought the circumstance that three of her brothers had perished on the field of battle whilst supporting his family, merited some attention on his part.

On my arrival in England I was sent for by the Duchess of Kent to Kensington. She wished to inquire about her son's health and course of study.

Before I took my leave she desired the Princess Victoria, now our beloved Sovereign, at that time about a year old, to be brought in, and I had the honour of kissing her hand.

It is not necessary here to enter into the history of the subsequent proceedings regarding Queen Caroline, except to state that soon after her arrival in England the Bill of Pains and Penalties was introduced into the House of Lords,[1] and it became necessary to send some one into Italy to collect evidence on her behalf. One of her Italian suite, the Chevalier Vasselli, was sent for this purpose; and the Queen, who had always been very kind to me, as she invariably was to all young people, asked me if I would like to accompany him. With my father's permission I gladly availed myself of this oportunity of visiting Italy. We travelled day and night, and arrived at the end of a week at Milan. It then became necessary to have some one to translate the statements of witnesses for the English solicitors and counsel employed in defence of the Queen at home. A Mr. Henry, who had been a judge at Demerara and afterwards at the Ionian Islands, was sent to collect evidence, and I offered to act as interpreter until some regular

---

[1] On July 5, 1820, by Lord Liverpool. It was entitled a bill 'to deprive Her Majesty Queen Caroline Amelia Elizabeth of the title, prerogative rights, privileges, and exemption of Queen Consort of this realm, and to dissolve the marriage between His Majesty and the said Caroline Amelia Elizabeth.'—ED.

interpreter should be sent out. I then stayed from July to the middle of October in Italy, living almost entirely in Italian society. I visited Milan, Verona, Venice, Trieste, Ravenna, Pesaro, and Rome for the purpose of seeing witnesses and translating their statements, sometimes by myself, sometimes in company with Mr. Henry and a solicitor afterwards sent out. I also spent some time with Bergami at his villa at Pesaro,[1] and with the Marquis Antaldi of the same place, a most estimable Italian nobleman ; and it was with regret that I returned home on a hurried summons from my private tutor at Cambridge, who informed me that if I missed the October term I should be thrown back a whole year in my academical course.

Thus ended my sojourn in Italy, which I have always highly valued on account of the familiarity which it enabled me to acquire with the Italian language and with Italian society. On my way back from Rome I fell in with the Austrian army marching upon Naples to put down the Constitution which had been established there.

It may be as well to mention here, without further allusion to the subject, that both from the

---

[1] Bartolomeo Bergami had been the Queen's favourite courier and valet during her foreign travels, and an attempt was made to prove that there had been a criminal intimacy between him and the Queen; but, like all the graver charges against her, it broke down.—ED.

evidence I obtained in Italy (which could not be made available) as well as from the evidence actually given in the House of Lords on the celebrated Bill of Pains and Penalties, and also from my own observation of Queen Caroline, with whom, on my journey to England and afterwards, I had many interviews, I was satisfied of her innocence of the crimes laid to her charge. She was very careless of appearances, or even may be said to have courted observation, as in the famous instance when it was alleged that William Austin was her child.[1] She was devotedly attached, and most warm in her kindness, to all young people ; but all I saw satisfied me that she was not guilty of anything beyond imprudence. Many of her Italian acquaintances, as the Antaldis of Pesaro and the Ercolanis of Bologna, were families as distinguished for respectability as any in our own country.

As for the Queen's trial, never was any trial against the meanest prisoner so shamefully conducted. The witnesses for the Queen in Lombardy and Venice were afraid to go to England on her behalf from dread of persecution by the Austrian Government on their return. Those only of the poorer class would make the venture, and it required several communications with the Court of

---

[1] A boy whom she had adopted, and who constantly accompanied her. There was no mystery about his parentage, save what was fabricated by slanderous gossip.—ED.

Vienna before Mr. Henry was allowed to despatch even these. It took a month to send over the first set, whilst the King's witnesses were sent at twenty-four hours' notice. As a specimen of the difficulty of inducing witnesses to give evidence in London I may mention the case of a jeweller in Venice who was prepared to swear positively that the Queen never entered his shop, in contradiction to one of the King's witnesses who said she bought a gold chain there and threw it round Bergami's neck; but when I asked him if he would go to England and repeat the statement there on oath, he replied that he dared not, for it would be utter ruin to him to do so. It was a great satisfaction to me a few years ago to hear a barrister of great ability, who had had large experience in Crown prosecutions, and who was highly conservative in politics, say that he had read the whole of the Queen's trial through, and was not only satisfied that the charges were not proved, but was convinced that she was innocent.

[Amongst my grandfather's papers I have found a series of letters written to him by Queen Caroline, most of them during the years 1819 and 1820.

I do not think any one could read them without being moved to compassion for the writer. They are the piteous record of the life of a homeless, persecuted wanderer. Her movements were continually watched and misrepresented by hired spies and

informers. Ambassadors and Ministers, English
and foreign, at every Court in Europe treated her
with studied insult, or with cold contempt and
neglect. And to this conduct they were instigated
by the Court in England. Every kind of impedi-
ment was placed in the way of her meeting Mr.
Brougham in France, as her legal adviser. And
when they did meet, as related above, at St. Omer,
even he was in favour of her accepting the mean
proposition conveyed through Lord Hutchinson,
which in plain English was a bribe of 50,000*l.* a
year to induce her to surrender all the honours to
which she was entitled, and tacitly to admit the
truth of accusations which she had always indig-
nantly denied.

My grandfather seems to have been the only
person who had the sagacity in this crisis to
perceive the true drift of popular feeling in England,
and to measure its force. He urged the Queen,
much to the annoyance of Mr. Brougham, to proceed without hesitation to England, telling her that
she might safely rely upon the generous support of
the English people ; though, perhaps, even he
scarcely anticipated the extraordinary rush of
enthusiasm with which she was actually received.
There were few, indeed, in the higher ranks who
had the courage to befriend her ; for, to quote her
words in a long letter which she addressed to her
husband in August 1820, ' to calumniate your inno-

cent wife was now the shortest road to royal
favour, and to betray her was to lay a sure
foundation of riches and titles of honour;' but the
mass of the people were true to her, from the day
after she landed at Dover when she was escorted
by multitudes to London in a kind of triumphal
progress, to the day when they compelled her
remains to be conducted with due honour through
the principal streets of London, in spite of the
military and police who tried to enforce the orders
of the Government that the body should be taken
by a more obscure route.

'Here lies Caroline of Brunswick, the injured
Queen of England,' was the inscription placed by
her desire upon her coffin ; and a careful perusal of
her letters and investigation of her career, must,
surely, force any candid mind to the conclusion that
the inscription was justified. Granted that she
was not a refined, or dignified, or highly educated
princess, yet she must be credited with some share
of ability, and no small amount of spirit and perseverance. It must be owned that she was persecuted with the most relentless animosity; and,
whatever her moral failings may have been, no
crime was *proved* against her, either in the course
of secret inquiries or of a trial which, though
public, could hardly be described as impartial.—
Ed.]

In October 1820 I went to Trinity College, Cam-

bridge. My private tutor was the Rev. George Mac-
farlane, only lately deceased. The tutor of my
side, as it is called, was the Rev. John Brown; the
Greek lecturer, Professor Monk, afterwards Bishop
of Gloucester and Bristol; and the lecturer in the
higher mathematics was Mr. Coddrington, who had
recently been senior wrangler.

I formed acquaintances amongst men senior to
myself rather than among men of my own year,
principally from having some Genevese and other
friends in the years above me. I thus became
well acquainted with Lord Macaulay, who was two
years senior to me; with Airey, the present
Astronomer Royal, who was one year above me;
with the lamented John Bethune, then Drinkwater,
well known in the Council of India; and several
others who have since achieved distinction. I did
not till later in life know Sir John Romilly, the
Master of the Rolls, who was also in the year
above me.

During my Cambridge career the suppression
of constitutional government in Italy by Austria, and
in Spain by France, had filled England with Italian
and Spanish refugees. The latter, if they had served
with our army during the Peninsular war, were
provided for to a great extent by our Government,
but many of them and all the Italians were in a
state of complete destitution. The connexion of
my father with Italians during the time of Queen

Caroline's trial occasioned many of the Italian refugees to visit at his house, and many Spaniards also became desirous of acquaintance. Among the latter were Generals Mina and Quiroja, Rafael Riego, Canon of Oviedo, brother of the ·general who had been executed in Spain, and Galiario, a distinguished member of the Liberal party and an orator of eminence in the Cortes. Galiario was intimately acquainted with our English literature, and of him I took lessons in Spanish. The principal Italians were General Guglielmo Pepe, the leader of the Neapolitan constitutional army, and afterwards in 1848 the defender of Venice ; and an aide-de-camp of his, Colonel Poerio, uncle of Carlo Poerio, whose sufferings under the nefarious administration of the late King of Naples are but too well known through Mr. Gladstone's touching narrative. Pepe and Poerio earnestly ·entreated my father to take steps for bringing the sufferings of their poorer countrymen to the knowledge of the public, and by my father's direction I gave notice through Poerio of a private meeting of all the Italians who might wish to attend at a room hired for the purpose in Marlborough Street. There, as arranged, I made them an address, and requested each to put down his name, address, position, and capacity for earning a livelihood. About 180 did this ; their number was afterwards considerably augmented, and finally my father procured the Lord Mayor's assent to a public meeting at the Guildhall for the relief of the Italians and such Spaniards as were unaided by the Government. A subscription of about 100,000*l.* was the result of these efforts. Several of the refugees could manufacture articles of taste, and our family sold more than 200*l.* worth of one particular manufacture alone for the benefit of some of the Spaniards.

To avoid the expense of a special private tutor during the long vacation, I read in London during my first vacation, but the result was prejudicial to my health. In the second long vacation I was troubled with most formidable attacks of giddiness from indigestion attributed to mental exertion, and for many weeks I could not even read a newspaper. The disadvantage also of not having a private tutor was further increased by my giving way too much to my own course of reading, which was not always that which would tell in the examinations. The consequence was that though I had obtained a scholarship in my first trial for that honour in 1822, and was placed in the first class in each year in the college examination, I had the mortification of finding myself 24th wrangler on taking my degree in January 1824, and several men who had been in the second class at Trinity were above me. In 1824 the examinations for honours in classics were first held, and I went again into the Senate

House, but the cold marble floor rendered me so ill that I was compelled to retire from the examination. In my second year I had obtained the second Declamation prize (a silver cup) ; the late · Mr. Hampden Gurney obtained the first. The custom was for the declaimers to be selected two and two, and they were allowed to choose a subject out of several submitted to them by the Dean of the Chapel, where (somewhat indecorously) the declamations were delivered. The theme which I and my opponent selected was whether the Revolution or the Restoration had conferred the greater benefit on our country. I of course took the side of the Revolution ; but I wrote my essay with great reluctance, thinking the whole proceeding rather a foolish one, and I was much surprised when I heard that I had obtained a prize. This declamation nearly cost me my Fellowship, as will presently be seen.

On leaving Cambridge in January 1824 I was not competent, according to the rules then in force, to try for a Fellowship before the following October. I did not like to lose all this time of preparation for my profession by going up to read at Cambridge, the more so as I did not expect to obtain a Fellowship in my first attempt. I therefore proposed to my father that I should begin at once to study for the Bar, and I was placed with the late Master Roupell to learn equity drawing. It was by mistake, and owing to ignorance on my father's part and on my own, that I was not first placed with a conveyancer. In the Trinity term of 1824 I was entered at Lincoln's Inn; Henry Brougham and Thomas Denman signing the recommendation required by the rules of the Inn. I devoted myself to my studies as a draftsman till the long vacation, and then began to read seriously for the approaching examination for a Fellowship at Trinity. In July, August, and September, I read through the ' De Republicâ ' and the ' De Legibus ' of Plato, and also twice read through the whole of Aristophanes, besides going again over the first and third books of Newton's ' Principia.' At the election of Fellows in October there were six vacancies, one being occasioned by the death of the Greek professor, Dobree, shortly before the examination. Contrary to expectation two only of the senior year were elected, and I, with three others of the junior year, were elected to the other vacancies. My success took me entirely by surprise. It was announced to me on the evening before the declamation by the present Dean of Salisbury,[1] one of the examiners. He called again, however, late at night to say he feared he had made a mistake ; nevertheless, next day I was declared to be elected. The cause of this hitch, which was not known to me for many years afterwards, was this. The Master,[2] it seems,

---

[1] The late Dr. Hamilton.—ED.   [2] Dr. Wordsworth.—ED.

had been alarmed by the supposed radicalism of my unfortunate college declamation in which I had quoted the line, ' the right divine of kings to govern wrong.' Now the election is by the Master and eight Fellows, and until the recent alteration of the statutes by the Royal Commission (of which I was a member), the Master and one Fellow could place a veto on the election made by the other Fellows, whatever the result of the examination might be. After the examination had proved that I was qualified for election, the exercise of this veto was discussed, and one Fellow was found to coincide with the Master's views, and hence Mr. Hamilton's fears that the election might be cancelled. I have since been informed that one of the Fellows expressed his intention, should this step be taken, of printing all the answers to the examination papers. Be it as it may, the veto was abandoned. No personal feeling was entertained against me on the Master's part, for both then and afterwards he was generally most kind and friendly towards me. He no doubt proposed to act on a sense of duty, and one can now hardly imagine the dread then entertained, by the Tory party, of Liberal politics.

In November 1825 I was invited to accompany a young man, who had just left Eton for King's College, a nephew of the present Bishop of Exeter,[1] on a journey to the South of Europe recommended

[1] Bishop Philpotts.—ED.

to him for his health. I gladly availed myself of the opportunity of revisiting Italy, and of obtaining some recreation after hard work. We proceeded by Paris and along the banks of the Rhone to Nice, thence by the Cornice road (at that time for the most part a mule road) to Genoa, and by La Spezzia to Lucca, Pisa, Leghorn, and Florence, and, after staying there some time, to Rome, and subsequently to Naples. We returned to England in May 1826. At Florence I made acquaintance (amongst other Italians) with Baron Poerio, the father of Carlo Poerio, an ex-member of the Neapolitan Parliament, and at Naples with General Florentan Pepe, the brother of General Guglielmo Pepe. At Bologna, too, on my return, I passed a day with the young Prince Cesare Ercolani, whom I had known in England after the Queen's trial. There, too, I was introduced to Professor Tommasini, a distinguished medical professor and practitioner, and to the Abbé (afterwards Cardinal) Mezzofanti, the celebrated linguist. I conversed with the Abbé in English, which he spoke without a grammatical error of any kind.[1] I also heard him speak in German, Italian, Greek, and Armenian;

---

[1] My father also on one occasion heard him speak English, and remarked to him that he was quite free from the mistake, so common with the Irish and Scotch, of misplacing 'shall and will,' 'would and should.' Mezzofanti replied, 'Oh, yes; I think I have completely mastered that difficulty. My rule is " *I* shall, *You* will." ' At that time he had never been more than thirty miles from Bologna.—ED.

and I afterwards met with an Illyrian monk who had conversed with him in the Sclavonic tongue, and a gentleman from India who told me he had conversed with the Abbé in Telagoo, the form of Hindustani spoken in Madras. All agreed as to his perfect mastery over any language which he adopted.

On my return to England I had the advantage of being placed in the chambers of the late John Tyrrell, Esq.; and I certainly feel that in these chambers, with Mr. Tyrrell's careful assistance, I laid the foundation of all such knowledge of English law as I possess. It was Mr. Tyrrell's custom to attend his chambers regularly at half-past six in the evening, and to remain there often till midnight, or one o'clock in the morning. He would take tea with such pupils as attended, and discuss any points of difficulty that arose in their examination of his papers, or would go through a course of reading and discuss the subject with them.

At the end of the year I was requested to remain till my call to the Bar about six months later, which I did with great satisfaction and profit. Mr. Tyrrell had been a pupil of Lord St. Leonards, and his school was that of Mr. Charles Butler which had to a great degree discarded the mass of verbiage, still too great, that defaced our conveyances of land. I recollect seeing some forms prepared by an eminent conveyancer of the opposite school, when transferred, on his retirement, to Mr. Tyrrell, cut down to one-fourth of their original dimensions. Whilst I was with Mr. Tyrrell he prepared and published his suggestions for the improvement of the law of real property, the result of which was that Mr. Tyrrell was added as a member to the already existing commission upon the law of real property.

I was called to the Bar on November 27, 1827. Lord Eldon had resigned the Seals but a short time before,[1] and Lord Gifford was dead.[2] Lord Lyndhurst was Chancellor, Sir John Leach Master of the Rolls, and Sir Lancelot Shadwell Vice-Chancellor. I occupied two rooms, part of a set of chambers at No. 3 Old Square, on the ground floor, which were sub-let to me by Mr. Wm. Lowndes, the author of ' Lowndes on Legacies.' I I had known Mr. Lowndes for some years, and felt it to be a great advantage to live in the same chambers with one who, in addition to a sound knowledge of law, was a first-rate scholar. He had been a pupil of Dr. Parr's, and still cultivated classical literature, and especially all that was connected with Greek philosophy. He wrote the ' Life of Plato,' in the ' Encyclopædia Metropolitana,' and possessed an excellent library, not only of ancient,

[1] April 30, 1827.—ED.

[2] He died September 4, 1826, aged only forty-eight. He was Master of the Rolls at the time of his death, and, had he lived, would in all probability have become the successor of Lord Eldon.—ED.

but also of modern authors, including some German
works, a language which, so far as reading it was
concerned, I had taught myself at Cambridge.
Both from the books and from the conversation of
Mr. Lowndes I derived great benefit.

During the last year and a half of my study for
the Bar, I had also received much kindness from
the late Basil Montagu, Esq., and his admirable
wife. I had been allowed free access to their
home in Bedford Square on any evening I thought
fit to go, when it was their custom to receive those
who had this privilege from eight to ten. There I
sometimes met Irving, and Carlyle, and Procter,
then better known as Barry Cornwall ; and others
of an older literary school, but less widely known :
also John Kemble and his gifted sister. Thursday
was the only day on which such receptions did not
take place, for every Thursday evening was spent
by Mr. and Mrs. Montagu at Highgate, in the
company of Coleridge. I had the privilege, through
Mr. Montagu's kindness, of frequently accompany-
ing him on these pilgrimages, and I entertain most
lively recollections of many an evening passed
there of the highest enjoyment and interest. It is
well known that Coleridge poured out all the
riches of his prodigious memory, and all the poetry
of his brilliant imagination, to every listener. I
was not only so addressed myself, but I heard the
whole of the poet-philosopher's favourite system of

Polarities—the Prothesis, the Thesis, the Mesothesis, and Antithesis—showered down on a young lady of seventeen, with as much unction as he afterwards expounded it to Edward Irving. I was also present at some discussions between Edward Irving and Coleridge, on subjects of higher and holier import, in which the poetical temperament of Irving shone forth, but not with the genial, all-embracing fervour that distinguished Coleridge. At this time Mr. Montagu was bringing out his edition of Lord Bacon's works, and he requested me to undertake the translation of the 'Novum Organum.' This I did, and completed it in the year 1826, and was always thankful for this opportunity of mastering that wonderful work.[1]

Shortly after my call to the Bar, I became well engaged in business as a conveyancer and equity draftsman, partly owing to my father's being so well known in the City, and partly to recommendations from Mr. Tyrrell to some of his clients when he was too much engaged to undertake the work himself. I remember standing in great awe of Sir John Leach, the Master of the Rolls. The first brief I held before him was merely a brief to ask for the payment to executors of the small arrears of an annuity (a few pounds), when the principal sum was about to be paid out on the death of the

---

[1] This translation has been separately reprinted since both by Pickering and others, and has been generally acknowledged to be the best extant. —ED.

annuitant to the parties entitled in remainder. This at present is a matter of course. Then, in strictness, a separate petition, costing more than the money itself, was formally required. I simply asked, as instructed, that this might be dispensed with, and the money paid. The answer from the Bench was, ' Sir, you might as well ask me to pay it to the porter at Lincoln's Inn Gate.' Happily there is not at the present day any necessity for dreading such a reply, nor is it believed that there is a judge who would make it.

The first occasion of my making any speech to a Court, was before the House of Lords, in the case of Westmeath *v.* Westmeath, where I was instructed by Mr. Lock, the solicitor for Lady Westmeath, and her infant daughter, Lady Rosa Nugent, to appear for the latter. After two counsel had been heard for Lady Westmeath, and Mr. Adam (who was my leader) for Lady Rosa Nugent, the House said they did not intend to hear any more counsel. Mr. Adam (meaning it kindly) said his friend Mr. Wood expected to be heard, and Lord Lyndhurst with his usual courtesy and kind consideration for young men said, ' Oh ! let us hear him then.' This was an inauspicious beginning, but I got through it tolerably well, and retained the confidence of Mr. Lock as long as that gentleman continued in business.

In the year 1827, just before my call to the

Bar, I happened to enter into conversation with Monsieur (afterwards Baron) de Billing, then an attaché in the French Embassy, with reference to the Battle of Navarino and the destruction of the Turkish fleet by Russia, France, and England. M. de Billing had long been a friend of mine. His father, a gentleman of Alsace, was residing at Paris in 1817, and was well known to my father, who met him at the houses of the Liberal party. His mother was an English lady; and he spoke English at this time with most remarkable fluency and freedom from accent, so much so that he usually passed for an Englishman in society. His son, the present Baron de Billing, was now occupying the same position at the French Embassy as his father then had, and was equally remarkable for his command of our language. M. de Billing was a man of great intelligence, and at this early period was a warm Free Trader, and supporter of constitutional government. He and I agreed that it was a mistake for the constitutional governments of France and England to assist Russia in weakening Turkey, and that their policy should rather be union between themselves in the support of Turkey against Russian aggression. M. de Billing expressed a wish that I should put my views into the shape of a letter to be inserted in the ' Times,' he under-taking to show it to Mr. Barnes, the editor. In compliance with this wish I wrote a long letter addressed to Lord Goderich, and signed 'An Englishman.'

[This letter occupies three columns and a half of very small type in the 'Times' of January 9, 1828, and, the length of it being so great, I have thought it sufficient to indicate its character partly by extracts, partly by a summary of the contents. It is entitled, 'A Letter to Lord Goderich on the Necessity of a close Alliance between England, France, and the Netherlands.' When the letter was published Lord Goderich had ceased to be Premier; but a note is prefixed to the letter stating that it was written before his resignation was considered probable, and that the writer now addresses it to him as the recognised head of a Liberal Ministry.

It is introduced by a quotation from the speech of Queen Isabella in Shakspeare's 'Henry V.' act v. scene 2.

> So be there 'twixt your kingdoms such a spousal,
> That never may ill office, or fell jealousy
> Thrust in between the paction of these kingdoms,
> To make divorce of their incorporate league;
> That English may as French, French Englishmen,
> Receive each other! God speak this Amen!

The letter begins by a severe criticism of the English policy in the treaty of Vienna, in which the dominant aim had been to depress France, instead of strengthening her tendencies to a constitu-

tional government, and generally supporting those
countries which were inclined to what the writer
calls the civilising, as opposed to the despotic,
principle. Of the former principle Holland and
the Netherlands were especially representative, and
' by a lucky hit, in the fervour of our spleen against
France, we fell upon the fortunate expedient of
consolidating these two countries, and subjecting
them to a sovereign who appears worthy of the
important charge thus reposed in him.'

The arrangements made by the treaty of Vienna
for guarding the frontier of the Rhine, were also
unsatisfactory. The frontier of the Rhine de-
manded the watchfulness of a military Argus.
France and the Netherlands might have sufficed
for the duty, but Prussia and Austria were entrusted with the most important fortresses. The
danger involved in this arrangement was not
imminent, as France and the Netherlands might
keep Austria and Prussia in check, but in the
distance lurked a much more powerful adversary.
' The wild ambition of Charles XII. first introduced
the barbarous Asiatic hordes of Russia into Europe ;
that of Napoleon has consolidated their power and
rendered them integral members of the great
European commonwealth ; yet notwithstanding that
the influence of commerce has communicated the
refinements of domestic life to the inhabitants of
St. Petersburg, and this influence has spread over

some of the western parts of Russian territory, that vast empire must as yet, even in its most favoured portions, be considered as scarcely emerged from infancy. The feudal spirit yet predominates; and the circumstances attending the deposition of the present Emperor's father, and his own accession to the throne, evince that want of stability in the Government, which is a marked characteristic of society at such an epoch.' By the treaty of Vienna, however, instead of Russia being confined within the bounds which had limited her territory until the treaty of Tilsit, Austria and Prussia were compelled to submit whilst their formidable neighbour crossed the Vistula and, by taking possession of the Duchy of Warsaw, commanded at once a direct road to Vienna and Berlin. 'From the Oder to the Rhine there is nothing which can arrest her progress; and were the question proposed to Austria in her present undeveloped condition, whether she would yield a free passage to the tide of barbarism in preference to the glory she might obtain by a conflict on behalf of civilisation, there can, I fear, be little doubt as to her choice.' This concession to Russia, the writer adds, was not merely vicious in principle, but led to that disastrous and disgraceful train of compensations (as they were termed) which had stamped indelible disgrace upon our country. 'Some pretext was offered for the spoliation of

Saxony by the firm adherence of its sovereign to
the cause which he had espoused ; but the im-
politic cession of the richest provinces of Italy to
Austria, and the cold-hearted barbarity which
sacrificed the unoffending and defenceless republic
of Genoa, leave room for only one consolatory
reflection in the proof they have afforded of the
sympathy which unites folly and wickedness, and
the confirmation of our belief in the opposite union
of wisdom and virtue.' The feelings of Frenchmen
had been exasperated by a continued attitude of
coldness and distrust on the part of the English
Government, combined with great severity of treatment, the enormous fine of 700 million francs
imposed upon her at the Congress of Aix, the tax
of 50 million francs to be paid to foreign troops,
and the periodical visits of the Duke of Wellington
to the Rhine fortresses.

On the other hand, our indifference to the
struggles for liberty in Spain and Naples—countries
in which the inert mass of ignorance and superstition
rendered those efforts as abortive as the convulsive
struggles of Enceladus beneath Ætna—had excited
the generous indignation of many Englishmen ; and
our alliance with Austria and Russia, after the resolutions taken at Troppau, Laybach, and Verona, was
felt to be as unnatural as the conjunction of the
dead with the living. The death of our diplomatic
Mezentius and the advent of Canning to power

opened a new and enlightened era. In domestic policy amendments of the law were effected which had been advocated in vain by a Romilly and a Mackintosh. 'Principles of Free-trade opened a new career for talent, and prepared the way for strengthening the tie of common interest, which can alone bind nation to nation in indissoluble friendship.' The Spanish colonies had been recognised in America, prompt assistance had been given to Portugal against the efforts of drivelling Spanish dotards. There was some hope of Prussia obtaining a constitutional government. In Austria and Russia, on the other hand, nothing more could be anticipated than the progress which the human mind must eventually make from barbarism to civilisation.'

Then turning to the south-eastern part of Europe upon which public interest at that moment was fixed, the singular spectacle presented itself of a people invested by their religion, their language, their past history, with the dearest and most enthusiastic memories of enlightenment, yet now groaning under the most execrable and debasing tyranny. The establishment of Greece as an independent or tributary republic, or the creation of a monarchy on the ruins of the Mohammedan Empire, would be an issue to which no one could object. But the writer deprecated any attempt to emancipate the Greeks by an alliance with a despotic and half civilised power, such as Russia or Austria. The success of all future arrangements for the settlement of that part of Europe must depend upon a strict and cordial ' union between the constitutional governments of Europe.' The writer concludes by saying : ' I am too young to be destitute of enthusiasm, and I dare to hope for a period when the exertions of our country, which have already diffused and protected civilisation throughout the whole extent of the new world, may be hailed in the old with generous applause and seconded by the ardour of surrounding nations, till the full tide of civilisation be poured over every part of the inhabited globe, and, traversing the empires of Austria and Russia, may meet with that current which already circulates around the southern part of the eastern continent, until des. potism no longer knows where to find a resting-place.'

The contents of this letter scarcely bear out the statement made by the writer many years afterwárds in his Autobiography, quoted above (p. 55), that he ' advocated a union between France and England to support Turkey against Russian aggression.' It seems rather to advocate the support of constitutional government in all parts of the world, and to express a jealousy and suspicion of a despotic power like Russia taking part in the emancipation of Greece from the thraldom of Turkish tyranny. No doubt there was a time subsequent to this when the writer thought, in common with many other eminent men and some distinguished statesmen, that the Turks were capable of reform, and that it was the interest of this country to protect the Ottoman Empire. He lived long enough, however, to become completely disabused of this fallacy, and to ridicule what he called ' the Russian scare ' as pusillanimous and ill-founded.]

Mr. Barnes, the editor of the ' Times,' expressed great satisfaction with the letter, and requested me to call upon him. Editors of the ' Times ' did not mix so much in general society then as they do in the present day. But Mr. Barnes was a scholar who had received a University education, and, though not well acquainted with the drawing-rooms of London, was intimately acquainted with public affairs. I found him in his modest habitation in Nelson Square, Southwark, and he asked me whether I should be willing to undertake writing for the press, assuring me of success in so doing, but kindly adding that it would interfere with my prospects at the Bar if I was really disposed to devote myself to that profession. On mature re-flection I declined the proposal, but felt encouraged by it in my exertions for self-support, and grateful for the candid advice given me by a man of such ripe experience.

In the year 1828, the first year in which I

practised, a wholly new business had arisen consequent on the passing of the Liverpool and Manchester Railway Bill in 1827. The Parliamentary
Bar was then a comparatively small body. Those,
indeed, who confined themselves to practising before
one or other of the two branches of the Legislature, might be said to be only two or three, Mr.
Harrison and Mr. Adam being the two leaders.
The principal business before committees had been
upon contested elections, with occasional contests
on canals, roads, harbours, and market bills, or
upon competing schemes for supplying towns with
water or gas. But the passing of the Liverpool
and Manchester Railway Bill was the signal for
larger speculations which have since resulted in
the prodigious development of railway traffic.

I received my first Parliamentary brief to
support, with Mr. Harrison as my leader, a new
branch of the Stockton and Darlington Railway.
The railway was then traversed by cars drawn by
horses, and had been the earliest used for passenger
traffic by that method. The intent of the bill was
to increase the coal traffic to the river Tees, and it
was vehemently opposed by Lord Wharncliffe,
Lord Durham, and other coal owners on the river
Wear. Amongst other objections Lord Wharncliffe
suggested before the committee of the Lords,
through Mr. (afterwards Baron) Alderson, that
according to the well-known case of Natusch v.

Irving, decided by Lord Eldon, a company formed for one purpose could not use its funds for an extended plan of operation. I was left to fight the battle with Mr. Alderson, and contended that the rule had no application to the case of a corporate body applying to Parliament for an extension of its powers. The committee requested Lord Eldon to be good enough to attend one of their meetings, and he decided in favour of my view. This decision led Lord Wharncliffe to introduce the well-known standing order which bears his name, by which no new application can be made to Parliament by an existing company for extended powers, unless three-fourths of the proprietors, present at a meeting convened for the purpose, sanction the application.

From this time I became extensively engaged in Parliamentary practice, and so continued till the year 1841. I did not, however, neglect my business in Chancery, which continued to increase ; for I always entertained a hope of sitting in Parliament, which is inconsistent with Parliamentary practice as a barrister, but had resolved not to do so till I was in independent circumstances as to fortune.

The changes which I personally witnessed in public opinion on the subject of railways were remarkable. At first the landowners opposed every line which passed through their property : within six years they objected to every line which did not pass through their property. In 1828 I was counsel for a company who proposed to make a line from London to Blackwall. The project was scouted as ridiculous, and unceremoniously rejected. In 1836 I was again counsel for a similar line against two competing lines, the only doubt being which of the three should pass. The com mittees also happily underwent great improvements. At first any member might attend, five being a quorum. It was a common practice for the five to enter and put down their names every morning and retire, leaving a chairman to hear all the evidence for many days alone ; and then perhaps thirty or forty members would come to vote on the preamble. Sir Robert Peel first reformed these proceedings, which have gradually assumed a far less objectionable shape.

In 1829 a very long contest took place on the bill promoted by the corporation of London for making the approaches to London Bridge, and for raising funds for that purpose by continuing certain taxes on coals brought to the port of London. The bill was vehemently opposed by the coal-owners, especially in the House of Lords. and only carried by the perseverance of the Duke of Wellington, then Prime Minister, who, with six of his colleagues, attended daily, and, on finding that delay was the aim of the opponents, actually obtained the leave of the Crown to keep Parliament sitting till the bill should be disposed of.

During these proceedings I had frequent opportunities, both in conversation and in the course of
the examination of witnesses, of observing and
admiring the cool judgment and penetration of the
Duke of Wellington. He would examine witnesses,
who came to depose to the inconveniences of the
proposed approaches, respecting the length of a
waggon and horses, of a load of timber and the
like, and the space required for turning, and constantly corrected their imperfect and inaccurate
knowledge of these subjects.

At the close of the session of 1829 I found my
way sufficiently clear to justify me in taking a
step which I had long ardently desired to take.
I became engaged to my present wife, Charlotte,
the daughter of the late Major Moor of the Bombay
army, author of the 'Hindu Pantheon,' and many
other works on interesting Indian subjects.[1] Major

[1] Major Moor entered the Indian army as a cadet before he was
twelve years old. The date was fixed in his memory by the fact of his
having witnessed the sinking of the 'Royal George' at Spithead in
1782 while embarking with his fellow cadets at Portsmouth.

From this early age he educated and maintained himself by his
own exertions. He served under Lord Cornwallis in the first campaign
against Tippoo Sahib. At the age of nineteen he was wounded by a
bullet which lodged in his elbow-joint and could never be extracted.
This injury ultimately compelled him to give up field duty and to
take service in the Commissariat. Having returned to England on
furlough at the age of twenty-one, he published in a quarto volume his
'Narrative of Captain Little's Detachment' which gave the first clear
account of Mysore, and Tippoo Sahib's government. The book is
repeatedly cited with much praise by Mill in his 'History of British

Moor resided on his property at Great Bealings, near Woodbridge, in Suffolk, and I had been more or less acquainted from childhood with my future wife.

We were married on January 5, 1830. Just before my marriage I went to reside in Dean's Yard, Westminster, where I continued to live till the year 1844. My business steadily increased, both in Chancery and Parliamentary practice ; but in 1836 an event occurred which, after occasioning much anxiety to me and my family, resulted in making me independent of my profession, and led to my entering on a Parliamentary career.

In the year above mentioned died Mr. James Wood, of Gloucester, an eccentric man, who con-

India.' On his return to India Mr. Moor entered the Commissariat at Bombay and supplied the army of Sir Arthur Wellesley on its march to Assaye. The energy and efficiency with which he discharged this duty are acknowledged in the published ' Wellington Correspondence.' About this time he suggested to the Indian Government the planting of the potato in Mysore, having noticed that the soil of that region was favourable to the plant. He selected and sent the potatoes for this purpose, and their introduction has saved the people of Mysore from more than one famine when there has been a failure of the rice crop. He further employed his leisure in researches concerning the history and literature of India. His 'Hindu Pantheon,' illustrated from his collection of bronze idols, is still considered a standard work on Indian Mythology ; and he was the first to disclose some of the most terrible social disorders of India in his treatise on ' Hindu Infanticide.' On his final return to England at the age of thirty-seven he settled on his own property in his native county of Suffolk, and acted for forty years as a county magistrate ; occasionally visiting London to attend meetings of the Royal Society, of which he was a Fellow, and of other learned bodies.—ED.

ducted business as a banker and draper, and by parsimonious habits had accumulated a property of about a million sterling. He left a will by which he gave all his property to four individuals whom he appointed his executors. One of them was the son of a lady of the name of Sermon, supposed to be his sole next of kin. This lady was his second cousin, and her son had been apprenticed to Mr. Wood. The other executor was Mr. Osburne, who had been for twenty years or more Mr. Wood's confidential clerk; the third was Mr. Chadburne, his solicitor; and the fourth was my father. Some years before this time Mrs. Elizabeth Wood, a maiden sister of Mr. James Wood, also residing in Gloucester, but not with her brother, had written to my father expressing her admiration of his conduct in reference to Queen Caroline, and desiring him to become her almoner, and to recommend such charities as he thought worthy of support. He knew nothing whatever at that time either of her or her brother, but answered her letter, and from time to time named several charities to which she contributed; and on one occasion, happening to pass through Gloucester, he called on her, and then heard for the first time of her brother's existence. In the year 1823 or 1824 Mrs. E. Wood died, and it was found that she had left her house in Gloucester to my father for his life, with remainder to his youngest son, Western Wood, whom she had never seen, but who happened once accidentally in his father's absence to have answered one of her letters. The bulk of her property she left to Master Stratford, one of the Masters in Chancery. My father was invited to attend her funeral, which he accordingly did; and on that occasion Mr. James Wood, to whom the deceased had left nothing, asked to be introduced to him. My father naturally supposed, from what he had heard of Mr. Wood's habits, that the latter would have been annoyed at his sister's disposition of her property, and especially of the house, which was worth about 1,200*l*. On the contrary, however, he expressed his great satisfaction at the gift, and his admiration of my father's conduct in reference to Queen Caroline; and a wish that he would occasionally visit Gloucester. In the autumn of 1824 my father took his family to the Spa at Gloucester, and having examined the house that had been devised to him in this singular manner, found it so good and substantial that it might easily be converted into a residence for some months in the year.

On the very evening of the first arrival of my father with his family at Gloucester, Mr. James Wood called, and I then saw him for the first time. Nothing could exceed the warmth of his demonstrations; and from that time, whenever my father visited Gloucester, Mr. Wood showed him every civility, and, indeed, gave in his honour the only entertainment he was known to have given in his life, at which I was present.

It was not, therefore, a surprise to any one that James Wood should have included my father amongst his devisees. In fact, he had on more than one occasion mentioned his intention to customers at his bank, who were anxious to know what would become of his property at his decease, it being well known that he had no near relative, and that, if he died without a will, there might be delay in winding up his affairs. The proof of this was of great value afterwards in the litigation that ensued.

Unhappily the will was prepared by the solicitor who was himself benefited under it. Unhappily, also, this solicitor was misled into other acts, after the testator's death, which threw suspicion on the document itself; and this led to a litigation, and to a most extraordinary and successful forgery of a codicil, as to the forging of which neither I nor my father ever entertained the smallest doubt. But the history of the transaction is too recent for an exposition of all its remarkable circumstances. It must suffice to say here that after Sir Herbert Jenner, as Judge of the Court of Probate, had rejected both the will and the codicil, the Privy Council established both. In the meantime bills in Chancery, injunctions, and all the usual course of law proceedings that takes place when a large stake is concerned, occurred.

The will and codicil were rejected in 1839, established in 1841, and a final decision as to the largest legacy in the spurious codicil was given adversely to the claimants of it by the House of Lords after my father's death. The time was a very trying one to myself, as upon me devolved the responsibility of privately advising my father in the litigation. The total costs must have been nearly 100,000l. on all sides, the bulk of which might have fallen upon my father to his all but ruin. Happily, however, he never swerved in his confidence in the cause, and his determination to contest it to the last.

In 1837, before there was any notion of a serious contest about the will (for my father was ignorant of any possibility of misconduct being imputed to the solicitor or any one else), he had accepted a baronetcy offered to him most handsomely by Lord Melbourne, and one of the first honours conferred by her present Majesty. Lord Melbourne told my father, amongst other things, that her Majesty was aware that she owed her birth in this country to his suggestion. He and Lord Darnley, in fact, received the whole of the Duke of Kent's revenues in trust for his creditors, the Duke, from the most honourable motives, retiring to Brussels, and receiving but a small amount of income. Owing to his Liberal politics he had never enjoyed the advantages of office conferred on other members of the Royal family, yet his debts were trifling compared with those of the Duke of York. My father, hearing that there was a prospect of the Duke having a family, wrote to him at Brussels to suggest his removing to England before the birth of the child who might probably become sovereign of this country. The Duke replied that a considerable sum would be necessary to enable him to make this change. No funds were in hand, and my father suggested to Lord Darnley that they two should give their personal bond to Messrs. Coutts for an advance to the Duke, taking their chance of his living long enough to enable them to be repaid out of income. The Duke and the Duchess were enabled by this means to come to England, and the advance was only just repaid at the time of the Duke's premature death.

The acceptance of a title rendered the vexation occasioned by the decision of Sir Herbert Jenner about the disputed will all the more trying. My father, however, bore the announcement which I made to him of that adverse event with his accustomed extraordinary coolness and self-possession. He went to the House of Commons that day, and several persons observed his manner to be as calm as usual. His only remark to me was, ' Well, we are right, and we shall have justice at last.' I happened myself, after hearing and communicating the judgment, to be obliged to argue a case of some difficulty before a Master in Chancery that day, and I have often recollected with pleasure that, though not possessed of my father's cool temperament, I argued it successfully.

I recommended my father to secure the services of the late Lord Campbell (then Attorney-General) and of Lord Kingsdown, on the appeal to the Privy Council, and it was greatly owing to their wonderfully acute and searching examination of the facts that justice was done as to the will. The success of the codicil remains as an example of marvellous audacity rewarded.

I went to the Privy Council in great anxiety to hear the judgment. My father was at Hatherley, in Gloucestershire. As soon as the result was known, I set off and travelled by rail as far as Cirencester, whence I had to post, and arrived at my father's house at half-past eleven at night. He was in bed and asleep, though he knew that the judgment was to be given that day. When I had roused him and informed him of the result, he simply remarked, ' I knew justice must be done.' When told of the success of the codicil he expressed surprise, but no more, and quickly fell asleep again.

In this year (1841) a considerable change was

made in the constitution of the Court of Chancery. Two additional Vice-Chancellors were created, and I found myself compelled to determine whether I would give up practising before committees in Parliament, or practising in Chancery; for the junior counsel in Chancery, having to follow their pleadings to whatever Court the cause might be attached, were compelled to practise in five Courts, besides the Court of Appeal, and this of course was impossible to combine with Parliamentary work. I had never relaxed my hold on Chancery business, and, though the Parliamentary business was three or four times more lucrative, I now resolved entirely to abandon it. This I did, and in the very first year my Chancery business was doubled.

In September 1844 my father died. Shortly before this I had applied to Lord Lyndhurst in the usual manner for a silk gown. I felt that my business at this time fully justified me in so doing, and I was not a little annoyed when I was passed over, my junior, Mr. Parker (afterwards Vice-Chancellor), being appointed. On my father's decease my duties as his executor were very heavy, and rendered the burthen of Chancery drawing insupportable. I mentioned to Vice-Chancellor Wigram my intention to have practised in his Court had the honour of Queen's Counsel been conferred upon me, and the necessity I felt of

retiring from the Bar, if I were obliged to remain
an equity draftsman, owing to the duties devolving
upon me as my father's executor. Up to the time
of my father's decease I had not received any
income from any source whatever, since my call
to the Bar, except my professional earnings, but I
had now become, although not rich, independent
of my profession. The Vice-Chancellor Wigram
most kindly mentioned the matter to Sir W.
Follett, then Attorney-General, and he with equal
kindness spoke to Lord Lyndhurst. Lord Lyndhurst immediately expressed his regret at what
had occurred, saying it was entirely by inadvert-
ence, and promised that on an early occasion the
patent of Queen's Counsel should be granted.
This promise was fulfilled in February 1845, and
from the date of my appointment till I became
Solicitor-General I confined my practice entirely to
Vice-Chancellor Wigram's Court and the Court of
Appeal, and was then usually opposed to Mr.
(afterwards Sir John) Romilly, which was the
commencement of a warm friendship between us.

Shortly after the termination of the Parliamentary session of 1847 a vacancy was expected
in the representation of the city of Oxford owing to
the bankruptcy of one of the members which had
occurred in the previous year. It was competent
for any member to move for a new writ on the
expiration of a year from a member's bankruptcy;

but as it was the sixth year of Parliament, and a
dissolution was certain, no one liked to come forward as a candidate with the chance of having to
undergo two elections in the course of one year.
It was suggested to me that this afforded an
opening for a new man; but the Liberal member
was firm in his seat, being justly beloved and
respected, and no one recollected an instance of
two Liberals being returned for the city of Oxford.
Moreover, there was a prejudice against any two
candidates coalescing, so that a fresh Liberal candidate would have to rely on the least known
supporters of Liberal principles as the promoters
of his interests. I went down, however, to Oxford,
where I was up to that time unknown, and was
warmly received by Mr. Alderman Sadler, the
chairman of Mr. Langston's committee, who told
me he could only introduce me to some gentlemen
to act as the committee of a new candidate, and
could himself do no more than give me his vote.
I thus found myself brought face to face with a
committee composed of the most advanced Liberals,
amongst whom was a dissenting minister. I felt
no difficulty as to my political principles, as I had
always been a warm friend to a large extension of
the suffrage, and vote by ballot; but my Church
principles, which were decided, might, I felt, be used
against me. I at once told my proposed committee
that there must be a clear understanding upon all

points before I came forward ; that probably they would hear me called a Puseyite, which I was not, for I declined to follow any individual's views ; but that my most valued friend was Dr. Hook, of Leeds, and that our sentiments on most Church matters coincided. I further told them that in my address I should avow my attachment to the Church, and at the same time state my entire disapproval of any political disability whatever founded on the religious opinions of the citizen of a free country; that, in fact, in Scotland I should be a dissenter from the Established Church, and should object strongly to being liable to political disabilities if residing there.

I had constant reason to rejoice at this explicitness. As it happened, Parliament was dissolved without a new writ being moved for Oxford, and I had but the one election, and that without opposition. I was twice afterwards elected—once on accepting the office of Solicitor-General, and again in the general election in 1852, and in each case without opposition; and the Liberal party have ever since returned a sound Liberal candidate with their old representative, Mr. Langston.

Parliament met in November 1847. The first words which I spoke in the House were in a debate which arose the following month upon the functions of the Ecclesiastical Commissioners, and from that time I never failed to stand forward to avow my deep attachment to the Church. On Sir J. Trelawney's motion for the repeal of Church-rates in 1849 I moved and divided the House on a resolution to allow the Dissenters voluntarily to exempt themselves by declaration, and I always refused to support abolition as a direct step towards abolishing the Established Church.

I resisted the bill proposed for allowing the marriage of a man with his deceased wife's sister in a speech made on February 29, 1850, the only speech of mine which has ever been printed; and on June 5, 1850, in a debate on education, I defended the National Society and upheld the doctrine that religion alone had promoted education in this country, and that the Church had taken far the largest and most active share of that duty. This I maintained in opposition to what I conceived to be an utterly unfounded notion that religious differences impeded public education.

But, on the other hand, I never hesitated to uphold complete political freedom independently of religious opinion. I did this on several occasions when it was proposed to modify the oaths of members, but chiefly in support of the rights of Jews to citizenship. The earliest speech which I made of any length was on the second reading of the bill brought in by Lord John Russell for admitting the Jews to Parliament (February 7, 1848). I afterwards, on June 12, 1850, moved for and obtained a select committee to inquire into precedents as to the oaths of members, and to inquire into the mode of administering oaths in Courts of Justice. On this committee—over which I, as mover, presided—Lord John Russell, Sir Robert Peel, Mr. C. Wynne and other eminent members sat ; and upon the strength of their report, which merely related the state of the several Acts of Parliament, and the precedents, especially that of the admission of Mr. Pease, the Quaker, on his affirmation, and the rule of Courts of Justice allowing every man to swear by what is most binding on his conscience, I, on July 26, 1850, together with Mr. John Abel Smith, took Baron Rothschild (who had been twice elected for the City of London) to the table of the House of Commons. Here he took upon the Old Testament the oaths of allegiance and supremacy, which do not contain the words ' on the true faith of a Christian,' and he then proceeded to take the oath of abjuration, omitting the words ' on the true faith of a Christian.' This being done, I moved that Baron Rothschild be allowed to take his seat. My argument was founded upon the fact that the Baron had sworn in the only way which could bind him ; that the law distinguishes between the matter to which the deponent pledges his oath, and the mode in which he pledges it ; that the whole history of the introduction of the oath of abjuration, and especially the enactment that a person sitting in Parliament without taking it is ' to be deemed a Popish recusant convict,' showed that it could not have been intended for any person other than those professing the Christian religion. I still believe the argument to be sound, although it. has since been otherwise decided by the ' House of Lords,' mainly owing to special enactments in relief of Jews from this oath having been made on special occasions. I was complimented on all sides for the speech, but the House declined to adopt the view. Nevertheless, these discussions, it may be hoped, had some effect in tending to the ultimate abolition from the Statute-book of the last fragment of persecution.

I also brought in and passed on two occasions a bill for relieving scrupulous persons who were not Quakers, Moravians, or Separatists, from being sworn in Courts of Justice, and to substitute an affirmation with the usual penalties of perjury, as in the case of Quakers and others. This bill was rejected each time in the House of Lords ; but the principle has since become law, as part of the Common Law Procedure Act.

I did not hesitate also to support my political views as a reformer. I voted on all occasions for reform to the extent of household suffrage. I spoke and voted more than once in favour of the ballot, and in March, 1848, I spoke and voted for the repeal of the game laws. My earliest success, however, in the House of Commons, was in February 1848. Mr. Rolt had been an independent Conservative candidate for Stamford in opposition to the two nominees of the Marquis of Exeter, but had failed. A petition was signed by one-third of all the electors complaining that the electors on this and every occasion had been so coerced by the Marquis that they prayed to be disfranchised. Mr. Rolt asked me if I would bring this petition before the House. I did so, and moved that it should be referred to a select committee. This was on February 12, 1848. I was then comparatively unknown, and in opening my motion I was supported and cheered only by members below the gangway which separates the more advanced Liberals from the supporters of a Liberal Government. However, Lord John Russell at length rose, and stated that the case was brought forward with such moderation, and was in itself so strong, that he must support the motion. Sir Robert Peel was greatly annoyed at this, and answered Lord John in a speech of some irritation, in which he, from error, misstated some legal propositions. I availed myself of this in my reply, which was loudly cheered by the whole Ministerial side of the House, and the motion was carried by a majority of one. The Government, however, referred the nomination of the committee to the Committee of Selection on

Private Bills, and I obtained a committee of nine, in which Mr. Horsman alone went heartily with me. Mr. Henley, Sir John Pakington, Mr. Stuart Wortley, and other strong Conservatives were thus opposed, in reality, only by myself and Mr. Horsman, though some rather moderate Liberals were also on the committee. Three elections were gone into, and the committee unanimously reported that, regard being had to what had previously occurred, they were satisfied the electors had voted under undue bias and constraint. Nothing more, however, could be done than to give this useful hint to the Marquis ; and, indeed, I was myself unable to give full attention to the committee, owing to the death of my mother whilst it was sitting.

In May 1849 Mr. Horace Twiss, Vice-Chancellor of the County Palatine of Lancaster, died. This Court exercises free equitable jurisdiction to any amount where the property and the litigants are in the county ; but there were so many impediments arising from its antiquated and unreformed state that it had become all but a sinecure. Lord Campbell, then Chancellor of the Duchy, with whom the appointment of the Vice-Chancellor rested, wrote to me to ask if I would undertake the office with a view to its reform. I replied at once that this was the only condition on which I would accept it, and that I must be allowed to resign if a bill for its reformation could not be passed. The

VOL. I.   G

salary was 600*l*. a year, which for a sinecure was just that amount too much; in fact, it came out of Her Majesty's privy purse, as the surplus funds of the Duchy form part of her private revenues.

I succeeded in passing a bill which had been prepared some time before by Master Duckworth, but had failed, being opposed by Sir E. Sugden, then in the House of Commons. This draft was brought up to the existing date, and the Court has worked well ever since. I resigned the office when I was appointed Solicitor-General in 1851, and was succeeded in it by Mr. Bethell, afterwards Lord Westbury.

On February 21, 1851, Mr. Locke King, in a thin House, carried by 100 to 52 against the Government his bill for extending the franchise in counties to 10*l*. a year occupiers. The Conservatives purposely absented themselves. I had voted in the majority : Lord John Russell resigned ; but, on Lord Derby's failure to form a Government, he returned to office. Shortly afterwards Lord Langdale retired from the duties of Master of the Rolls, and the Attorney-General, Sir John Romilly, succeeded him. To my very great surprise I was asked to call on Lord John Russell on the subject of succeeding to the office of Solicitor-General. Lord John received me very cordially and said : ' I ought to tell you at once that I intend to bring in a bill for extensive reforms, otherwise I should not have made you this offer.' I replied I was very glad he had said this, as I should not otherwise have accepted the office. In truth I felt very strongly on the subject; and the Chartist movement in 1848, although abortive, had exhibited very ugly symptoms. Even the large body of workmen employed on the Houses of Parliament, 300 or more in number, had declined to be sworn in as special constables, saying they would not go out against 'their order,' though they would preserve the property from harm. Many like circumstances had come to my knowledge on the memorable April 10, 1848,[1] when, together with the late Mr. Brunel, I had the command of the special constables who were entrusted with the protection of the streets between Great George Street and Downing Street, both inclusive, the whole of the district being under the late Honourable John Talbot, Q.C.

In March 1851 I thus became Solicitor-General, and about the same time began acting vigorously on a commission, of which Sir John Romilly, when Attorney-General, had procured the

[1] The day fixed by the Chartists for carrying their monster petition in a vast procession from Kennington Common to the House of Commons. Half a million persons were expected to join in the procession, and the public were filled with apprehensions of violence. London was guarded by a strong body of special constables, besides police and military, and the intended procession was proclaimed illegal. Deterred by these preparations the Chartists abstained from attempting to execute their plan.—ED.

appointment, for reforming the Court of Chancery. The present Lord Chancellor Lord Westbury, Lord Justice Turner, Mr. (afterwards Vice-Chancellor) Parker, Mr. W. James, and others, took more or less active parts in that commission, of which Mr. Chapman Barber was the effective secretary. Sir James Graham and Mr. Henley were also most useful assistants as members of the commission to the professional members of it. Sir John Romilly presided. The effects of that commission are well known to the profession. The expense and delay of the Court have been prodigiously diminished, especially by the abolition of the Masters' offices. The Master of the Rolls and the three Vice-Chancellors, with the assistance of their chief clerks, now do the whole work formerly performed by ten Masters and their chief clerks, and do it much more speedily. The procedure also was greatly improved. Sir John Romilly had before this passed an Act for improving equitable procedure in Ireland, and had introduced and carried the Encumbered Estates Bill for that country which has worked a social revolution of inestimable value there.

As Solicitor-General, under the direction of Lord Truro as Lord Chancellor, I had caused the bills to be prepared by Mr. Chapman Barber which, owing to the resignation of Lord John Russell's Government, were afterwards passed during the

Chancellorship of Lord St. Leonards, who gave the weight of his hearty concurrence to the proposed measures.

In like manner the Act for the amendment of the Patent Law, which had been prepared by Sir A. Cockburn, as Attorney-General, and myself as Solicitor-General, and which actually passed the Commons in 1851, was again brought forward and carried by the new Government in 1852.

Whilst I was Solicitor-General a meeting of all the equity judges and of distinguished members of the Bar was held at Lord Truro's, when it was resolved to found a new Court of Appeal in Chancery, and to establish two new judges, to be called Lords Justices of Appeal, who, together with the Chancellor, should form the full Court, whilst the two Lords Justices together, or the Chancellor alone, could sit as a separate Court. This bill I brought in and carried, and also a bill for abolishing several superfluous offices of the Court of Chancery.

In the spring of 1852 Lord John Russell resigned office,[1] and I of course ceased to be Solicitor-General. Shortly before Christmas in that year, Lord Derby having resigned, a new Ministry was formed by Lord Aberdeen. I went into the country for my Christmas holidays, not having

[1] The Government was defeated by a majority of eleven in a division on the Militia Bill.—ED.

expected to be offered any connexion with the new
mixed Government ; but in the middle of the night
I received a message from Lord Aberdeen request-
ing to see me immediately in town. On visiting
the Earl I was offered the option of the Solicitor-
Generalship, which Lord Aberdeen said he should
prefer, or the vacant Vice-Chancellorship occasioned
by Lord Cranworth, the Vice-Chancellor, accepting
the Great Seal. Lord Aberdeen added that Lord
John Russell had wished him to make the latter
offer. The fact is that Lord Truro had previously
offered me the Vice-Chancellorship which was
afterwards accepted by Vice-Chancellor Parker,
and I had been disposed to accept it, having found
the work of Solicitor-General almost too much for
my health, and a great interference with all domestic
comfort. I spoke to Lord John Russell on the subject,
who requested me not to give up the Solicitor-
Generalship, and I at once said that a word from
Lord John (for whom I always entertained the deepest
respect) was enough. On his own resignation
Lord John wrote me a kind note, expressing regret
for his interference, and with equal kindness begged
Lord Aberdeen to renew the offer of the Vice-
Chancellorship, which I accepted, and was sworn
in just before Hilary Term 1853. In truth my
Solicitor-Generalship had been rendered specially
irksome by my having for forty-eight nights to
fight the battle of the Ecclesiastical Titles Bill

against the Irish members. I heartily approved of the bill, and thought, and still think, it was a most becoming declaration of national adherence to the faith ; but the irksomeness was occasioned by the mode in which the warfare was carried on by some of the Irish members, and its protracted duration.[1]

I have now sat for nearly eleven years on the Bench, during which time I have had to decide many arduous and important cases. On one occasion only have I written my judgment. My reason for delivering unwritten judgments is twofold : first, that I find such writing to be positively injurious to my health ; and, secondly, that the delay which it would occasion would be more injurious to the suitor than could be compensated by any supposed clearness in the judgment.

I did not think it proper to notice the remarks made upon my judgments in this respect by a Lord Chancellor, for the tone of the remarks rendered any notice undesirable ; and on principle I still adhere to the practice of delivering unwritten judgments.

---

[1] This bill was occasioned by what was commonly called the Papal Aggression, which consisted in a decree of the Pope for dividing England into dioceses, to be ruled by bishops taking their titles from English towns. The bill prohibited the assumption of these titles. The first reading was carried by a majority of 332, and the second by a majority of 343. It was stubbornly contested in committee, as mentioned above, by the Irish members, and by some Conservatives who thought it did not go far enough. The third reading was carried by a majority of 217. See also *Life of Dr. Hook*, vol. i. p. 287 sq., and 456 small edition.—ED.

[The remarks here referred to were made by Lord Chancellor Campbell in December 1860, in giving judgment upon an appeal from the decision of Vice-Chancellor Wood in the case of Burch *v.* Bright. The case is described in the 'Saturday Review' for December 29, as one which 'arose out of a partnership dispute, in which complicated accounts had to be gone into with reference to the working of certain patents, the different partners taking very diverse views and giving very conflicting evidence as to the understandings and agreements by which their interests in the patents were to be determined. The whole dispute was one of those tangled and tiresome wrangles to which no one but a judge could endure to listen. The Vice-Chancellor made a decree deciding some of the disputed points and referring others for further inquiry; and this decree Lord Campbell affirmed in every particular, holding, not only that the results which were arrived at were correct, but that in leaving the remaining matters to abide the issue of further investigation, the Vice-Chancellor had taken the only course which the state of the evidence left open to him.'

The comments which the Lord Chancellor made upon the form of the Vice-Chancellor's judgment were to the following effect. 'I am of opinion that the decree appealed against in these suits ought to be affirmed without any variation. I think that by the declaration which it contains, and the inquiries which it directs, complete justice will be done between the parties. I have come to this conclusion after attentively listening to the able arguments at the Bar addressed to me on either side, after having carefully perused the written pleadings, the depositions, and the multifarious documents in evidence, and after having laboriously travelled through the decree and the judgment of the Vice-Chancellor, occupying forty-six pages of a huge quarto volume closely written. Considering my long experience as a judge and the position which, however unworthily, I have the honour to fill, perhaps I may without impropriety venture to say, with the most profound and sincere respect for Vice-Chancellor Wood, that I should have disposed of this appeal, not only with less labour to myself but more satisfactorily and more confidently, had his judgment been more condensed. My attention has been diverted from the main question in the case by elaborate and minute disquisitions as to the bearing of contradictory evidence on subordinate points, and by following the devious paths by which the final conclusion is at last reached. Judgments of such prodigious length, instead of settling, have a tendency to unsettle the law, and instead of sending away the defeated party contented, I can say from my own experience since I have presided in this Court that they rather generate appeals. For although the decree be right, some of the various reasons given for it may be questionable, and a false hope is excited that, impugning these, the decree may be reversed. The verdicts of juries are generally acquiesced in, perhaps because they are given without reasons. An equity judge who has to determine questions of fact cannot follow this course, but there is no necessity for his stating from his tribunal all that passed through his mind during his deliberations, with all his doubts and his waverings. I will further venture to declare my hearty concurrence in the opinion frequently expressed by one of the most distinguished of my predecessors (Lord Brougham), that when, on account of the importance and difficulty of the case, judges after having heard it argued at the Bar take time to consider, they will do well by delivering a written judgment. The judgments even of Lord Eldon would have been still more valuable had he adopted this practice, imitating the example of that illustrious judge, his brother, Lord Stowell, who by his written judgments has composed a code of international maritime law admired and respected by all civilised nations.'

This lecture of Lord Campbell's created no small sensation, and was severely commented upon, with one exception, in all the leading journals of the day. Amongst lawyers it excited not only surprise, but something like consternation, and the equity judges conceived that it would be neither just nor prudent to let it pass without some serious remonstrance on their part. This could be done with all the more effect because the judge himself, who had been the subject of the Lord Chancellor's reproof, maintained an absolute and dignified silence.

The following protest, therefore, was addressed to Lord Campbell by Sir John Romilly (the Master of the Rolls) and the Vice-Chancellors Sir R. T. Kindersley and Sir John Stuart :—

'December 22, 1860.

'Dear Lord Chancellor,—It is with deep regret that we feel called upon to address you in consequence of the words reported to have fallen from you, on Thursday last, in giving judgment in a case of appeal from the decision of Vice-Chancellor Wood ; in which you appear to have commented on the mode adopted by him in giving judgment, both in that case, and generally in cases brought before him, as distinguished from the value to be attached to his decision.

'We are all of us ready and happy, at all times, to receive from you any private advice as to the mode in which we should conduct the business entrusted to us, and we shall endeavour at all times to profit by your suggestions ; but advice given in public assumes the form of a rebuke, and when this is delivered by the Lord Chancellor of Great Britain from his judgment seat it acquires a most solemn character.

'Every judge has peculiar modes of expressing the conclusions he has arrived at, and the trains of reasoning which have led to them, and it is scarcely possible that these should not be susceptible of improvement. But this is, we believe, the first occasion on which any judge has commented on the manner adopted by any other judge in delivering his judgment, as apart and distinct from the value of the reasoning, and conclusions to be found in the judgment delivered.

'We trust that your lordship will forgive us for expressing the alarm we feel at the adoption of a course which, if persisted in, can scarcely fail to interrupt the cordial relations which have hitherto distinguished the intercourse between the judges in this country, both at law and in equity, and the apprehension we entertain lest this should lead to a diminution of the respect hitherto paid by the public to the persons who preside over the judicial tribunals of this country.

'We have the honour to be,
'With great respect,
'Yours, very sincerely.

'P.S.—We have written and sent this letter without any communication with the Vice-Chancellor Wood.'

To this letter the Lord Chancellor replied in the following terms :—

'Torquay: December 27, 1860.

'My dear Master of the Rolls,—I have read with the most respectful and kindly feelings the remonstrance signed by yourself and the Vice-Chancellors Kindersley and Stuart, against the observations I made upon the judgment of Vice-Chancellor Page Wood in the case of Burch *v.* Bright.

'I am sincerely obliged to you for communicating to me your sentiments respecting what may be fitly said by a judge in a Court of Appeal touching the judgment of the Court below. I am sure you will not be offended if I with equal frankness express to you my sentiments on this delicate subject.

'I think that the appellate judge would be guilty of a breach of public duty, and would disgrace himself, if he were, from his tribunal, to make any irrelevant remarks which could be construed into a censure of the Court below ; but I think it belongs to the appellate judge to comment freely on the judgment he has to review, and the manner in which it has been given.

'Such a right I have often known to be exercised in the House of Lords, and in the Judicial Committee of the Privy Council—Courts of Appeal in which I have for many years practised as counsel and sat as a judge. I should not like to repeat the observations which I have heard from Lord Eldon upon some of the judgments of the Court of Session in Scotland; and I believe that he was in the habit of complaining that the judgments of Sir John Leach, when Vice-Chancellor and Master of the Rolls, were too short, as they did not sufficiently inform him of the reasons on which the decree appealed against had been pronounced.

'If anything which fell from me on the occasion you refer to was at all inconsistent with the respect or courtesy due from one judge to another I most humbly beg pardon, and I should be willing to apologise publicly for what I said. But surely if Lord Eldon might complain that a judgment was too short, I might be excused for complaining that a judgment was rather too long; adding that if it had been shorter I could more satisfactorily have disposed of the appeal. I by no means presumed to say that when a judge, after hearing a case argued at the Bar, has taken time to consider, it is his duty to deliver a written judgment; but I thought that I had a not unfit opportunity of again declaring the opinion which I have expressed before, both in public and in private, that this is the preferable course.

'I assure you that when I was transferred to

the Court of Chancery I considered it a great felicity in my lot that I was to be associated with judges for whose learning, talents, principles, and manners I had such a high respect, and it has been a source of much gratification to me that hitherto we have all acted so harmoniously together.

'I have the honour to be, my dear Master of the Rolls and Vice-Chancellors, with the utmost esteem and regard,

'Yours, very sincerely,

'CAMPBELL.']

Both before and since my elevation to the Bench, I have been very actively employed on commissions. I first sat upon a Commission for the Improvement of Church Leasehold Property, in which Sir John Shaw Lefevre took a prominent part. This was before I had entered Parliament. The recommendations of that commission have been carried out, partly by a bill which I passed when Solicitor-General, and partly by subsequent legislation, nearly in the very mode recommended. I was a member of the Cathedral Commission, and of the Divorce Commission, on the recommendation of which the Divorce Court was established. I concurred in this on the ground that virtual prohibition of divorce to the poor, whilst it was allowed to the rich, was an insupportable anomaly. The commission steadfastly set its face against altering the ground of divorce. I was personally acquainted with many cruel cases affecting men of moderate means, and the great influx of business to the new Court arose much more from unremedied injunctions than from wanton laxity of conduct.

I was chairman of a Commission for inquiring into Legal Education, the recommendations of which I still wish could be effected; the establishment of a Law University, of which the Inns of Court should be colleges; and the granting of a degree of M.L. or Master of Law, which magistrates and others might avail themselves of without the expense of a call to the Bar. Considering the numerous legal appointments in the colonies, I think that education should be indispensable in the barrister, and tested by examination.

I sat on Commissions for Chancery Reform, as has been stated, and for the Consolidation of the Statute Law; on the Commission for inquiring into the Accountant-General's Office in Chancery, the Commission for inquiring into the difference of practice between English and Irish Courts of Justice, and the Commission for inquiring into the Patent Laws.

I also acted on one of the Commissions for reforming the Statutes of Cambridge University, when I laboured anxiously to limit the duration of Fellowships, so as to make them a support and encouragement whilst a career is being sought, and not a premium upon indolence.

Lord Cranworth, during his Chancellorship, requested me to act with Lord Wensleydale and Sir Lawrence Peel, on a Commission for determining the long pending claim of the Crown of Hanover to some of the Crown jewels in the possession of Her Majesty. This claim was raised, and a commission appointed to investigate it, in the time of William IV. The commissioners were Lord Lyndhurst, Lord Langdale, and Sir Nicholas Tindal; but the death of the latter put an end to the commission before they had reported. The new commission, by its report, adjudged as to some few jewels that the Court of Hanover had made out its claims, and they were immediately restored. It was at the anxious desire of Her Majesty that the new commission was appointed.

It happened to be necessary to examine the will of George III., and it was found to be in the possession of a highly respectable solicitor ; for the sovereign alone cannot leave his will in public custody. It remains with his executors, and passes to their executors in succession. This is an anomalous state of things, and should be rectified : it arises from the sovereign's testament not being susceptible of probate.

As regards my connexion with the work of the Church, I may mention that I have been on the Committee of the National Society since the year 1834, and that I belong to numerous other

Vol. I.   H

Church societies. I am convinced that the Church alone, from its organisation, from the wealth of its members, from its endowments and its parochial subdivisions, has the means of bringing home religious instruction to the people. I have resided nearly thirty years as a householder in the parish of St. Margaret, Westminster, which is united to that of St. John for the maintenance of the poor. When I first knew the district the two parishes together had but two churches, one dilapidated chapel of ease, five clergymen, and about two hundred or three hundred children at school. They now have ten churches, twenty-six clergy, and more than ten times the original number of schools; and a fund for paying additional clergy which is permanently endowed with more than 25,000*l*. All this has been effected by working the parochial system. Miss Coutts, Archdeacon Bentinck (a canon), and the daughters of the late Bishop Monk (also a canon) have respectively founded three churches, and Miss Coutts has further built a school and parsonage, and endowed the incumbent; but the rest has been done by purely local exertions. Canon Wordsworth originated the Westminster Spiritual Aid Fund, the fund for paying curates, and himself raised 12,000*l*. of that fund.

I have taken an active part in establishing a free library in the district under Mr. Ewart's Act.

This Act has been largely used in the north of England, and also in many large towns in other parts of the kingdom ; but in the metropolis there is only one free library, though several attempts have been made to' establish one in other districts besides Westminster. Here it has thoroughly answered during the four years that it has existed ; the monthly visits are nearly 3,000, whilst 4,000 persons take out books for reading . . .[1]

[1] At this point the narrative suddenly breaks off with the words : 'I really can write no more.'—ED.

CHAPTER I.

LIFE AT WINCHESTER AND GENEVA. CORRESPONDENCE,
A.D. 1818–1819.

THE foregoing narrative, lucid and interesting though it is, and in some respects minute in its details, would form, if taken alone, but an inadequate picture of the writer's character and life. The high religious principle, indeed, the ability, the industry which always distinguished him, could not fail to be traceable in any sketch of his career; but for a revelation of the inner man, the thoughts, the feelings, the sentiments which constitute the real character, we must look elsewhere. And this want is very thoroughly supplied by his correspondence with the friend of his life, Walter Farquhar Hook. From boyhood to old age the two friends communicated to each other their whole mind, and whole heart, upon every event and every subject in which they were interested. From the beginning to the end of their intercourse nothing was reserved, nothing dissembled ; there was no suspension of intimacy, however temporary ; there was no estrangement, however slight. There was the similarity in principles, in tastes, in interests, and dispositions without which intimate friendship can hardly exist at all ; but there were also those dissimilarities which, within certain limits, tend to strengthen the tie between two human souls, causing as they do a reciprocity of gifts, and leading often to differences of opinion and sentiment which stimulate thought, and suggest matter for serious argument or playful banter, without impairing affection.

Thus both were warm-hearted, and of eager temperament ; but while Hook was naturally impetuous and irascible, his friend was invariably sweet-tempered and kept his enthusiasm under the control of a calm and sober practical judgment. Hook imparted his religious opinions and his passionate love for English literature to his companion—benefits which the other requited by endeavouring to excite in his friend a taste for scholarship, and an ambition to attain a high position at school, and at the University. In this he partially succeeded ; but he could not impart his own aptitude for philosophical and mathematical studies, or for the acquisition of modern languages. Hook, indeed, had a remarkable antipathy to everything foreign, especially French, and cared very little for travelling; while his friend was passionately fond of the latter and enjoyed intercourse with foreigners, partly owing to his great linguistic skill, partly to his social disposition, and his eagerness to acquire information. Speaking generally, it would be true to say that of the two friends my uncle had the more powerful intellect, was more accomplished, more widely read, and more evenly balanced in temperament; but the other had a certain fire of energy, a depth of human sympathy, a fund of peculiar humour, and a touch of eccentricity which enabled him to exercise an extraordinary influence over other men. He had, in fact, qualities which have more affinity to genius than what is commonly understood by great ability or superior talents. The contrast in outward appearance between the two friends as youths must have been curiously striking. Hook was tall, gaunt, pale-faced, red-haired; while my uncle was short, and small limbed, but inclined to be stout, and of a ruddy complexion.

The correspondence begins in the year 1818, when Hook had left Winchester for Oxford, and ends in 1875, the year of his death. Out of this long series I have endeavoured to select such letters as are interesting and instructive in themselves, and illustrate the life and character of the writer. A few have already appeared in the 'Life of Dr. Hook' published a few years ago,

and others should be read in connexion with
letters from Dr. Hook, and Lord Hatherley's letter
to the editor, printed in the same work. The only
long break in the series occurs between the years
1820 and 1828 when my uncle was at Cambridge,
or beginning his professional career in London, and
his friend was at work in his curacies, first at Whip-
pingham, and then at Moseley. I have searched in
vain for any letters belonging to this period. They
were probably swept by mistake into the great
conflagration of manuscripts which was made when
Dr. Hook left Leeds.

The story of my uncle's life falls naturally into
four divisions. I have devoted a chapter to each
of these periods, annexing the correspondence
which belongs to it. It may be noted as a
singular circumstance that the earliest extant
letter of the future Lord Chancellor is one which
relates his share in an act of insurrection against
authority and order—the Great Rebellion at
Winchester.

The language of rapturous affection for his
friend by which these schoolboy letters are distinguished may seem extraordinary and almost
unnatural in a youth of seventeen or eighteen ; but
I have heard my uncle say that no tamer expressions would have satisfied the demands of Hook's
fervid disposition, and the custom being once

established of addressing each other in such high-flown terms, it became quite spontaneous and genuine.

Hook, moreover, was very fearful lest residence abroad should in the smallest degree alienate his friend's affections from himself or shake his allegiance to Shakspeare, and he watched for the least symptoms of failure in fidelity to either with the keen eye of a jealous lover. Hence the letters of December 18, 1818, and January 10, 1819, in which the writer with an earnestness and solemnity partly pathetic, partly amusing, and also with a lucidity and precision significant of the future lawyer, justifies some criticisms which he had dared to make on the great poet, asseverates at the same time his inviolable fidelity to him, deprecates his friend's hasty judgment, and implores him not to execute his threat of breaking up the Shakspearian society which he had founded, and burning the badge of the order.

Few letters from Geneva have been preserved save those of which portions are, printed in the following pages ; but the original collection must have been a very large one, as the friends seemingly wrote to each other every week. It indicates no small exuberance of bodily strength and mental vigour on the part of the writer that besides studying, as he says he did, ten hours a day, he was able to pen such long letters, and to compose a tragedy, 'William Tell,' and other poems, to which allusions are occasionally made in the correspondence.

THE REBELLION AT WINCHESTER.[1]

May 15, 6 a.n.a.[2]

My most beloved Walter,—I would not write to you till to-day because nothing was settled before to-day. We had the day before yesterday a letter from Gabell advising that Wood junior[3] should be sent back, and saying that I went because I would not say that I had been intimidated, and therefore he could not keep me. He added at the end of his letter ' by your eldest son's departure Winchester loses one of its brightest ornaments.' I would not tell anybody else of this because they would think me vain, but I always tell you, my dear Hook, of everything. Wood junior returns to-morrow, and my father has written to Gabell asking him to take me back till the end of the half year. I am sure if I go back I shall be miserable. My father is vexed because, not having been at a public school himself, he

---

[1] See *Life of Dr. Hook,* vol. i. p. 18, and 608 small edition.

[2] *i.e.* A.D. 1818 : a.n.a. signifies anno nostræ amicitiæ, 'the year of our friendship.' All the early letters between the two friends are dated in this way.

[3] Western Wood.

does not know much about them, and so cannot be persuaded by the arguments of all my other relations that there is no disgrace in being expelled in such a cause. As for me, I would not have been out of the rebellion on any consideration ; and I am sure we are all much obliged to you at Oxford for drinking the healths of the rebels.

I believe I gave you an account of everything prior to our seizing Etheridge's[1] keys on Thursday after ' bells,' at a quarter to four o'clock. We then entered into college, and, with the assistance of some college fellows ready for the purpose, rushed into the porter's lodge, and, having pinned Dickins to the wall, secured all the keys of college. When the great gates had been shut a minute or two, D. Williams saw us all armed with cudgels, and came down. He made some harangue ; but we told him that it was not at all owing to his conduct that we had taken up arms, but to the tyranny of Gabell alone, which our souls could no longer brook. We further told him that he should have free ingress and egress, and that his friends also, if not too numerous, should be admitted into college. We then with scobs[2] and faggots blocked up his door which leads

---

[1] The butler. This former letter has been lost.

[2] A Winchester word for a piece of school furniture, which was a desk and box for books combined.

into quadrangle, for in case we were forced from that space without quadrangle, extending from the stables to the great gate, we meant to enclose ourselves within middle gate and the gate in the seventh chamber passage. We also blocked up the passage into quadrangle from Clarke's and H. Huntingford's apartments, neither of whom was then at Winchester. Our men were divided into eight regiments. I was lieutenant of one. These divided among themselves the divers duties of watching, breaking open doors, &c. Soon after we had secured ourselves, Wigget, who commanded at commoners' gate, sent to say that Gabell, Puffers, some servants, &c., were at the door trying to force it. Bailey and Wigget were nearest to the door, the former holding the key on the outside. Gabell said : 'Bailey, you had better open the door.' W.: ' Sir, you have no chance.' G. : ' Wigget, you are no longer prefect.' W.: ' Sir, I could have told you that, for if we had not broken out prematurely, the prefects would have sent you a paper of resignation, which was by mistake left in commoners.' This was the fact. Mr. T. P.: ' Let me in, let me in ; I will fight any six.' Dobson at the gate behind Wigget : ' I wish we had you in here, we would break your head for you ; only if we let you in others would come too.' The party then left the gate. In the meantime the Warden had sent down a paper saying that the last rebellion arose from no grievances being stated, and begging to know ours. We said we would send them up next morning ; because we thought it would seem like fear to send them up at first. After Gabell, &c., had left the gate they came round to the Warden's bow-window and took down our names. I was not on duty there, but I went to show myself, as did all the rest, that my name might be taken down. We then nailed up the Warden's door. I got the first nail myself and struck it in, the noise bringing the ugly phiz of Lissmore out of the window. Malet then said : ' Let me strike, as I am stronger ; ' which I did. Lissmore said he knew Sir Alex. Malet's name, and the Warden declares, as I understand, that he will bring him before the House of Peers unless he has ample satisfaction. I forgot to tell you that parties with many flints from quadrangle were placed on the top of the tower over porter's lodge, which commands all college, and at top of the towers over middle gate. I was sent with a party to reach college chapel tower. After breaking open some doors (as keys broke in the locks, they were so rusty) I ascended, second fellow, to the top of the tower, and saw Gabell and Puffer in commoners' court. There were three loud universal cheers when this point was gained, and laurel branches and flags (our handkerchiefs) displayed. Soon

after we gained the top of hall. We remained
unmolested during a great part of the day. At
seven in the evening, Barnard, the brother of the
Prebendary, putting his head out of window with
Hollis, said he only wanted to ask a civil question.
It appeared afterwards to be a question civil in
law only. We let him in, much against my wish ;
but Porcher and Ward were the first day's captains (two captains were chosen daily from the
council of twenty, of which I was one), so that he
was let in. He stayed an hour palavering, and
said he must read the Riot Act, but he would give
us a night to consider, and would come at seven
in the morning. We set watches for the night of
two hours a company ; but most of the leaders
watched more. I watched at the great gate, of
which I kept the key, till half-past one. Then I
went into chambers, where there were comfortable
fires all night, threw myself on a bed, and at two
got to sleep, and slept till four. I then watched
again till the time of our marching out. In the
morning, at seven, came the magistrate (many of
us wished again to keep him out), and said we
were committing a felony in keeping the keys, and
summoned us in the name of the King, adding
that, if any were found in arms, should the
soldiers enter, they would be sent to prison.
Some were rather frightened at this. We again
sent up our terms, which we had sent up once

this morning, containing our grievances, which I mentioned, I believe, in my last. They were refused ; but Urquhart, at the window, asked for a parley. He said that Gabell did not want us, and we might all go. The magistrate, too, said that if we went out he cared no more. We all then marched out at nine o'clock, to go to the ' George.' In the churchyard we were met by a body of about twenty soldiers, who, notwithstanding B.'s agreement, charged us. We had thrown away our cudgels in college, so they easily took Jones and Fredericks prisoners. However they afterwards liberated them and invited them to dinner, saying the attack was a mistake, as they did not know Barnard's agreement. Then Gabell wanted a conference in commoners. We all of us went there. We went up to know who were to be expelled. He soon after called up Porcher and Malet and sent them off ; then Wigget, Hyde, and Morris, and then me. He would not expel Copleston and Martin ; and though they came up and dined up in town, and had given their honours that they would share the fate of all, they basely went down to commoners. Well, when we were expelled, all the windows in college and commoners were broken at leave out. Almost all commoners came out, and a great number then set off directly for their homes. Jones headed a party of thirty over college wall. We dined about six, at the 'George,' many having gone home, some having been forced back, and some having broken their honour by going back. We slept at the 'George.' In the middle of the night West-combe came to see me in bed, and asked me to get up, which I did. Then he wanted to persuade me to return, saying that all the college boys had re-turned but those who were expelled, and that Gabell would receive me again if I returned with him. I said I was very much obliged to him for being so friendly to me, but that my honour was dearer to me than my life. He behaved in a very gentlemanlike way, and said that he could not press me, since it was on a principle of honour that I refused. He then went away. Abbot, ——, and our two selves went home in a chaise. I hear from Winton that many have returned, and that Gabell has made eight boys prefects, but that these prefects are much bullied, and that boys are daily being expelled. My dear Hook, I do not think Gabell will take me back, and I hope not. I have now told you everything I remember.

Adieu, God bless you! Thus prays your ever affectionate friend,

WILLIAM.

London: May 18, 1818.

My dearest Hook,— . . . Certainly I should have thought that if my father sent me back I was in some degree acquitted of my promise. But, besides that, I could not bear to be seeing Gabell, and the being under his power, after having thus rebelled against it. Moreover, he inflicted corporal punishment on the college prefects, which I should esteem such a disgrace that I would rather be expelled forty times. I was sorry, my dear Walter, to find you disapproved of the rebellion. I must confess, upon cool thought, it does not appear to me that any boys are justified in using violence against their masters; but surely if any were, we were. You forget that his giving so few remissions for commoners speaking, his giving no holiday for Leopold, and none for Hombourg's marriage, though other public schools have a fortnight additional holidays, and his nearly expelling a prefect for the usual practice of setting a watch, all happened this half year. Much do I thank you for refuting such foul calumniating lies (I must call them so) as were spread about concerning me. You always act so friendly a part with me: you are a true, dear, dear friend.

The reason I am in such a hurry is that I am hardly in time for post. I have delayed, waiting for Gabell's letter, which was sent to the City.

VOL. I.   I

He will not take me back; but now my father has got my brother taken back, he is almost, if not quite, appeased. I am soon to go to Geneva, which I now hear, though I knew it not before, I should have done had there been no 'row.' My good friend, my uncle,[1] is there, who said in a letter that the English there are very dissipated, but that several young persons, saying they would avoid English society in order to learn French, do not mix with them. I certainly shall be one of these. But, alas! it grieves me that we shall not meet now for some time. My dear Hook, do not grieve too much at this. I am to go soon, but I know not when, and I know not how long I shall have to stay; and thence I shall go to Cambridge. . . .

I trust, my dear friend, that I shall be able to avoid bad society at Geneva. Oh, I pray to God that I may! My uncle will stay there till I get to him. He is an uncle whom I know to be capable of giving me excellent advice, and therefore he will be an amazing advantage to me. I hear the system of teaching is excellent, and they always examine you the next day as to what the lecture was about on the preceding day, so that you must always be attentive to the lectures. Mathematics are very much taught, and there are also lectures on law which will be useful to me; for all law is in some manner connected. Besides, I shall obtain

[1] Mr. Page.

an accurate knowledge of French, and shall perhaps be enabled, if I find time, to learn Italian. The only thing, my dear Hook, that grieves me is that I shall be so very far removed from you whom I love, whom I adore. It seems fated that we should not meet; but I love you beyond measure; believe me, I love you.

God bless you! From your adoring friend,

WILLIAM.

ON THE EVE OF DEPARTURE FOR GENEVA.

London: May 22, 1818.

My dearest Friend,—This is probably the last letter which I shall send you from this place. I shall most likely leave for Geneva to-day or to-morrow. Perhaps I shall go alone, but that is not settled yet; because there is a young person of the name of Read (or some such name) whom my father wishes me to go with, if he leaves London soon enough. Of course, as you may imagine, I vote this a very great nuisance indeed; for I know nothing at all of this person. . . . Pray do not be desponding: we yet may meet and be happy one with another. I pray God that it may be so. . . . I hope that I shall be able to hold firm to my religion, to which at present I feel myself entirely devoted, and by God's help I think I shall so continue. Pray for me, my dear Walter, that I may not fall into temptation. Do not be

I 2

so melancholy; the disappointment, I am sure from my own feelings, must be grievous, very grievous; but we must submit with patience, and with a hope that we shall soon meet one another once more. I long to hear from you an account of your studies, and, as your collections must now be over or fast approaching, how you have succeeded, or are likely to succeed in them. Oh, my dear friend, do attend, I beseech you, heartily to your studies, for I have set my heart upon your getting first-class honours! It would be such an honour to you through life, that I should rejoice at it as much as in my own. For nothing can possibly give me greater joy than any honour or advantage accruing to my dear and only friend. Therefore I entreat you, if you have any love for me, to prosecute your learning diligently; for I know you have considerable talents, and will, I think, make a due use of them. You will think that I am running on in too prosy a style; but, to tell you the truth, I feel by no means in a lively humour. . . . Do pray let us write often, that thus we may as far as possible atone for our absence. It will be a long, long absence, longer than any that we have yet undergone. But, wherever I go, no absence shall ever be able to efface from my mind the fond remembrance of my dearly loved Walter. I cannot, my dear, good friend, write by any means a long letter now, as I am going off in such a hurry; but, however, do not think that my love is scant. If I were to measure out the length of my letters by my love, I should have to write whole volumes.

God bless you my dearest, dearest Hook!

First Letter from Geneva.

June 8, 1818.

My dearest Walter,—I fear that you will think I have been very negligent; but I was forced to delay my letter because my uncle has been making an expedition to various mountains of the Alps in which I have accompanied him, so that I was always either walking or in a vehicle. . . . My uncle has now left this place, and I am now fixed in my *pension* (as they call it in French), in which I have been about three days. At present I have about three chapters of Tacitus to translate every morning into French; and there is a mathematical master with whom I shall study three times in the week at this house, and also go to his house three times in the week at six o'clock in the morning, an hour which I have chosen myself as it will give me more of the day. At present I am thus only preparing myself to be admitted into the Auditoire, for which one examination will take place in August, and another in October. My chief difficulty is my not having as yet a thorough knowledge of French, which, however, I hope to have in three weeks' time. I can understand it sufficiently to know what the people say, but cannot talk very fluently myself. There are three other persons at this *pension*, and a number of little boys about eight or nine years old, who only dine and sup with the family. One of three, who have, like myself, a room to themselves to sleep and study in, is an English-man, but as he very seldom will talk in English to me, I must, of necessity, soon learn French. The family consists of an old, very good-natured gentle-man, who is my master, two of his sons—one about twenty-five, the other nineteen—and his four daughters, of whom the two eldest are very amiable ; the other two are very young and do not talk much. We are allowed to do our exercise when we like, and at all other times to walk about unless it is the hour of the mathematical or any other master. Our hours are very regular. We breakfast at eight : at least if you choose to come down then you find it ready, or you find it there if you prefer it half an hour later. We dine at twelve, we drink tea at six, and sup at nine, and, unless there is a party, go to bed at ten. No parties can be kept up later than midnight without special leave from the chief syndic (four syndics are the governors of the Canton and Republic of Geneva), who will not give permission, except the party is on account of a marriage, or some such great occasion.

I see very plainly that if a person likes he can be very idle here. However, as I am very anxious to enter the Auditoire in August, I only go out at eleven to bathe in the lake (for the weather is more oppressively hot than I have ever felt it in England), and to walk after seven in the evening, when we have done tea, till supper-time, because the evenings are so very beautiful, and if I did not go out at all I should certainly be ill. When I get into the Auditoire I shall study mathematics, algebra, &c., which will be of immense advantage to me. Nor shall I neglect Latin or Greek, for the gentleman with whom I am, whose name is Du Villard, is the Professor of Belles Lettres at Geneva, and has too much affection for his favourite classics to neglect them. Besides, I read them very much by myself, dividing my time between them and study of the French grammar. I have got here my Æschylus and Sophocles, and my Homer, an Herodotus, a Longinus, a Cicero's 'Orations,' an Horace, a Juvenal, a Tacitus, a Virgil and Ovid, a Xenophon's 'Cyropædia,' the ' Funebres Orationes,' and an old Greek Testament of yours, which I found being kicked about at Winchester. I have not brought many English books; but I could not deny myself old Shakspeare, which, together with the *Spectator*, makes my English library.

My dear Walter, I have given you this full account of myself because you have always told

me that you delight in hearing all that concerns
me, and so, having vanity enough to think this
possible, I always take you at your word. Pray,
pray do the same with me : let me know all about
you, and especially let me know if there are any
hopes of your coming here. Oh, that there may
be ! nothing could make me so happy here as the
presence of my dear Walter. You have no reason
to think that there is any one here to supplant you
in my unalterable affection. The Englishman is
not very agreeable, and the two Frenchmen are
lively enough, but do not much abound in sense.
One of them is a Parisian, and speaks with a most
excellent accent, so that I shall be enabled by him
greatly to improve my French. My dear, dear
friend, how much I want somebody to communicate
my thoughts to ! Separated by such a distance
from my relations, I feel more than ever the want
of that invaluable blessing, a kind and good friend.
But how could you say at the end of your letter
' parted for ever ' ? My dear, dear friend, I see no
reason to think of such a thing : such a thought
would make me perfectly miserable, and I beg that
you will not entertain it yourself. Your verses are
very good, and to me very valuable, because I
know that they flow from the heart. . . . I wish
very much I was back in England ; but still, though
at such a distance from home, I must prefer this to
Winchester. Here we are treated like gentlemen ;

there we were not.   Here I can be as much by myself as I like ; there I never could be alone, but still,
though amidst such a crowd, always felt myself alone
and destitute, because that one person whom alone I
could love was absent.   By-the-bye, I have not told
you that to my great annoyance Porcher in London
asked me to write to him once in two months, as
he thought I should like to hear of news from
Winchester.   However, that matter is soon settled :
it shall be first once in three months, and then not
at all ; so that this does not cause me much dis-
quiet.

May you be happy ! and that he may see his
dearest adored friend soon is the prayer of your
devoted   WILLIAM PAGE WOOD.

Geneva: September 6, 1818.

I have broken, as you see, the rule of once a
week, as it is nearly a fortnight since I sent my
last letter.   But Thursday and Sunday are my
only writing days, all the rest of our time is so
much occupied.   I was going to write to you on
the Thursday before last, but I was prevented—I
must confess, in rather an agreeable manner—by the
arrival of my dear father, mother, and sisters. . . .
My father only stayed here till Tuesday last : he
then set off for Chamounix, and intended to proceed
as far as Milan.   He will return in three weeks'

time, and will make some stay here if the Parliament does not meet in October ; and I am sure I hope it will not, for I shall then be able to see him much more than before. For our vacation begins on October 1, and we shall then have four weeks with only Latin and Greek to do, which will be nothing, after such complicated studies as before, and there will be two weeks with nothing to do at all. I could seldom find time to see my father before four o'clock in the afternoon, so that you may conceive we are rather busy, and I was then forced to put off the writing out of some lectures, until my relations had gone. You may easily imagine what a great pleasure it must be to have the society of my relations here, since I am entirely without a friend in this place. There is not one person here that I like more than another, and not one that I would trust with the most unimportant secret. How I wish that my dear, dear loved friend were here, if only for a day! it would give me such infinite pleasure. . . .

I have had a letter from my eldest brother, and he says that Gabell, in the character which he sent home, said ' that he heard I was in Switzerland, and hoped that I should do well, for that he should always be glad to hear of my welfare.' This liking which he seems to have had for me may make me appear perhaps very ungrateful ; but let me assure you, Walter, that I thoroughly weighed beforehand whether it would be ungrateful in me to join the rebellion, and I thought that certainly the injustice of Gabell in general (though, perhaps, not to me) was such that I ought not to refuse concurrence in any action which showed him that we could not submit to it without indignation. Indeed, had I been roused by a sense of private wrongs, I should have thought myself much less justified, since I should have shown myself selfish. Even now I feel, as I always have felt, gratitude to Gabell for his particular kindness to me; and now that I have shown him that I have not a slavish spirit, I would give anything to have it in my power to do him a benefit. I wish since I am now upon this old and, I dare say to you, stale and disagreeable subject (which I beg pardon for stupidly introducing), that if you see Mr. West-combe you would thank him as much as possible, *most heartily* from me for his kindness the night before I left Winchester.[1] . . . He showed himself to be a man of feeling (for I know that he only wished my advantage) and a man of strict honour. I mention this because if you could find an opportunity of thanking him, you would do me a great favour, as I do not think that I performed that duty sufficiently at the time.

Perhaps you will say, ' Why do you thus bring up such old stale things, instead of telling me what

[1] See above, page 112.

you are doing at Geneva?' But, indeed, were I to
tell you that, it would be nothing but a dull weekly
routine of lectures. I do these lectures generally
by myself. Now and then, if there is a hard one,
the Frenchman of our *pension*, who is not very
bright, comes and begs that I will do it with him.
When I have no lesson I read either Latin and Greek,
since we do but little of either, or our friend—yes,
friend—Shakspeare. Sometimes I take a boat
upon the lovely lake, and generally, when I can
squeeze in two hours of spare time, indulge in a
swim, for the water is so delightful that I seldom
stay in less than three-quarters of an hour at the
very least. The other day I performed rather a
feat in swimming the lake and back again, a distance of a mile and a half or rather more, without
stopping, and passing through several currents
which cross the lake, amongst which is the river
Rhone itself, which enters the lake in a most dirty
condition at one end, and goes out a most heavenly
blue colour at the Geneva end. . . . God bless you,
my dear, dear only friend !

PROTESTATION OF FIDELITY TO SHAKSPEARE.

Geneva : December 18, 1818.

My dear Walter,— . . . You must have some
strange prepossession against me with regard to the
French plays, for at present I detect nothing but sins
against Shakspeare. I reverence the great poet as

much as I always did and always shall. The expression *lutulentus* seems to me, on second thoughts, considerably too strong;[1] but I do not think that anybody of any taste can think that much is added to the dignity of tragedy by the porter's speech in 'Macbeth' or the porter's speech in 'Henry VIII.' I merely cite two flagrant instances of *quod tollere vellem*. I do not think that he who would try to defend such passages as these, or others which might be selected, is a true friend to the great poet, for in my opinion they were written to amuse the people, and Shakspeare had a finer and nobler mind than to think that they could be any ornament to the piece. Far be it from me to be fastidious on his anachronisms, as on the 'seacoast of Bohemia,' for such defects do not at all take off from the interest of the piece. And even those parts which are not ornaments, and might have been omitted, I do not regret that Shakspeare wrote, for I think a great genius always writes in a bold, irregular manner. One might say in comparing the French poets to Shakspeare, as in comparing Homer to Virgil, that Racine (for instance) never falls so low as Shakspeare, nor does he ever mount by any means so high. For my part, I was always fond of native genius uncramped

---

[1] I have not found the letter in which this epithet occurs, but the present letter indicates pretty clearly how it had been applied to certain passages in Shakspeare.—ED.

by rules. The very reason why I said I thought
Corneille the best of the French poets is because he
lived before that time when the unities and the
Greek models were insisted upon ; and, therefore,
his unfettered genius could better display itself.
I like Homer ten thousand times more than Virgil,
and Shakspeare ten million times better than all
the French poets put together. Far from burning
my ribbon, I have regarded it as a badge of the
most noble order, and I feel myself conscious that
I have not changed one tittle of my opinion of St.
Shakspeare since I took the oath of the order, nor
have I fallen into a single heresy against the
doctrines of that oath. I always defend Shakspeare
to the utmost of my might, nor do I admit to
any but yourself that there is a single blemish
in one of his works. You say, too, in the end
of your letter, ' those who think that much is
to be taken away, &c. ; ' but if you look at the
quotation you will not find anything like the word
' much.' I willingly recant *cum flueret luculen-
tus*, which is more applicable to the Germans ;
but I think he who says that Shakspeare wrote
every passage with the idea of ornamenting his
piece, and nothing with a view to gratify the
vulgar, is an enemy instead of a friend to the divine
author. . . .

My dear, dear Walter, how happy would it
make me if you could by any means contrive to

make a little trip here before next summer! We shall have a long vacation from June till August— that is to say, vacation at the Auditoire—though I shall still have to pursue my lessons of Latin and Greek with M. Du Villard. However, I fear you will not be able to execute this project, and I will speak no more of it, because I believe that you would, of yourself, be ardent to come here if you could. For, notwithstanding you have formed one impossible idea, that of my deserting Shakspeare, who, with you, shares my friendship (yes! and old Shaky always will), still, you will not, I trust, form the *very* impossible one that I could ever cease to have you continually present to my thoughts.

We have got about thirty Greeks here who have run away from the Grand Signor. I should like very much to know them, as they are very well instructed in ancient Greek, and their conversation is said to be very entertaining. They were immensely rich, since the head of the family had more than two millions of English money ; and they have managed to save one million.

By-the-bye, have you read the new work of Lord Byron, the ' Curse of Minerva ' ? I think I never read such an infamous publication or one more worthy of being burnt by the hands of the common hangman. . . . I must finish my letter, but not without assuring you that I love you and Shakspeare, if possible, more than ever ; and I am, as truly as ever, your most affectionate, devoted, and only friend, W. P. Wood.

P.S. The long-threatened letter of H. has not yet arrived, and I begin now to repose in security. Nor have I received another from Porcher. Indeed, I took the most effectual way not to receive any, as I did not choose to answer his last.

Fidelity to Shakspeare vindicated.

Geneva : January 10, 1819.

My dear, dear Friend,—I thank you much for your last long letter. You are determined never to understand what I say about Shakspeare rightly ; you always think that I have such an absurd idea as to compare him with French authors in the first place ; in the second, you say I do not like the English style of plays ; and in the third, that I do not think Shakspeare a model of a much greater perfection than any author that has yet appeared. These charges are very heavy ones if well founded, but I am glad that with a safe conscience I can declare them to be utterly groundless. As you have been able to form such ideas, you must think my taste, little as it was, much debased, and I must have sunk much in your opinion, if not in your affection ; therefore, I am sorry that I ever entered upon the topic. Let me only explain my meaning in regard to the porter's speech in ' Macbeth.' I do not mean that I dislike a mixture of comedy and tragedy ; I only meant that I did not think the speech very comic, or, at least, that I thought it of a low comic order. Rather than break up a society the foundation of which is attended with such dear, such sweet recollections, rather than be degraded from an order of which I have not yet felt myself unworthy (although you think me so in wishing to burn your ribbon), I assent to every opinion of yours, which, if well sifted, differs not, I think, much from my own. For you allow that, as a human being, Shakspeare must have some fault, only that he is nearer to perfection than any other— an opinion which I have always held and still hold most tenaciously. I have only had the audacity to point out what seemed to me the nearest to a fault in perfection. You allow that there must be some fault, but do not admit this to be one ; and much, indeed, must my audacity be punished if you mean to disgrace me by burning the order. As I said before, never have I mentioned my opinions to any one else ; but, having always been accustomed to open every thought of my heart to you, I have thus offended you with regard to this point. But to show you that I have not broken my oath which I swore on my honour (which, I believe, you will think unstained), I here swear to it again, adding

further, upon the same honour, that you may no
longer mistake my opinion, first, that I value the
French trash so little that without the least pain, on
your wish and probably without your expressing it,
I shall never read another French play ; second,
that no kind of style can in my opinion come up
to the English style, at least of those few styles that
I know. The French is much too stiff and cold ;
the German rather too enthusiastic ; and the Greek,
in my poor opinion, rather too pompous ; that is to
say, one always finds in their plays the language of
princes, and not enough of natural life. Third, that
I honour, and adore, and love Shakspeare not one
whit less than when I first was admitted to this
honourable order ; that I consider him, as I always
did, a model for every English writer ; and would
that I could imitate in the slightest degree the
grand model ! I consider him as perfect as a
human author can be. But as I see that there
always has been some fault in every great building,
some defect in the best government, and some sin
in the most virtuous man, so I think there must be
some fault in the best author.

I have thus, I think, clearly stated, *upon mine
honour*, my opinion. I flatter myself that I love
Shakspeare no less than you, although you will not
believe it, and tell me that you prefer a German's
or an Italian's love to mine, whilst I am sure either
of these would commit greater offences than mine,

and would find far more faults than I have done, since they have national prejudices of style to combat.

I cannot say that I feel much flattered with the compliments you thus kindly bestow upon me, and, as I think, most undeservedly. I beg you will not burn your ribbon till you send me an answer. Besides, if any one burns it, it is for me to do so ; for if, to my great grief, you persist in wishing to reject me as a heretic from the order, of course I must submit to the harsh sentence, and not force you to quit an order of which you are the founder. You and H. will then remain the sole knights, though I well know that he is tenfold more heretical than I am.

Thus I close for ever this discourse ; and do not think, my dear, dear Walter, that I am at all angry, though at the same time, believe me, I say in earnest that which I have said, and above all that great would be my sorrow were you to expel me from that society which I entered with so much joy. . . .

You will now soon be returning to Oxford and will soon have to undergo your examination or ' little go.' I have no fear, as I do not doubt that it will be honourable to you. I only am a little inclined to believe that you cultivate other muses in preference to those of Herodotus, and that your tragedies, &c., interfere with your studies. I my-

self feel the delights of authorship, but above all
in poetry, for I cannot leave off when I have once
begun, and consequently ' William Tell ' is nearly
finished.

[N.B. Nothing of the French kind in it. . . .]

I have stolen from the night to write this ; and
as it is now near midnight and we get up very
early here (almost like Winchester), I must conclude. My dear Walter, may God bless and preserve you this night and for ever ! and oh ! may
your love to me remain as firm and undiminished
as mine ever will remain to you, that of your
devoted-to-death friend,

W. P. Wood.

EXHORTATION TO INDUSTRY.—RECREATIONS AT GENEVA.

Geneva : February 16, 1819.

My dear Walter,— . . . I am now anxiously
waiting for the decision of your ' little go.' You tell
me that you have been very idle, but I hope that you
only slander yourself as Malcolm in ' Macbeth.' If
you have been so, let me entreat you to amend for
your sake, your parents', and mine. In your plan
of study I was thinking another hour might be
gained in the morning. Seven hours is what I
always find sufficient for sleep, and I have got a
clock with an alarum on purpose to wake me.
However, I do not know what time your chapel
takes ; so perhaps I am now talking without know-

ing anything about the matter. For my part, I generally study ten hours a day—from eight in the morning till twelve, from one to six, and from seven to eight. This is the best plan during the months of January and February, because there are often balls to which one goes about half-past eight and stays till twelve. I now have become a famous waltzer, and begin to show off in the Russian or quick waltz which is the principal dance here. We also dance several German and Italian dances which are very pretty. I find the French *contredanses* very easy. But if I talk more on this subject you will begin to think me a dancing-master, though I assure you the dancing-master here thinks it no ignoble business. He calls himself professor of dancing, and one day, when I made a bad step, told me that if I did such a thing again I should be a disgrace to my country. He is a little man of Piedmont, for the Genevese are too grave for such light occupations. As our professor of botany will make a journey in March, we shall be examined by him before his departure, so that I am getting up my botany as fast as possible. This is rather convenient, as it will take off beforehand a tolerable load from the great examination. I forget whether I told you that I am following a course of law of M. Rossi, who was a professor of law at Bologna, and is reckoned very clever. I like his manner very much, for he enlivens a study which of itself is but dull with all the brightness of an Italian imagination.

Your flattery (for I must say it was such) at the end of your letter must have been intended to conciliate me so that I might not scold your idleness. However, I repeat again and again that if you are idle you must quickly amend, or soon it will, perhaps, be too late, and you may never acquire those habits of attention which are so necessary for any one who devotes himself to the study of the law.[1] But you will begin to think me a proser, and perhaps, too, a little impertinent for presuming thus to advise my elder and superior. However, the little ant grovelling upon the earth sometimes gives a lesson to man the master of it.

FRIENDLY CRITICISMS. ROSSI'S LECTURES ON ' ROMAN HISTORY.'

Geneva : March 2, 1819.

My dear Walter,— . . . Geneva is very gay now, and I always try to get over my business by eight or nine o'clock that I may have the pleasure of relaxing myself by a ball after a day of hard study. I have become quite a waltzer, since few quadrilles, or as they are here called country dances, are danced. However, I believe the season finishes by the middle of this month, and I confess that I

[1] It was at this time intended that W. F. Hook should make the law his profession. Vide *Life*, vol. i. 19, 49, and small ed. pp. 14, 38.

prefer the relaxation of bathing in this delightful lake in summer to all the *soirées* of the winter. Besides, in summer we always make one or two tours on foot amongst these beautiful mountains, and how I wish that you could make one here with me ! How delightful would it be to wander together in some of the most romantic parts of this most romantic country !

I see that you are still a little in Escott's company, by your taking in the paper with him, and I wish that you would learn with him, for, though it may not be very agreeable, I think it might be very advantageous to you. I am glad, however, that you have had enough power over yourself to set to work in earnest. Your greatest fault, I remember, was to like the modern classics to the utter exclusion of the ancient, not forgetting another fault which I know not whether you have yet reformed, that of despairing at the least little check that thwarts your wishes. These are the only two faults that I know in you, and they are not of a very grave nature, although the consequences might be grave, especially of the last, even in a moral point of view, if you indulge too much in those desponding ideas which are sometimes traceable in your letters, as when you say that you are sure you never can be virtuous, &c., while you know at the same time, to use a strong expression, that 'it is all a lie.' However, forgive me for having so long trespassed upon your patience by a complete sermon, not to mention the impertinence of my advising and correcting, or rather thinking to correct, one who is my senior in mind as well as years. . . .

How often in thinking of the beauty and the interest of Italy which I hear frequently extolled, being as it were at the very gates, since here begins the famous road of the Simplon, have I figured in my mind a vain imagination of the happiness I should feel could you and I, just at my leaving this place, wander together through that celebrated and delightful land! It is a mere fairy castle without foundation; yet how delightful it would be to meditate together upon that wondrous wreck of human grandeur, whether one considers the stately palaces, the forums which resounded with such eloquence, the temples where triumphant heroes seemed to command the gods themselves, all now crumbling to dust; or whether one considers the wreck of mind, those orators whose souls of fire have subsided into the false brilliancy of modern wit, those heroes who, not content with defending their country, sought to outstretch her wide limits in their gigantic projects, now dwindled into men who submit alternately to Austria and France! The thing most ridiculous is that the inhabitants of Rome still say, 'When we were masters of the world, &c.;' whereas I should have thought that a modern Italian would not mention the name of Rome without blushing.

Talking of the Italians reminds me of the lectures of Signor Rossi, which I find excellent. He has begun by sketching the origin of human societies, has then conducted us to the gates of Rome, and will to-night begin a more detailed account of the Roman law which he will bring down to the discovery of the Pandects, and will then compare it with the Teutonic law which the English kept, when the greatest part of the Continent received the Pandects. Rossi is a great sceptic. He believes scarcely a word of the history of the first 500 years of Rome; thinks it probable that Romulus never existed, certain that he did not give a name or a Constitution to Rome, which in the first case would have been called Romula (a circumstance which has often struck me), and as to the second he shows clearly that all the first institutions of Rome were derived naturally from the state of primitive society. He thinks that the Romans were probably a colony from Cære, since, as you may remember, their wonderful respect for that town, against which they always hesitated to declare war, and to which they sent their gods after the burning of the city, has never been satisfactorily explained. Of course he treats as fabulous the arrival of Æneas; he disbelieves the account of the origin of Rome from a set of robbers, and the story of the Rape of the Sabines. He thinks that Numa is perhaps only an allegorical being, as his name signifies Divine inspiration. All this is founded upon many plausible, not to say good, reasons, which the limits of a letter will not permit me to describe. I make extracts at every lesson, as I have learnt that practice from being obliged to write down all that the professors say at the Auditoire, and these extracts I copy out; so if ever you like to take the trouble of perusing them, you will be able to do so. His style is very luxuriant, as the Italian style at present generally is.

CHAPTER II.

LIFE AT CAMBRIDGE—BEGINNING OF PROFESSIONAL LIFE—
MARRIAGE—DIARY AND CORRESPONDENCE, A.D. 1828–
1847.

MY uncle's letters to his friend from the year 1819
to 1828 have been lost, and we are consequently
deprived of the most faithful mirror of his mind
during that period. His Autobiography, however,
sufficiently indicates how steadily the work of
education and preparation for the career which
lay before him was being carried forward.

His early education, indeed, owing to the
peculiar circumstances in which he was placed
after he left Winchester, had been liberal in a far
more real sense than the ordinary technical meaning of that term.

The wide range of his studies at Geneva, his
intercourse with foreigners, his acquisition of
modern languages, the curious episode of his
journey to England in the suite of Queen Caroline,
his employment as an agent in Italy to procure
evidence for her on her trial, must have made him
in some respects a man of the world at an age
when the experience of most youths has been
confined to home and school.

He went up to Cambridge the accomplished
and cultivated man, rather than the schoolboy
trained merely in scholarship and mathematics.
His father had been excessively vexed by his share
in the rebellion at Winchester, and, not having
himself received a liberal education, was unable
fairly to estimate his son's powers. He was consequently delighted by the visible proof of ability
which he soon displayed at Cambridge in obtaining a scholarship at Trinity. I have heard my
mother say that she never saw her father, who was
a remarkably self-contained, reserved man, so completely overcome with emotion as when he received
the letter announcing this piece of success. His
son's comparatively low place in the final mathematical tripos was no doubt a disappointment,
though easily to be accounted for by the three
causes mentioned in the Autobiography : first, his
dispensing with a private tutor from motives of
economy ; secondly, the state of his health ; and
thirdly, a disposition to discursive reading which
no doubt greatly enlarged his mind, but at the
expense of some of that minute technical knowledge which would be most valuable in a mathematical examination. This failure, however, was
amply compensated by success in his first trial for
a Fellowship in 1824, when he was elected over
several other men who had been placed above him
in the tripos, although the greater part of the

previous six months had been spent in reading for the Bar rather than for the Fellowship.

His six months' tour in Italy with Mr. Philpotts in 1825–26 strengthened his hold upon the Italian language, of which, as well as of French, he became a consummate master ; while his literary and philosophical interests were quickened and developed, after his return to England, by his intercourse with the Basil Montagus, and his introduction through them to the society of S. T. Coleridge and other eminent literary men.

From November 29, 1828, to March 6, 1829, he kept a Diary, copious extracts from which are inserted at the close of this chapter. It is a record of most prodigious industry. From it we learn that in the compass of these three months, although the larger part of his days and evenings were occupied in the practice and study of the law, he read, amongst other works, Warburton's ' Divine Legation,' considerable portions of Hooker, Collins on ' Free Thinking ' and Bentley's ' Reply,' Bentley's ' Phalaris,' Bird's ' Inquiry into the Human Mind,' Cæsar's ' Commentaries,' parts of Homer, of Greek Plays, and of Theophrastus, besides novels and other light literature. Not only did he find time to read all these works, but to write the criticisms and reflections upon them contained in the Diary, and long letters on a variety of subjects to his friend.

Undoubtedly, however, such reading and writing was only the recreation of his leisure hours, and most of his time and thought was devoted to the law. To this he was actuated not only by a sense of duty, and by a natural ambition to rise in his profession, but by an ardent desire to marry. He was deeply attached to his future wife for seven years before he ventured to declare his attachment, for he considered that it would be dishonourable to entangle her in an engagement before he had acquired a position of complete independence. It was not till the middle of the year 1829, when he was earning about 1,000*l*. a year at the Bar, that he felt justified in making a proposal of marriage, and even then he thought it right to ask his father's consent to the step. This he did by letter, which his father, owing to the preoccupations of business, kept in his pocket for several days without answering. The painful anxiety, not to say agony, of mind which he underwent during these seven long years of toil, and self-restraint, and suspense, lest the prize for which he was labouring should after all be lost, can only be measured by the intense devotion of his whole life to that prize after it had been won. When he was Lord Chancellor, having to return thanks for his health being drunk at a dinner given in Trinity, Cambridge, on the occasion of opening the Cavendish Laboratory, he combined in one epigrammatic sentence a most happy and graceful compliment to his college and his wife. 'The day,' he said, 'on which I became a Fellow of Trinity was the proudest and happiest day in my life except one, and that was the day on which I ceased to be a Fellow of Trinity.'[1]

Never, indeed, were the heartstrings of two human beings so completely intertwined. Neither husband nor wife was able thoroughly to enjoy any pleasure without the society of the other, and there can be no doubt that he valued her company more than that of the most distinguished or most interesting person in the world. All his arrangements for vacation tours were made with a special view to her comfort and enjoyment, and his decision in 1852 to accept a judgeship rather than the office of Solicitor-General was unquestionably determined by his thinking that the demands of the latter office upon his time in the evening subjected her to too much loneliness. On the first occasion that he stayed on official duty as Lord Chancellor at Balmoral he was invited to remain for a few days beyond the term of his official attendance ; but he

---

[1] Professor Westcott was so much struck with the saying that he suggested to the Rev. B. II. Drury that he should turn it into a Latin epigram.

The following is Mr. Drury's version, which he has kindly allowed me to insert here :—

'Ille dies vitæ mihi felicissimus in quo
Ordinibus vestris consociatus eram.
Quid loquor ? ex isdem felicior abstulit hora,
Inque magis grato fœdere vinxit Hymen.'

declined on the plea that he was anxious to return home, as he and his wife had never been so long separated. The excuse was one which thoroughly commended itself to Her Majesty's approval, and she was graciously pleased on the next occasion to invite Lady Hatherley to accompany her husband. The two sonnets which he composed and presented to his wife every year on the anniversaries of her birth and of their marriage (of which several are printed at the end of this memoir), are not only very remarkable memorials of the unfading glow of his affection, and of the deep religious feeling which was blended with it, but evince very considerable skill in the art of verse-making.

The long interval between his marriage in January 1830, and his entrance into Parliament and public life in 1847, was a calm yet exceedingly active period. His professional business steadily increased, and he was often detained at his chambers till a late hour of the evening ; but he filled up the interstices of his time by reading history, theology, and philosophy, and by pouring out his thoughts to his friend in the letters of which the extracts printed at the end of this chapter are of course only samples. Two or three remarks may be made upon these letters.

I. The rarity of any allusions to politics. This was partly, no doubt, owing to a certain difference between the friends in their political views; but also to the predominant interest of the writer in religion, theology, and moral philosophy, believing, as he did, that there were no subjects which more profoundly and vitally affected the springs of all human action. Probably few men ever lived who were more thoroughly familiar with every part of the Bible. He had always been a regular and diligent student of it, and after his marriage it was his invariable custom to read three or four chapters daily with his wife, by which method they read through the whole of the sacred volume every year.

II. The deep sense of sinfulness manifested in these letters is very remarkable. The expressions, indeed, of self-accusation which he occasionally employs in some of his most confidential letters far exceed in severity any to be found in those which I have thought proper to publish. Dr. Hook used to think that he was at one time almost morbid on this point. If so, the defect was not outwardly apparent; but all who knew him well were aware that the modesty and meekness, which constituted one of the chief charms of his character, were mainly due to his deep conviction of the need of an Atonement, and to his humble and absolute reliance for salvation on the merits of his Divine Redeemer. He was more embarrassed, and at times even distressed, by the praise which was so

VOL. I.   L

continually bestowed upon him than any man of whom I ever heard.

III. In close connexion with these characteristics he seems at times to have been quite oppressed by a sense of his comparative uselessness. But just as a sense of sin is one of the surest conditions of an advance in holiness, so a sense and a dread of uselessness acted upon him as an incitement to those works of charity and benevolence in which he was continually engaged, in Westminster and elsewhere. His principal anxiety respecting the great accession of wealth to his father, consequent on the death of the eccentric miser of Gloucester, was that it should be well used. Writing to Dr. Hook on this subject in April, 1836, he says: 'I can only ask your prayers that this accession of worldly means may be a real blessing to my father. I have witnessed so much his goodness of heart in the assistance he has at all times afforded to others, even when he was himself in some difficulties, and have so much reason to acknowledge his kindness to us all in giving us education, involving him in great expense, in order to enable us to make our own way, that I have but little fear that this increased wealth will be employed by him for good.'

The protracted and costly litigation respecting the will by which this wealth was bequeathed to his father, and the anxious and responsible task which devolved upon him in connexion with it, have been recorded in the Autobiography; but it is from other sources that we learn how immediately after the final issue of the contest in his father's favour he, began to make other persons share in his own good fortune. In a letter to Dr. Hook announcing the result of the final appeal, October 1841, he writes : 'I have this day sent a cheque to Glyn's to your account with the Becketts' bank. You will put down the 100l. in the manner mentioned in my last note, and the remainder you will employ as you like. I know of no other objects that have greater claims upon me than your church, except one in my own parish now building, and another which I hope will soon be begun, and one also at Woodbridge, in Suffolk, the place of my early bringing up ; ' to all of which he indicates his intention of contributing.

When Sir Matthew Wood came to reside at Hatherley Court, in the little parish of Hatherley, near Gloucester, about fifty years ago, he started a school with a fairly efficient teacher in a cottage on his estate, and maintained it up to his death in September 1843. Mr. Wood, knowing that it had been his father's intention to build a school and a teacher's residence, lost no time in carrying the project into effect. In May 1846 he opened in person the new school, called Sir Matthew Wood's School, which, with the teacher's house, he had built at his own cost on a site near the parish church. It was incorporated with the National Society, and a certificated master was engaged. Mr. Wood defrayed all the expenses of the school, amounting to about 100*l.* a year, down to the year 1879, when he endowed it with a capital sum of 3,300*l.* I am indebted for this information to my cousin, the Rev. H. W. Maddy, who became rector of the parish in 1856 ; and for some further details in connexion with this subject I cannot do better than quote the following passage from his letter to me : 'From 1846 to 1879, with only two exceptions (one of which was owing to pressure of work when he was Lord Chancellor), he annually visited the school. Each child, without exception, was examined by him in secular knowledge, some three or four hours being given to this work. On many occasions he kindly and patiently listened to no less than twenty or thirty recitations by the scholars. The day of his visit was always looked forward to with peculiar pleasure, and regarded as a red letter one in the school year. He always concluded his annual examination with a very careful testing of the religious teaching. His catechisings were always listened to with the deepest interest and delight, both old and young present feeling that they were being addressed by a singularly humble-minded and deeply religious Christian man, and being shown how helpful the true teaching of the Anglican Church was in real life. It was my privilege to hear more than twenty-five of these catechisings, and I can thank God for the opportunity.'

In one of the letters which are inserted at the close of this chapter, bearing date April 22, 1836, he relates that he and his wife had become teachers in the Sunday schools of St. John's parish, Westminster. This labour of love they carried on till the year 1877, when advancing age and increasing infirmities warned them that it was time to retire. The touching letter to Archdeacon Jennings, announcing their intention of resigning, will be found in its proper place.

The first extract which I have given from his Diary is a part of the first entry; but only a small part. The day was the anniversary of his birth, and he began his Diary with a deeply devout address to God, which occupies several pages of manuscript, and is too long and of too private a nature for publication. He pours forth his gratitude for the 'numerous and continual mercies which I have received from infancy to the present hour.' Amongst which he places first, ' that I was born of Christian parents, and trained up early in habits of piety.' And last, ' that I have been enabled to attain the independence which I have ever regarded as the chief of earthly blessings.' There is a prayer ' that I may not be elated in heart by the recollection of these and other sources of joy and thanksgiving, or attribute to my own worthiness in Thy sight that which Thou hast so bountifully bestowed on me and mine.' And there is a declaration: ' I do most heartily from mine inmost soul promise a more perfect obedience unto Thy will· henceforth, until that awful moment arrive when I must give an account, as well of my past actions, as of the fulfilment of this present vow.'

Such was the spirit in which he entered upon that period of his life of which the following selections from his Diary and letters will supply a full and faithful picture :—

' *November* 29, 1828.—This day is, I believe, the anniversary of my first brief, as well as of my birth, and I have, by my father's interest, earned about 600 guineas in the course of the past year. There was a considerable degree of good fortune in this, particularly in my Parliamentary business, which constitutes more than two-thirds of the whole. I must not, therefore, expect equal success this year ; but, with the assistance of my Fellowship, independence is at least secured for some years. Happiness (as far as this world is concerned) must, I fear, be delayed some time longer. I have decidedly made no way in obtaining any further clients by displaying unusual ability, but I do not think that I have lost the good opinion of any who have entrusted me with business, by betraying incompetency. Sure I am that I have exerted all the powers which I possess, as far as any individual case has presented itself to me, though I fear I have not made the best use of the time allowed me for the improvement of these powers. . . . I have long been struck with the dreadful state of our sanguinary code of criminal law. The broad fact is apparent to almost any one who can think at all that an indiscriminate infliction of the severest punishment upon crimes differing materially in their consequences, both to society and to the moral character of the perpetrator, must not only fail to deter, but, where any additional object can be attained, actually stimulate the offender by offering a premium for the commission of the greater enormity, in the shape of an increased chance of profit upon an equal hazard of failure.' (After criticising at great length the existing laws, and various proposed amendments, the writer proceeds.) 'This subject has long hung heavy upon my heart, but more especially so since the following circumstance oc-curred to me : I had left one evening the sick bed of a young and near relative, then little expected to survive an attack from which it has pleased God to deliver her. Although unshaken at the prospect of death she had yet made the natural remark, " It seems hard to be called away at five-and-twenty." I had walked home with her words yet sounding in my ears. On my return at an early hour the next morning, eager to hear whether the past night had left any room for hope, I was obliged to pass by the Old Bailey, and the mob which surrounded me warned me that an execution was about to take place. I could not help inquiring the circumstances, and learned to my horror that six victims of our accursed system of penal law were about to suffer death, of whom the eldest had not reached the age of five-and-twenty, and not one of them had been guilty of blood. Yet here was a crowd uttering coarse jokes, and rushing with savage ferocity to witness the perpetration of a legal enormity which was to desolate six families, whilst I had felt overwhelmed with grief at the anticipation of the possible loss of a young relation, dying in undisturbed tranquillity of mind, and surrounded by kind friends who would find and bestow consolation in reflecting upon the promises held out to us by our blessed Redeemer! . . . I trust that I shall never forget the scene, nor the feelings which it inspired.'

'*November* 30. . . . I read after breakfast a little of Pistorius's comment on Hartley, having during the last six weeks perused the " Observations " of the latter. Neither the author nor the commentator appeared to me to be more happy than their predecessors in reconciling fatalism with morality. It must be clear to everybody that

fatalism leaves us just as we are, and that it is impossible to extract any rule of conduct from it.
Hartley's "Rule of Life," which is truly beautiful,
and contains many valuable suggestions, is no
proof of the contrary. If he says that his rule
is a part of the pre-ordained system, the same
might be said by any other moralist of any other
rule. There is a fine instance, however, in Hartley's noble sentiments and morality of the folly
of the common supposition that this or that doctrine must infallibly lead to this or that result,
and consequently the book is only fit for the
flames. There is a very close connexion between
Hartley's doctrine and Spinoza's, and yet the
former deduces his proof of revelation from that
which, in the hands of the other, has become pure
atheism. Again, startled as we may be by the
latter word, the morality in the "De Libertate
Humana" of Spinoza is most noble, and his conduct, I believe, corresponded with it. In common
justice to every author his whole doctrine and its
consequences must be taken together.'

'*December* 1. . . . Made considerable way in
Williams's reports, which I am reading in order to
fortify myself with the ammunition of cases, without which our artillery of general principles is of
little practical use. This course of reading was
recommended me when I began to study the law.
It would then, I think, have been useless. I have

now, I hope, pretty well digested (thanks, above all,
to Blackstone in the first instance) the crude mass
of principles which form the basis of our juris-
prudence, where, by dint of playing the civil against
the feudal law, we should ere this have been in a
glorious state of confusion, but for the separation
of our Courts of equity from those of common law.
I now with pleasure find that there is but little to
which I am a total stranger in any of the reported
cases I am reading, and can therefore suffer each
case to amalgamate with those similar to it in my
memory, and to combine with them in establishing
principles, which I trust I may bear in mind when
the dispersed particles which formed it are dissolved.

'Of light reading I have read some of the
correspondence between Warburton and Hurd,
which is very interesting. There is a freedom
and openness of thought and heart in the former
which contrasts much to his advantage with the
oily smoothness of the latter. Warburton is
"veteris non parcus aceti," it is true, but you
know the worst at once.'

'*December* 2. . . . Read a little more of Warburton's correspondence. The latter speaks highly
of Malebranche, and makes a very just observation
on the hasty malevolence which runs down an
author for a single folly. I have also read some
more of the commentary of Pistorius. His ex-

planation of the mechanical philosophy is very ingenious and clearer than that of Hartley, from being selected and brought into one point of view ; though I would by no means detract from the great beauty of demonstration in Hartley, with which all his propositions are linked almost imperceptibly together. I cannot, however, say that I am satisfied with either. Take Pistorius, for instance, on repentance. Should I repent as much of a jump by which I broke my leg, as of a lie or other moral offence; or, rather, can I be said to repent of both ? The feeling is so different that different words ought obviously to be resorted to. Then, again, what forces us to exclude certain motives so as to be actuated by others only ? Do we not deliberately exclude them ? Can I not at will start an idea, or train of ideas, totally unconnected with the last preceding idea ? This is the whole question, and, as far as experience can inform me, I answer in the affirmative. What other criterion can I take ? I read Archbishop King's " Origin of Evil " last August, and confess I very much liked it. I do not deny that absurdities can be pressed in his arguments, but the subject is not free from absurdities taken either way.'

' *December* 5. . . . One decided objection, in my opinion, to the moral consequences of the doctrine of necessity is the impossibility of inferring the existence of a Deity. We are so formed as only to reason from analogy; take away all free-will from man, he can understand it in nothing else; there will be but an infinite series of events, and no origin of all things. All reasoning as to design (Paley's watch, &c.) is done away with; the " watch " is a mere concurrence of the mechanical motives inducing the maker to form it, and is no proof of design according to the necessitarian, for man can have no design. Our notions of the Divine attributes are but extensions to infinity of properties with which we are acquainted; and if we know nothing which originates, neither can we suppose anything of that description; everything will be in time; and here, I think, the grand objection lies that there is no distinction made between the conceiver and the conceived; the thinker is nothing but a mass of thoughts without anything to link them together.

'I do not think that Hartley's proof of an originating Being offers any solution; he only exhibits the difficulty by saying that if you account for one member of a finite series by the preceding you are not advanced; but if you may go back to eternity you may still go back by finite beings just as the velocity of a body may be finite, though acquired in falling to a given centre from an infinite distance. Philosophical free-will is said to be mere chance—madness, &c. This may be if exercised contrary to God's will; but then there is a choice allowed

of not being mad or desperately wicked, &c., and
we only contend for that choice which may be the
very thing rendering our following God's will
virtuous ; and this is the only way to me of reconciling free-will with regulated order.'

' *December* 11.—Went to Coleridge's with Mr.
and Mrs. Montagu and Irving in the evening. I
was pleased with a reply of the latter to a lady
who complained that Blomfield, the Bishop of
London, had preached a sermon for a female orphan
school in which he had enlarged on the old topics
of the influence of women on society. " My dear
madam, these old truths are old because they are
fundamental, and they are the truths which must
be impressed on our minds ; they cannot be urged
too often. . . ." We found a large party at Highgate,
and Coleridge was very entertaining. He read us
a fine passage from a manuscript on the foolish
objection to theory and demand for facts. " Such
men," he observed, are " preparing their souls for
the office of turnspit at the next metempsychosis."
But I cannot go along with him in rejecting
Bacon's theory of induction as the groundwork of
an insight into general laws. Coleridge has indi-
cated this in the " Friend," and quoted a ludicrous
passage from Hooke, who requires ten times more
from the philosopher than Cicero did from the
orator. Bacon may have gone too far in his zeal
against hasty generalisation. If, indeed, a man

love his own fame better than truth, he will, when he has once generalised, twist every fact to his own theory; but we must have data to guide our imaginations; we must assume theories, and deduce results from our assumptions, which we compare with those deduced from experience, and thus attain the correct result. . . . Coleridge appears to attribute invention to a species of inspiration, which I suspect will be found to be vouchsafed only to those whose minds are well stored with facts. It is a species of gipsy prophecy in some cases, and we are astonished because we know not the individual's habits of observation. This, too, would account for the same theories being invented in different parts of the globe. Could any but a first-rate mathematician have hit upon the general laws of fluxion?'

'*December* 13.— . . . In the evening read a considerable part of Plato's "Phædo." The doctrine of the relative nature of our ideas is one of the greatest importance in my opinion, as a key to the chief metaphysical difficulties in our inquiries after the sources of our knowledge, &c., but is not applicable to the purpose for which Socrates is made to enforce it—viz. the eternal nature of the soul. It is obvious that a law of the soul itself cannot give us any information as to its essence, any more than the law of gravity can inform us of its cause. The contrast expressed by "dying and living " might with equal propriety be expressed by the act of " being and not being," and then the conclusion against the argument is at once apparent. . . . I heard a man of talent, the other day, inveighing against public speaking and poetry, as imperfect modes of expressing our ideas. I question whether algebraic expression of all our thoughts would conduce to our happiness.'

' *December* 16.—Conveyancing in the morning. Read some of Tyrrell's suggestions for the amelioration of the law of real property. I confess that he appears to me to deserve considerable credit for the pains he has taken. He has not only pointed out difficulties—a task very easy—but has suggested sound remedies. It is to be feared that the aristocracy will not consent to many important alterations, the abolition of tenures, &c. ; and the commissioners, therefore, must act like politicians ; they must propose, not the best laws, but the best which the majority of the world, or rather of the ruling powers, will accept.'

' *December* 17.—Finished Hurd and Warburton's correspondence. On the whole it is not very worthy of two Christian bishops. There is too little meekness and general kindness to all men. Old Montaigne has well remarked that if Christians were what they profess to be, we should have the necessary conclusion, " Sont-ils si bons, si doux, si charitables ? Ils sont donc chrétiens." Much might be written on the application of Christianity to everyday intercourse. Politeness in the usual acceptation bears the same relation to genuine Christian kindness as honour does to more important moral doctrines. A man of perfect politeness may wound the feelings of his neighbours, and even make such occupation his amusement, if he does but observe certain conventional forms; just as the man of honour may seduce his neighbour's wife or daughter, provided he shoots the husband afterwards, or gives him a chance of doing the same to the seducer.'

'*December* 18.—In the evening with the Montagus and Irving to Highgate. Coleridge was in full vigour of intellect, and his conversation, which took a theological turn, as is generally the case when Irving is there, was brilliant and at the same time of great depth and interest. . . . Coleridge's sentiments are formed on the Lutheran exposition of the Gospel scheme, which he considers to be derived from the exposition given by St. Paul and St. John, the two most gifted apostles. He conceives a genuine faith is the gradual substitution of Christ's reviving influence which causes the natural man to throw off as it were, by successive sloughs, the mortal vices. He conceives that an internal Church which "cometh not by observation" is preparing in the minds of men; whilst an external Church must at the same time, by its salutary

influence on the mind, keep up the internal action
which would otherwise gradually wear out; that
this was the scheme ordained from the beginning
of our earth and the very object of its existence, at
least after the fall ; that the Jewish prophets looked
forward to an eternal life by redemption, as the
expressions of Ezekiel, for instance, " that the
wicked man turning away from his wickedness
shall save his soul alive," have otherwise no
meaning, being certainly physically incorrect ; that
evil is merely subjective, not objective ; that it is
falsehood, the devil, who is a liar from the beginning, wishing to reconcile the impossibilities of
being at the same time a creature, and yet equal to
the Creator.   He finely illustrated the subjective-
ness of evil producing objective good by supposing
the parts of a machine in a manufactory . to be
animated, and anxious to tear and bruise each other,
and the manufactured article, which, at last, however,
arrives at perfection by this very means.   This, it
is true, leaves untouched the origin of evil, and
perhaps favours too much the doctrine of necessity.
Irving is, I think, a fine, high-spirited enthusiast ;
but enthusiasm is very dangerous ; its least fatal
effect is vanity, which may overcome us in our
very humility and self-abasement.   But let me not
criticise others ; God knows I have enough to condemn in myself.'

' *December* 21. *Sunday.*—St. Margaret's Church.

At night read several chapters of Epistle to the Romans. Correctly understood, they state no more than this: that if a man have faith he must be good ; from which it would logically follow that if he. be not good he cannot have faith ; but the first is a most dangerous doctrine for those who are not used to reason, and should never be cited except to be explained.'

'*December* 23.—In the evening amused myself with a little of Bentley's " Phalaris." How unfortunate that erudite men are so seldom gifted with his splendid logical force and pungent wit! He plays with his adversaries before he vouchsafes the death-stroke. The *cui bono*? may perhaps be asked of this learning. I know not any other answer than that, if it be worth while to know anything, it must be worth while to know it well, which, indeed, is the only real knowledge. The detection of fabrication is manifestly of great importance to the Christian world; though, for my own part, I should go so far as to say that, if none of the present Gospels were written at the time alleged, their internal evidence is sufficient proof of a Divine revelation, whether committed to writing at once, or handed down by tradition. " Never man spake as He spake," is the fact upon which we might base our faith, combined with the unexplained, uncontradicted account, traditionary or otherwise, of the Resurrection.'

' *December* 24.—Equity drawing in the morning, and part of the evening at an abstract. Read Theophrastus on courting popularity (ἀρέσκεια), on loquacity, on newsmongers, on impudence, on meanness. Many of the traits are very delicately touched, and are as applicable at the present day to ourselves as they were two thousand years since to the Athenians ; so much does man resemble man, whatever interval of time or space separates us. The λαλία is not kept sufficiently distinct from the ἀδολεσχία ; by the latter appears to be meant talking on a variety of subjects from a fondness for gossiping ; the former sheer talking for talking's sake . . . In the ἀρέσκεια the asking for the children after dinner, and finding out that they are as like their father as two figs, brings us quite home.

' Being Christmas Eve I read the first chapters of St. Luke, and I also continued to read the Epistle to the Romans. The ninth chapter is certainly very difficult. Butler's analogical reasoning is, I think, valuable in these cases. It shows us that the difficulty is equal whether we be Deists or Christians. Now it may be said that this is only shifting the ground ; but surely it is a point gained if we can show that nothing but fatalism, or atheism, or perhaps, indeed, nothing but the latter, can explain the difficulty ; for we then increase the opposing difficulties which bring us back to the point whence we started, either as Deists or Christians. A system of belief is, in fact, necessary for us as agents ; no man was ever practically sceptical, for, as Montaigne says, if he were, he could converse only in interrogatives. That belief, therefore, must be adopted which exhibits the fewest difficulties. In the case in question our notion of moral virtue is certainly shocked by the supposition of the election of Jacob from the womb. Yet are not men born in every species of rank in life, of virtuous or vicious parents, who will, of course, subject them to their own habits and conditions of life, healthy or diseased, rich or poor, and so on ? The free will of God must be our only criterion of right or wrong. If I had time I would enter into a proof of my notion that it is the fixed truth which constitutes all that we are to aim at, either in physical or moral researches—the only fixed point from which our calculations can be formed as to future consequences. It is this fixed nature of God's will which renders every deviation from what we have previously regarded as His will shocking to our reason ; but we must be satisfied that we do not clearly understand one of the questions when such uncertainty arises. The rewarding of the labourers at the eleventh hour is a paraphrase of this doctrine.'

'*December* 27.—Read at night St. John's last chapters, preparatory to my taking the Sacrament of Holy Communion to-morrow.'

'*December* 28.—Thanks be to Thee, Almighty God, that Thou hast vouchsafed unto me again to approach Thy Altar. Forgive, I beseech Thee, through the merits of Thy blessed Son, the repeated violation of my most solemn internal resolutions; and may the Spirit of peace, which He hath promised to those who trust in Him, so powerfully operate on my affections and thoughts as to eradicate all self-conceit, efface all impurity, and strengthen that faith which hath never been extinguished although dimmed by worldly vapours, until I acquire the blessed frame of mind which may render me ever a meet partaker of this Thy Holy Institution here, and of Thy eternal joy hereafter! Hear me, Almighty God, Father, Son, and Holy Ghost. Amen.

'Read at night the beautiful thirty-first chapter of Job. The reproof of Elihu is one of the most wonderful chapters in the Old Testament, and so also is the last chapter in the book. Read also several of St. Luke's parables.'

'*December* 29.—Law in the morning. In the evening read some of the characters in Theophrastus. That on ' blackguardism '—for I know no other word for βδελυρία—is a curious picture of

manners.   How can Casaubon translate ἀναισθησία
by *stupiditas*, when all the characteristics are
those of the absent man ?—a very different character
from the stupid. I am not aware that the Latin
word expressed absence of mind, nor can I at this
moment recall any word in that language which
does. It must be allowed, however, that there is
scarcely a sufficient difference in some of the
characters given by Theophrastus ; yet where in
nature they are so nearly intermingled, it is difficult to keep the shades wholly distinct. There are
some decided colours in the rainbow, but there are
others which blend with these, and form new com-
posite lines. The ἀναισχυντία and βδελυρία are akin,
and so is the latter with ἀπόνοια.'

'*January* 8, 1829.—Reading election law in the
morning. In the evening went to see the tragedy
of " Rienzi." What a noble subject ! It has often
struck me as a fine theme for tragedy, which was,
perhaps, the reason why I was disappointed with
Miss Mitford's. This is no presumption on my
part. Our fancy often soars above our powers of
expression ; and I should have written a much
worse play, though I should have imagined a
better one. The only powerful passage is that in
which Rienzi announces the union which will be
effected by the common hatred of the Orsini and
the Colonna towards himself ; and there are some

dramatic strokes which tell well. The scenes between Rienzi and Angelo and that between the former and his daughter are the most effective. What an example does Rienzi's history afford us of the impossibility of creating anew feelings which have once perished! He galvanised Rome, but he could not recall her to life. We may philosophically adopt the political fervour of Alcæus, and say with soberness that

οὐ λίθοι οὐδὲ ξύλα
οὐδὲ τέχνῃ τεκτόνων αἱ πόλεις εἰσιν, ἀλλ' ὅπου
ποτ' ἂν ὦσιν ἄνδρες αὑτοὺς σώζειν εἰδότες, ἐνταῦθα καὶ
τείχη καὶ πόλεις.[1]

What connexion had the Romans of the fourteenth century with the conquerors of the world? Of all which sprang from the fervid ambition of the latter a few mouldering ruins alone remain in the yet uneffaced labours of the architect, or the more precious relics of the orator or the statesman; but the mighty energy of will cannot be generated by those frail and silent monuments. The consciousness of surrounding weakness gave the first impulse to the cupidity of the hardy and

[1] This passage, which is not quite correctly quoted in my uncle's MS., occurs in Aristides II. 273; who, however, refers to the saying as having been originally uttered by Alcæus, and afterwards adopted as a kind of proverb.

The line in Alcæus to which Aristides alludes is doubtless the following :—

Ανδρες πόληος πύργος ἀρεύιοι.—Fragment 20.

daring settlers on the Palatine. They struggled for existence; they fought for the flocks and herds which grazed upon the neighbouring pastures, for the corn and the vine which enriched the soil. The conquered became one people with the conquerors, who were anxious only to secure support, and joined with the former in the cultivation of the united territory. At such a time was Cincinnatus called from the plough to the Dictatorship. But the rich, though distant, plain of Campania extended itself before the eyes of these martial agriculturists, and they longed for the enjoyment of plenty, unaccompanied by the necessity for labour. Wealth then began to be accumulated, and their projects aimed no longer at competence, but abundance. The physical wants being thus supplied, imagination began to play its part; then came ambition with its innumerable attendant virtues and vices, from which moment, were I disposed to write an essay, I could trace, I think, the future fate of Rome down to the present day, and show its agreement with the general laws which society has hitherto followed.'

'*January* 10.—Finished Roe's book on Election Law. I have now made some way in Reid's work on the Mind. I can, I think, sufficiently trace all his errors up to their source; namely, his ignorance of the principle of comparison which is the characteristic of our mind, and is in fact the only means of the development of its powers. One sees from his very first observation on sensation, and the belief, as he terms it, suggested by it, that he does not feel disposed to admit the fundamental axiom that, if we had but one sensation, we should have none, or, to speak less paradoxically, that we cannot have one sensation. We must be able to discriminate in order to be conscious. An anecdote of Biot affords an illustration. The French astronomer, accompanied by Guy Lussac, ascended into the clouds in a balloon. They were both much alarmed by the balloon suddenly becoming stationary, as they thought. They threw out ballast, but this appeared to have no effect; they let out the gas, still they remained suspended in mid-air. At last their alarm was transferred to a totally different cause upon their perceiving, as they emerged from the clouds, that they were descending at a fearfully rapid rate, and had been doing so in fact for some time, but when in the clouds could not discover their motion for want of any fixed object with which to compare it. Hence we may gather that the idea of motion, as well as of tangible figure and extension, are deduced from the comparison of two or more sensations, as may easily be shown. But I hasten to Reid's great mistake, that of supposing that visible figure can exist independently of colour. Mr. Fearne has demonstrated this to be a palpable absurdity ; but without vanity I may say that I have considered this as a self-evident truth ever since I read Berkeley, which was, I believe, in the year 1820 ; and I began a paper when I was at Cambridge, which I still possess, the object of which was to show that we cannot have any one sensation alone, or know that anything is hard, soft, &c., without having two or more sensations to compare, whence the proposition as to visible figure immediately flows. How can a figure be visible on a red surface unless the lines marking, or rather trying to mark, it be of a different colour from the marked surface? How could a blind man ascertain the existence of any tangible figure traced on a polished surface, unless the surface were raised, roughed, or otherwise distinguished to his finger ? But all this, again, is a fit subject for an essay.'

' *January* 11. *Sunday.*—St. Margaret's Church. Learn from Billing, who has just returned from France, the extraordinary agitation of the public mind which now exists there. He has promised to lend me Cousin's lectures on Plato.

' At night read the beautiful passage in " Paradise Lost " of the revolt of Satan and the faithful firmness of Abdiel. Such may I be, O God ! but how ill prepared as yet am I for that purity of faith ! The introduction of the passage from the Psalms, " this day have I begotten Thee," coupled with the preceding " on a day," &c., is not happy ; though it is clear, from the verses immediately preceding and succeeding, that the hyper-Arian sense which might be attributed to the expression was far from Milton's mind.'

'*January* 14.—Conveyancing. In the evening read half of the third book of Cæsar's " Commentaries." It is indeed a fine monument of his powerful intellect. It is a clear and masterly sketch of his military operations, as far as I can judge of such matters, and at the same time wholly elevated above the low vanity of exaggerating his achievements by dilating unnecessarily upon the formidable nature of his opponents. He had no reason to exaggerate. Well may Bacon say that the exploits of Cæsar and Alexander are grander than the feigned adventures of Amadis or Arthur ! . . .

' Whilst speaking of Cæsar's noble and ingenuous narrative I am brought back to the consideration of the curious psychological question of motives to action. To almost every excellence might an application be made of the line descriptive of the truly benevolent, who " do good by stealth, and blush to find it fame." I have heard of a powerful comparison of virtue in this respect to Eurydice ; if you look back on her, she flies. It is hence the great object of the Christian religion to prevent all thoughts of our own merit ; and surely, however difficult the doctrine of the Atonement may appear to some, it will not be denied by

the Unitarian himself that it produces a beneficial
effect by tending to subdue that pride which irresistibly follows the contemplation of our own worth.
Yet that school would refer all notions of worth
to the securing to ourselves the enjoyment of the
greatest and most durable pleasures, and thus perpetually turn our thoughts to the complacent contemplation of our superior abilities, inasmuch as
virtue becomes mere talent, and vice miscalcula-
tion. Is this calculating system that which is
usually found to produce happiness in its more
usually visible forms? I think not. The child
caresses you, and this certainly generates love on
your part, and ensures, so far, the happiness of the
child. But had the child calculated on this effect,
would it have been as happy in the result? or had
you known of such calculation, would the result
have been obtained? I think I may answer,
Assuredly not. No! the principle of love is, I am
persuaded, a something primary, a part of our
existence which is in itself pleasurable and at the
same time irresistible. It is this which appears to
me to have been man's natural state in Paradise,
and which will be his state hereafter ; and this love
is described by St. Paul (our translation has it,
" charity," from the Latin *caritas*, "dearness"), as
not being puffed up and as enduring for ever.

   ' I have wandered widely from Cæsar ; but, if it
were not too long a task, I think I could show that

the enjoyment of talent is destroyed by the frequent contemplation of it in the possessor, and sinks into an enjoyment depending on the breath of others, which may be withheld for the express purpose of creating a mortification they feel they have the power to inflict; real talent forming, almost unconsciously to itself, the very same approbation; and as South beautifully expresses himself, when speaking of will and reason, it may then be said to triumph, though drawn on as the chariot in the procession of a Roman conqueror.'

'*January* 17.— . . . Evening at home, and looked through Scott's "Heart of Midlothian" again. There is more true pathos in the character of Jeannie Deans, the combination of her sublime virtue with her humble simplicity, than in any other novel which Scott has written.'

'*January* 21.—My dear mother's birthday. Long may she live to enjoy our congratulations on its return ! How much do we—how much do I— owe to her ! A very large proportion of that high moral feeling which distinguishes the middle class of married Englishmen may be traced to their having known the blessings of a home under the care of kind and affectionate women. God forgive me all my wickednesses ; I feel them powerfully at this moment and deplore them, but had I never known the care of a mother I had been yet worse.'

'*January* 25.—I heard to-day an excellent sermon, from my friend Hook, at the Chapel Royal —the subject well selected—the conversion of the treasurer of Queen Candace, with an application to those who make wealth or politics the business of life.

'After church walked with Hook and his uncle Theodore. The perpetual flow of humour in the latter, with occasional rallies of genuine wit, make it impossible to feel any anger towards him whilst in his company, yet never was the character of one

> Qui captat risus hominum famamque dicacis,

more completely exemplified,

> . . . dummodo risum
> Excutiat sibi, non hic cuiquam parcet amico.

What, then, can political opponents expect? Yet is he more to be pitied than condemned. His vivacity renders him morbidly brilliant, and his keen sense of the ridiculous converts his exuberant spirit into satire. There appears to be no ill-temper in him, and I believe that for the moment he would be shocked at the idea of inflicting pain, but he would offend the next instant; and when, through the medium of the press, he can attack, without hearing any complaint from the sufferers, and is at the same time flattered by the encouraging laugh of his own coterie, he is regardless of all consequences. I can easily imagine that he would feel great pleasure in tying crackers to the coats of the mourners at a funeral, without stopping to inquire whether they were parents following a deceased child, or undertakers' assistants merely hired for the solemnity.'

'*January* 29.—In the morning finished the Report of Vernon, as far as to Lord Nottingham's death. Read some of Lord Guildford's decisions. The inferiority is striking.

'In the evening with B. Montagu to Coleridge's. He had been seized with a fit of enthusiasm for Donne's poetry, which I think somewhat unaccountable. There was great strength, however, in some passages which he read. One stanza or rather division of his poem, on the "Progress of the Soul," struck me very much; it was, I think, the fourth, in which he addresses Destiny as the "Knot of Causes." The rest of the poem seemed the effusion of a man very drunk or very mad.

'Coleridge launched forth at some length upon Bacon's inductive method, at the request of Montagu. I think he clearly failed in his attempt to depreciate experiment. The instances he selected— namely, the continued observation of the heavenly bodies, which led to nothing more than the Ptolemaic system, till Kepler's time, and his still more favourite one of the isolated nature of the facts attending magnetism and electricity till the present day—may tend to show that the *experientia literata* is nothing without a master-mind, which Bacon himself asserts; but if Coleridge means anything, he must mean that Kepler could have equally demonstrated his laws by one single observation, as from the result of the observations of ages; a proposition which cannot be maintained. The fact is, we consider too little the effect upon us from infancy of the knowledge of our age. A child of eight or nine knows more of the figure of our earth when you show him a globe, than any philosopher of early antiquity. It becomes a fixed truth in his mind, and he looks upon it as a datum whence he can reflect, instead of spending a life in satisfying himself of the fact. But go back a little further, and think what must have been the efforts of those men who invented letters, the fruits of whose labours are fully reaped by many a child of four years old. Thus is our labour in experiment abridged; and, however Hooke and others, by carrying the system to extremes, may have deformed and caricatured the inductive philosophy, there is no other method of discovering truth, as distinguished from the dreams of those who, like the schoolmen, deserted nature in its objective form, to amuse themselves with the creatures of their own imagination. To use Coleridge's favourite simile, the human mind may be the kaleidoscope, but it is a dull instrument if there be no extrinsic object to work upon. He was happy in one image, not so much as an illustration, but as a pleasing touch of fancy. He said that Nature had for ages appeared to wish to communicate her stores of higher knowledge by the phenomenon of the compass, but that she was too distant from us, and we could only watch the trembling of her lips without catching the sound.'

'*February* 2.—Reading law in the morning, and also the greater part of the fifth book of Cæsar's " Commentaries."

'In the evening read a part of Warburton's " Divine Legation." The dedication is a very fine onslaught upon the desperate folly of those who, by perpetually sneering, cease to enjoy one elevated thought. . . . The slightest point in common between two objects is sufficient for the ribald scoffer who neglects all differences if he can find one point of resemblance for his wit to fasten upon ; or rather in the differences, contrasted with the one point of resemblance, he finds the necessary material to excite laughter. Thus the gown and bands of a preacher put upon a monkey would no doubt make a ridiculous figure ; but one is far from inferring that the monkey and the preacher are in reality equally absurd, and so long as the *contrast* only excites laughter, the laughers may be most innocent ; but when the sneerer would endeavour to make you laugh again upon seeing the preacher in his pulpit, by insinuating some *resemblance* between him and the ape, then he becomes mischievous, as anxious to overthrow all calm reflection.'

'*February* 4.—In the evening read Bishop Hare's[1] tract on the " Difficulties and Discouragement attending a Study of the Holy Scriptures." It undoubtedly was ironical, as Warburton represents it in his preface to the " Divine Legation," and intended as a satire on the bigots of the day; but, from the laboured apology for Whiston and Clarke, one would naturally be led to conclude that the author was an Arian. The only doubt as to whether any part of the book be serious, must arise upon the first difficulty mentioned, namely, the language and various readings of the Scriptures; yet I cannot believe that so deep-thinking a man as the author appears to be, could really have felt much difficulty in this matter, except as wielding the argument against those who insist on minute dogmas, depending on a few doubtful texts. To such persons it may be formidable enough; but the *spirit* of the Gospel must be as intelligible as that of the " Iliad " or " Æneid," and its general facts as clearly stated; and, in spite of the various readings of these two books, I suppose no

---

[1] Francis Hare, Bishop of Chichester 1731-1740; great-grandfather of Julius and Augustus Hare. See my *Memorials of the See of Chichester*, p. 300.—ED.

one ever doubted that the one began with the quarrel between Achilles and Agamemnon, and ended with the burial of Hector ; and the other began with the voyage of Æneas, and ended with the death of Turnus.'

'*February* 5.—This evening read through Collins's " Discourse of Free Thinking," a book of more wit than weight. The absurdities of some divines are ingeniously brought together, though their genuine talent is not unfrequently misrepresented by the quotation of single passages, as for instance from Jeremy Taylor's " Friendship," to show that it is not inculcated by Christianity. . . . The commencement of his Third Satire is the best answer to himself. " I have frequently observed," says he, " in conversation, that men are more led by certain difficulties and objections, which they pick up, to reject what is certain and true, than they are to admit anything for true by virtue of a proof *à priori*." This observation is just, and will satisfactorily account for the usual mode of attack made by the impugners of Christianity, who ferret out every objection by piecemeal, and carefully avoid looking at the compact system of the whole, or listening to any defence which is made of it as a whole, or attempting, *à priori*, to demonstrate the impossibility of the Revelation. Let those beware who have to deal with insinuations of this nature ; and if they are beset by such puny assail-

N 2

ants, let them return the small shot of particular
difficulties, and ask them to account for the belief
of a most barbarous people (as these gentlemen
usually represent the Jews to be) in one God,
whilst the mass of their neighbours were plunged
in idolatry, or the sage few in Pantheism ; their
preservation of pure forms of prayer and adoration as exemplified in the Psalms, written chiefly by
one who is represented as the vilest of the human
race ; the coincidence of the fifty-third chapter
of Isaiah with the life and death of Christ ; the
acknowledged beauty of Christ's moral doctrine, He
being born of low parentage amongst this debased
and ignorant people ; the conviction wrought by
His propounding the most exalted purity to this
brutal and ridiculous race—for such, indeed, Mr.
Collins considers the Jews, and even pities Jose-
phus for being the historian of those to whom so
great a philosopher, as he himself would term
Jesus Christ, first thought of preaching. When
these difficulties have been digested, others might
be propounded, if such be the petty mode of warfare
which is preferred.'

' *February* 5.—In the evening went to Coleridge's. He discoursed somewhat mystically on
some points of Christian philosophy. Speaking of
the πνεῦμα ζωοποιοῦν, for instance, of St. Paul, he
conceives it to be a something not requiring the
understanding as a condition of life, but as being

in itself a source of life ; but how shall we comprehend that which he admits we cannot in the very terms of his proposition? . . . We discussed the King's speech, which was delivered to-day at the opening of the Parliament, and agreed as to the gross absurdity of the insertion of the bishops and clergy as detached from the Church, in the recommendation for Catholic emancipation. The event, however, forms an epoch in our history.'

' *February* 6.—Read a great deal of Warburton's " Divine Legation." His bold system of assertion is quite appalling, and one conceives it to be sometimes impossible that he should be the dupe of his own spirit of paradox. His character of Bayle [1] is finely drawn, though it is not a little amusing that he should lament the paradoxical habits of that acute philosopher. What can exceed the absurd assumptions introduced to prove that the fifth book of the " Æneid " is a description of the mysteries— a position so ably and humorously exposed by Gibbon?'

' *February* 8.—Ulphinston dined with us, and gave us some curious details of the Russian manners, especially the extent of the slave system, a large proportion of the shops, even at Petersburg, being kept by the slaves of the aristocracy. That vast empire appears as yet to have reached only the first stage of civilised government. How far

[1] Book I., section 3.—Ed.

the communication with more advanced States, which circumstances have extended to a degree unknown in the history of the other governments of Europe, may have an effect in modifying the usual progress from aristocratic monarchy to a temporary despotism, and thence to real liberty, remains yet to be seen.'

'*February* 9.—Law in the morning. In the evening a consultation with an old practitioner, in order to settle the draft of a lease of a salt mine. Heaven defend me from such twaddling in future as I was doomed to experience.'

'*February* 10.—Two hours more this morning with my venerable opponent. Drinkwater came in to inform me of the concoction of an Anti-Catholic petition at Cambridge, and we agreed to go down, with as many others as would join us, to oppose it.'

'*February* 11.—Went to Cambridge. We left, seventeen of us, at a quarter-past six in the morning, by two Paddington coaches, drawn by four horses each, nine having left on the preceding evening. We arrived at Cambridge at five minutes past one o'clock, and, at a little after two, had the satisfaction of hearing that the Anti-Catholics were defeated in the Upper House by fifty-two to forty-three, seven of our party only being members of that House. This we looked upon as a great triumph, especially as several clergymen had come up to vote against emancipation. The master and vice-master, together with one chapel reader, were the only persons at Trinity who voted for the petition, and amongst these were all our most celebrated men. We dined in Hall, and, leaving at twenty minutes to five, reached town at half-past eleven, much delighted with the triumph of Liberal feeling in our university. In the Lower House we should have been two to one. It appears strange that the impure mixture of religion with politics should have created so much confusion that twenty or thirty years must elapse ere the errors of our government in Ireland should be generally admitted after having been forcibly pointed out. Yet it required nearly the same time to effect the abolition of the slave trade, and our wonder ceases. . . . How vain is it that Christ so repeatedly stated that His kingdom was not of this world, else should His servants fight! But the still, calm voice of reason will ever at last be heard, and the writings of wise and good men strike root into the dense heap of prejudice till they gently heave it from its foundation, and we may trust in God that no effort towards His glory is finally thrown away.

'*February* 13.—Read a good review on Bentham's " Rationale of Evidence" in the " Edinburgh," by Macaulay : the first part rather pedantic and puerile, but the latter worked in a very masterly manner. Bentham's mind affords an instance of the effect of the utilitarian philosophy in generating universal suspicion—the exact reverse of the Gospel, which leads to universal love ; and assuredly legislation and religion act upon directly opposite views, and stimulate us by opposite motives. The legislator considers human nature in all its depravity, and restrains it by punishment. The teacher of religion seizes all that is pure and noble, and bends it to his use, making man happy and virtuous by telling him that he may be, and naturally wishes to be, so.'

' *February* 17.—Reading "Preston on Fines : " heavy work ; but I fear that the learning on these subjects, as it is facetiously called, will be requisite throughout our generation, should the things themselves be abolished, as it is to be hoped they may. I really know few branches of knowledge more capable of the good of innovation without the evil than the civil law. In morals and in religion the good and bad are so entwined by the tendrils spreading and uniting, though from widely distant roots, that you can scarcely extirpate the one without injuring the other ; but what shock could the human mind sustain if fines, recoveries, &c., were cut up, both root and branch ? As for titles being shaken, you can always protect the past whilst you legislate for the future.'

' *February* 18.—Called on Buckle, who lent me

a volume taken from the " Asiatic Transactions," and containing papers by Sir W. Jones on the Hindu Religion and Philosophy. How extraordinary must the enthusiasm of that great man have been which could lead him to devote his brilliant talents to the heavy labour of discovering the particles of meaning which lie hid under the rubbish of Indian poetry ! His translation from the " Bhagavad Gita " shows the lamentable mass of folly which must be waded through to arrive at any meaning ; for allegorical enigmas are but folly to succeeding generations who have forgotten their meaning, and surely no eloquence can be attributed to the fictitious tales of the support of the world on a rhinoceros horn, &c., &c. The first purana of the " Bhagavata," of which there are eighteen in the whole, consists, says Sir W. J., of 14,000 stanzas (Hindu chronology). In the tract where this occurs, by-the-bye, I think that the Hindu chronologers fairly overturn their own theory by proving too much, and at once defeat the conclusion on which Voltaire so everlastingly dwells. If Voltaire can really believe that the Hindus are justified by tradition in recording facts which took place in the reign of Vaivasarata (whose great-great-grandfather was Brahma), only 3,892,888 years from the date of Sir W. J.'s essay (1788), we can only say that he seems indeed to be one who could strain out a gnat and swallow a camel ; and he might perhaps have been delighted with the conversation between Valani and Vyasa, who, as a learned Brahman assured Sir W. J., did meet and talk together, though their ages differed by 864,000 years, the Brahman observing that the lives of the   [1] were preternaturely protracted. It is, indeed, much to be wished that the pioneers of literature would open the Eastern field to Europe. The skill of such a chief as Sir W. Jones is lamentably wasted in the attack, which I do not mention as in the least depreciating the results of his wonderful industry, but as regretting that his no less wonderful intellect was not wholly occupied upon matter ready prepared for its exertions.'

' *February* 19.—Read the earlier numbers of Cousin's lectures on the Mission, as he terms it, of the eighteenth century in completing the overthrow of the middle age system ; a work which was begun by the religious reformation of the sixteenth century and the political revolution in England in the seventeenth, till completed by the French Revolution. The Platonic school of the sixteenth century attacked Aristotle as the means of getting at the principle of authority ; and all synthesis of the past ages was overthrown by Bacon and Descartes in the seventeenth century, who recommended the commencement of a pure analysis. The latter, however, too hastily began a fresh synthesis, and

---

[1] The word here lacking is illegible.—ED.

the eighteenth century turned back to renew its analysis, and is distinguished in the author's opinion by the fact of its not having produced a single theory.

'There is great power in M. Cousin's style, but too much, I think, of a spirit of system; and the manner in which he frequently asserts that such and such events could not have happened otherwise than they did, is almost ludicrous. Yet it is by a similar mode of argument that the fatalist proceeds, who would be as much puzzled as M. Cousin if called upon for a prophecy of future events from present data. Cousin treats Bacon very unfairly, whom he accuses of having devoted his whole power and attention to physics. Had he never read the "Essays," or seen the sketches for "Histories of the Passions," &c., or the analysis of mind in the "De Augmentis"? The "Novum Organum" is known to be an unfinished work; yet is not the first half of it dedicated to the most valuable observations upon mind, which would in all probability have been followed up by an experimental treatise similar to the hints for physical observations in the second part?'

'*March* 3.— . . . During this week I have finished the second volume of Warburton's "Divine Legation." I do not by any means feel convinced that he has answered the texts brought against him, as to the promulgation of the doctrine of a future state, much less that there are not other passages to be found. He must have found some difficulty in Dr. Balguy's objection, referred to in one of Warburton's letters to Hurd, as to the true God having ordered so important a fact to be concealed.

'There is considerable force, in my opinion, in Warburton's arguments as to types, and their double sense. His definition is ingenious; an allegory in moral doctrine assumes the form of a double sense when it is important that both the present and a future generation should be benefited, the moral import to the present generation affording one sense, and the evidence of Divine power, when the second sense is verified, establishing conviction with posterity. Thus sacrifices, for instance, were types; whilst many of the actions of the prophets, as Ezekiel's shaving and dividing his hair, &c., are only symbols. Such is his course of argument; and when you add that he confines the same to a strictly double and not a manifold sense, it is at least a logical argument free from the contradiction in which the writer of this bold assumption is frequently involved, but still subject to considerable difficulty. The appendix to Volume II. is a masterpiece of wit, though not exactly in the style of a Christian clergyman. The unfortunate Tillard was scarcely a worthy adversary for the gigantic powers of Warburton. The latter's account of Job affords some amusing instances of his broad assumptions, and at the same time of his acute ingenuity.'

'*March* 4.—Read part of a lecture of Guizot's on the " History of Civilisation," which he divides into social and individual. He conceives that England excels in the first only ; Germany in the second ; France, of course, unites the two ; and to France, therefore, he devotes his attention. His remarks on English authors are somewhat superficial. He condemns Bacon, for instance, as being too practical, and not devoting any part of his philosophy to abstract questions, or the human mind. M. Guizot himself deals much in vague generalities, which he seemingly conceives to be the *beau ideal* of philosophy.

'Read to the end of Book V. of Cæsar's " Commentaries," in the middle of which book I had deserted him some little time since.'

'*March* 5.—Went to Coleridge's in the evening with Montagu and young Edgeworth, a brother of Miss Edgeworth, who appears to be a young man of some talent.[1] Coleridge wandered into metaphysical depths and mazes, talking of the characteristic of reason or the pure idea being the impossibility of defining it ; its definition involving contradictions, &c. &c. If he means simply to say that that which understands cannot itself as a whole be understood, I can agree with him ; other-

[1] See Mozley's *Reminiscences,* vol. i. page 40.

wise I should feel some difficulty, when no proposition is offered, to assent. His illustrations were
occasionally very beautiful. I like also his idea
of truth, of its being an eternity, as it were, in itself,
which we cannot feel ere we arrive at perfect
conviction. . . .

'This night in the House of Commons. Mr.
Peel, in a speech of four hours, introduced the
important measure of concession to the Roman
Catholics. All disabilities (except in connexion
with the Universities) are to be removed, so as to
admit them to every office but those of Lord
Chancellor of England, or Lord Chancellor or
Lord Lieutenant of Ireland. The two former
exceptions are owing to the difficulty about Church
patronage. A bill to raise the electing qualification from 40s. to 10l. is, however, to accompany
the measure, and will, I fear, render it unpalatable,
although I have no great opinion of the present
system of voting (*i.e.* not by ballot) of a body of
men who are at the beck either of the landlord or
of the priest.'

'*March* 6.—In Court a great part of the morning. In the evening read a great part of the sixth
book of Cæsar. His account of the Gauls and
Germans is very interesting. The seeds of feudal-
ism were, I think, even then thickly sown; the
Gauls, however, being much further advanced in
the career of civilisation than the Germans, who

were as yet mere nomads. It is curious to observe
that the Gauls admitted their inferiority in military
effort to their neighbours, and they appear to have
been in that state when men are not sufficiently
advanced to acquire the cool courage and confidence
inspired by superior knowledge, but yet so far
acquainted with luxury as to be unwilling to
sacrifice their ease to military glory. The account
of the beasts in the Hercynian forest is singular.
The Uri must be Bison. He speaks of Unicorni—
a mistake, I should think, for some elk, of which
single horns may have been shown to him ; and as
for the animal without joints in its legs there must
be some grand mistake. He only speaks from
report.'

[The next entry in the Diary is dated July 22,
and begins as follows :—]

' It is long since I have pursued my original
design of committing my transient thoughts to
paper. Occupation and idleness have both contributed to this neglect. I fear, too, that I have
not always been sufficiently at ease within to
venture upon the task.'

[The last sentence no doubt refers to the hopes
and fears by which he was agitated before he
ventured to declare his long-cherished but long-
concealed attachment to her who became his wife.
A passage written in cypher follows, and with this
the Diary comes to an end.]

To the Rev. W. F. Hook.

EDUCATION.—PROFESSIONAL SUCCESS.

Lincoln's Inn:
St. Shakspeare's Day, April 24, 1828.

. . . I heard last Sunday at my brother's church an admirable and truly liberal sermon of the Bishop of Lincoln, on the subject of the education of the poor, in which he considered the foundation of the prejudice existing in some minds against any improvement, or as they would term it innovation, in the minds of the lower classes, and declared his opinion to be, that where the parent took care that religious instruction invariably accompanied the development of the intellect, no danger could be apprehended from any extent of information. I have rambled on upon this subject, and perhaps said more than we can agree upon ; but our controversy has always been gentle, as will, I trust, ever be the case, from the harmony that reigns in all our deeper sentiments. The adoration of the same God, when sincere, must, I think, unite all hearts in one common sympathy. It is thus that Christ's doctrinal and practical precepts are indissolubly knitted together ; and may the time come, though it appears as yet but too distant, when the faith shall never be conceived as separable from the love inculcated by the Gospel !

I am writing this letter to you, my dear friend, from chambers, and, as I know how much you sympathise with all my good or evil fortune, cannot resist giving you some account of my proceedings at the Bar. I have been much more successful than I had any right to anticipate. I had already cleared about 150*l.* since I was called, which for a young man is very great. I am at present engaged on two committees; one on the Stockton and Darlington Railway in the Lords, the other on the East London Railway in the Commons. We have 10 guineas every day for an attendance of about three hours, so that you perceive I am in a fair way of becoming, what I may comparatively term, rich. One thing I do hope that I have secured, and that is an independence ; for should I fall off in my profession for a year or two, yet my fellowship will never exceed 200*l.* a year. I write this on St. Shakspeare's day, as a day of good omen, but cannot, I fear, send it in time for the post. I am rather disturbed and agitated at present by the circumstance of the young lady of whom I have spoken to you being in town, where I hope she will only remain a fortnight. I perhaps lie to you, and, if so, surely to myself, in saying *hope*; but my reason, if not my will, tells me it is the right term ; for where I have no right to declare that which I feel, it is not only better, but more desirable, to avoid all risk of doing so. It is, however, in vain

that I reflect on God's numerous blessings ; I am
still wretch enough to murmur internally at an
evil infinitely less than those to which thousands of
my fellow creatures are subject and from which I
am exempt, but I trust that He will pardon rather
than punish this weakness.

To the same.

HARTLEY'S PHILOSOPHY.

Lincoln's Inn : November 20, 1828.

. . . Almost the only book which I have
wandered to, out of the profession, has been
' Hartley on Man.' What a pity that so excellent
and amiable an author—one, too, whose reasoning
is just beyond refutation, and whose acuteness in
tracing the minute shades of thought and feeling
is unrivalled—should, by the assumption of hypothe-
tical physical data, be led to conclusions which
certainly embarrass, if they do not shake, the understanding ; and although to him they were not as
a stumbling block, for his faith really appears to
have been steadfast, as if founded on a rock, yet to
others, of whom there are a sufficient number
always at hand, they afford an opportunity of
unsettling all moral and religious notions by the
annihilating of responsibility ! One useful lesson
may, however, be deduced from the work, namely,
that we ought to judge of the motives and feelings

of the author by his whole work. We have no right, and it is most uncharitable, to select any particular passages and assert that they lead to such and such conclusions, for the purpose of condemning an author who expressly rejects such conclusions, and denies that in his mind they can arise from the premisses. Surely his own practice will not be governed by deductions, which others make, and he himself repudiates ; and of what but his actions have we a right to judge ? What I have said, however, by no means contravenes the indisputable right of exhibiting very glaring absurdities by way of necessary inference from principles advocated by others, as long as we content ourselves with thus exposing the unsoundness and danger of the work, without casting the least reflection on the intention of the author, who either candidly owns that he overlooked, or sincerely declares that his mind cannot adopt, the reasoning by which you have endeavoured to refute him. When, again, men are found acting upon their principles in such a manner as to present them to the absurdest deductions in their actual practice, it is very difficult to separate the doctrine from its promulgator, and the ridicule or aversion bestowed on the one must necessarily be reflected on the other. We must, then, learn to pity that evil which proceeds from the degeneracy of good feeling, and endeavour in charity to reform pure

depravity.   I must confess that the most mischievous sect I am acquainted with is that of the
utilitarian philosophy.   I would that I had time to
sift their sophistry to the bottom, not with any
vain hope of being able to produce any effect on
others, but with the assurance of at least readily
defending my own opinions against these varying
and shifting supporters of the coldest and most
heart-desolating system ever inflicted upon mankind.   Yet do I know several who in sincerity
adopt it, and I fear render themselves very unhappy
by its adoption, whom, however, I cannot and ought
not to condemn, whilst I fervently hope that they
may live to change their opinions.   The worst of
the evil is that, by annihilating the generous sentiments of youth, the theory leaves but little hope
of a return to such feelings in our age.   Paley has,
I fear, contributed much to the spreading of the
nearly allied system of universal philanthropy.
The resting of our happiness in religion only
appears to me to be manifested very briefly, thus :
Admitting that by the instruction of parents and
actual experiment we are led to reject that which
is pernicious to the body, and are so far temperate ;
and that which pains the mind, and are so far
sufficiently humane and benevolent to get rid of all
disagreeable objects of misery and suffering (which
is by no means the case) ; admitting also that we
should by reflection alone acquire sufficient energy

to repress our sensual passions, and that we should be led by compassion rather to relieve than to thrust out from our thoughts the distresses of others ; yet, after all, is there more provided for than that which is simply within our own power ? What are we to do in order to remove all those pains which, both in body and mind, unavoidably beset us in this world ? and if a future world be admitted, a position not inconsistent even with atheism as Hartley has shown—for we might exist eternally in that hypothesis (if we ever exist at all by it)—if, I say, a future world be admitted, what can we desire from experience to assist us in securing happiness there ?   Must not revelation lend its aid both to console us under what we may comparatively term undeserved suffering here, and to give us the full assurance of happiness hereafter as a consequence of a certain line of conduct to be adopted upon earth ? . . .

To the same.

LABOURS OF THE LEGAL PROFESSION.

Lincoln's Inn : January 2, 1829.

. . . I have been much engaged during the last month in a very laborious and one of the least profitable of the departments of the law.   I believe I mentioned to you that a cousin of mine had offered to send me the whole of the conveyancing for which he should require the advice of counsel (he

is an attorney in Devonshire). As I have given
myself out as a conveyancer and equity draftsman,
the common plan of beginners at the Chancery Bar,
and my time is not fully occupied, I have under-
taken this business, which is one of the most useful
in conferring a competent knowledge of the law,
and possesses at the same time the advantage of
securing me about 300*l.* a year independently of
other clients. It is, however, not only laborious
when you have no pupils to assist you in the
drudgery, but always makes me rather nervous in
consequence of the importance of accuracy in
opinions as to title, and in the forms of deeds, &c.
From the rapid interchange of property in these
days, the conveyancer can no longer flatter himself with the hope of his mistakes remaining undis-
covered till he is peaceably deposited in his grave.
At every fresh mortgage your handiwork is submitted to the searching eyes of some individual
who considers the detection of an error as the
establishing of his own reputation for sagacity. . . .
The conclusion of your letter struck me with
agreeable wonderment. Can any good thing come
out of Cambridge? I have not met with Mr.
Rose's [1] work, for in fact I have not read much of
anything but law during the last month, but I will
endeavour to procure it. Talking of Cambridge, I
have just received my dividend thence, which had
a narrow escape, having with the others been in

---

[1] Rev. Hugh James Rose.

Remington's bank a fortnight before Rowland Stephenson's departure. It strikes me, my dear friend, and I am sure you will accept my offer in kindness as it is meant, that you may, in entering upon your new living,[1] be desirous of having some ready money in hand ; and here are 200*l.*, which I shall not at all want, at your disposal for as long a time as you please. You will not, therefore, be unkind enough to refuse me this pleasure if it be really of any service to you, or scruple to say if more were wished, either now, or at any other time ; for I shall always, be assured, open all my circumstances to you as I would to a brother. I have now spent the first year of my life in which I have not considered myself as encroaching on my own family, and, with God's blessing, hope to possess health and good fortune enough to continue independent, and I trust I shall never wish to heap up riches.

To the same.

RELIGIOUS REFLECTIONS.

Lincoln's Inn: February 19, 1820.

Your last long and kind letter interested me most deeply ; and though I regretted the depressed tone which characterised it as written in a moment of depression, I felt much satisfaction in once more experiencing the glow which seems to animate my whole frame, when the tender and grateful recollec-

---

[1] Holy Trinity, Coventry.

tions of the happy days of our boyhood are brought vividly before my imagination. It is indeed melancholy for us to reflect upon past pleasures which can never be renewed in the same shape; but then it is a melancholy which is in itself soothing, such as, I thank God, I cannot determine from experience, but such as I can suppose to be the recollection of a friend lost to us upon earth, when we shall recall every kind thought and act, and look forward with a Christian's confidence to a happy reunion. We cannot expect that the buoyancy of spirit with which we enjoyed the passing hour without dreaming of the future, should attend us throughout our career on earth, for the experience of increased disappointments, as we advance in life, renders such blindness impossible; but may it not be the benevolent intention of our Creator to warn us, as soon as our maturer reason is capable of reflection, that we are not to fix our affections or repose our trust upon any perishable creature? True it is that He has hallowed human attachments by informing us that they would vainly pretend to love the Invisible Author of our being, who have never cherished affectionate feeling towards their brethren, and it is by the genuine kindness of the heart that a peasant can evince a more perfect comprehension of the Gospel spirit than a philosopher; yet we are forbidden to set our affections on things beneath in an exclusive sense, and are told that where our treasure is, there will our hearts be also. We know where that treasure ought to be; would God that we could always be mindful of the knowledge vouchsafed to us! I did most earnestly, my dear friend, pray for God's assistance upon your efforts in your new sphere of duty; to wish to be good and pious is greatly to advance to the attainment of our object. ' Ask, and it shall be given unto you,' is the promise of Him who cannot deceive. I am, indeed, aware, from sad consciousness of my own unworthiness, that to ask in the sense which alone can be attributed to that promise is at times most difficult, and that God will not listen to the murmuring of our lips if our heart be far from Him. He trieth our innermost thoughts, and to Him is laid bare the foulness which we dare not ourselves look upon.

Do not, my dear friend, do not, I beseech you, refer to me as to one who is fitter than yourself to offer up prayers to Him who is of purer eyes than to behold iniquity; such praise wounds where you intend to gratify. I am as miserably weak as any poor being can be; all that I dare to say is that I have not yet felt myself so abandoned by God's good Spirit as to be able to stifle the deep remorse which I feel for frequent offences; may I never become desperately wicked! I know my own weakness too well to suppose this to be impossible, but yet feel such confidence in God's mercy as not to deem it probable. Above all things, how fully do I agree with you as to the efficacy of prayer in supporting us under all the temptations which here surround us! How mistaken does the Deistical opinion as to the propriety of offering *thanks* only to one God appear, even if we reason from common experience alone! Must we not wish for that which we ask in our prayers, and will not the fervour of the latter react upon the wish which excites it? Again, the frequent contemplation of blessings enjoyed which would form the subject of thanksgiving would, by perpetually reminding us of the advantages we possess, generate a secret feeling of self-complacency and pride, whilst in our prayers we acknowledge our feebleness, dependence, and humiliation. The Pharisee used thanksgiving only; the publican ejaculated his short but fervent prayer, and went down to his house justified rather than his haughty fellow-worshipper. We, however, rest not upon this reasoning. In the very parable I have alluded to, but more directly in many other parts of our blessed Lord's instructions, we are commanded to pray; and what is there which should lead us to conclude that prayer is not a mode appointed by the Ruler of the Universe for obtaining His good and greatest gifts, in the same manner as bodily exertion is requisite for acquiring a supply of temporal advantages?

Our Saviour Himself appears to condescend to

reason thus with His disciples when He asks them why it should be more improbable that God should give to them who seek Him, than that man should render to his fellows the services they request of him. We have as much right to expect our neighbours to give us supplies of food, raiment, &c., unasked for, as that spiritual grace should be granted to those who adopt not the required means ; for it would not be a sufficient answer to say that God knows all our wants, which man cannot, since it leaves this difficulty : Why were not men so created as to know each other's wants and to feel the disposition to relieve them?—a question which we have no right to ask; it is enough that experience shows us such is not the case ; and it is a fine analogy from that experience to say that the same reason which prevented such a formation of men's minds produced the necessity of prayer ; that reason cannot, in our present state, be offered to our minds under any more immediate form than as being God's will, which should satisfy vain curiosity. I am much obliged to you for your recommendation of Whately's book, which I shall procure, for the whole subject of the essays interests me. I have been lately reading War-burton's ' Divine Legation,' one of the most illogical books I ever met with, but the learning and talent it displays make amends for many defects ; I do believe that the author was a sincere Christian,

and I think his book too much out of the common
way to do much mischief. The dedication of the
first volume to the freethinkers is well worth your
reading. It is a short and masterly exposure of
the nonsensical expression of ridicule being the
test of truth. I am about to read Hooker's
'Ecclesiastical Polity' regularly through, which
will, I fear, take me some time. What do you
think of my being one of the party of twenty-six
who went to Cambridge to oppose the Anti-Catholic
petition? I really considered that it would be a
disgrace to the University, and for that reason felt
it my duty to go down. I know you will not
quite agree in this; but only two out of about forty
of our college, who voted, supported the petition,
and, with the exception of Dr. Wood, scarcely a
man of known talent.

To the same.

MATRIMONIAL CONGRATULATIONS AND PROSPECTS.

Great George Street: March 20, 1829.

I did not receive your letter to-day till I
returned home, too late for the post. I am unwilling to let another depart without offering,
though in few words, my heartfelt congratulations
to you on your success in the most important of
all earthly pursuits, and I pray that that success
may ever be a source of recollections as pleasur-

able as the feelings which it must at this moment excite in you. I do not doubt that the object of your choice must be virtuous and amiable, and am willing to admit of her returning your affection as a proof of her talent and discernment ; but the less I write the better. What can the cold effusions of a pen which has been dipped in legal ink the livelong day, what can they contribute to the rapture of a successful lover ? I thank you heartily for the last paragraph of your kind letter (and how kind, I felt most warmly, was it in you to write to me at all !) I will not be jealous, and shall hope that, as you have promised me, I shall acquire a new friend instead of losing one. It has ever been my earnest wish to see you happily settled in life. I know that on all accounts you must have most anxiously desired it. Thank you for your affectionate wishes on my behalf. I am fortunately at this moment much occupied, and it is only from such occupation that I can form any hope ; nor have I any justification for those wilful and almost impious murmurings, which sometimes exist in thought, though they never, I trust, escape my lips. How many are there who, with far greater powers of mind and energy of spirit, are left to struggle in the profession which I have embraced, whilst, by the circumstances in which I am at present placed, I have been enabled to advance more rapidly ! Still I feel that I am dependent upon the interest which can be made for me. I have not lost, but I have not yet *made* any way myself, and, until I feel more confidence in that respect, must not mislead another by false suppositions of future advantages that may never be realised. But how much have I written already of myself in a letter which must be short, and which should only be dedicated to the expression of my delight at the happiness of my dearest friend ! There is no one thing, my dear Hook, which has made me more earnestly long for a partner of all my thoughts who should be constantly with me, than the consciousness that had I not possessed, in such a friend as you have been, the means of giving vent to the feelings of my heart, I should have either sunk under their vehemence, or, by the constraint I experienced, should have degenerated into a cold and selfish, or irritable and dissatisfied being, miserable and the cause of misery to those around me. As it is, I but too often lament the want of one who can rejoice and weep with me, and am sure that our hearts have so many points of resemblance that you must have experienced this aching void. Gladly do I anticipate that you will never again be subject to that misery.

To the same.

MATRIMONIAL PROSPECTS.

Tenby : September 3, 1829.

. . . . I can scarcely look forward to the future
without some superstitious dread ; yet do I feel
blessed with the assurance that no evil of this
world can deprive me of the rapturous thought
that I have been loved by one so good, so purely
virtuous ; this will be my consolation in the utter-
most misery that I may be doomed to suffer here,
and still more do I fervently pray that I may
deserve such attachment, that I may never for an
instant forget the awful trust reposed in me by
one so much better than myself, but strive daily
to cherish in her the piety and goodness which
must lead her to an eternal union with the only
God, for so shall I fit myself for the right performance of my own religious duties.

To the same.

PREPARATION FOR MARRIAGE.

Lincoln's Inn : November 25, 1829.

I am much obliged to you for your merciful
treatment of me, though, indeed, you only let me
off on the plea of insanity. . . . In the first place,
I have had rather more business than usual in
Chancery matters, and some of them perplexing

enough. Then I have had a house to furnish—
many weeks having passed, indeed, in preliminaries
—and I have only now just obtained possession.
Then I appear to-day as an author, having published a pamphlet (with my name) in the shape of
a letter to the commissioners on 'Real Property,'
in favour of a General Register. It would to you,
I fear, be almost unintelligible, such is the state of
our law ; but I will, if you like, reserve a copy for
you. This letter was begun and printed by the
advice of my quondam master, Tyrrell, who is one
of the commissioners ; but that is not to be spoken
of, it being, in fact, a defence of the very and only
reasonable course which they have adopted against
the attacks of one of the old school. You thus
see that I have had enough work upon my hands.
Then you will remember that I have now another
correspondent—a rival with you in my affection.
You will be very glad, my dear Hook, to hear
that our marriage is now fixed for the first week
in January. I shall leave town about a fortnight
before that, and so take only a fortnight's holiday
afterwards. This, you see, renders any scheme of
reaching you impracticable. I think, as the shortest
road to any abiding place, we shall go to Southend,
which will render it unnecessary to pass through
town, and will also be near London if I should be
obliged to return earlier than I anticipate. By
being so near we may manage to steal a little

more time, if my clerks do not send me word of there being any papers in chambers. I shall only be able to get the dining and bed-rooms finished before our return, but our drawing-room and the whole house will, I hope, be ready before the spring. In the midst of all this sort of bustle I cannot collect my thoughts sufficiently to write to you as I would write; to express all my deep thankfulness for the past, and confidence for the future. Everything, indeed, now smiles upon us; I hope we may be strengthened to bear any reverse. You, too, my dearest friend, enter, not unfrequently, into my thoughts, when I reflect on the immense addition to my own happiness which has been vouchsafed me in that of all who are near and dear to me. . . . I do, as you may suppose, most ardently long for that rest and tranquillity which after all this bustle, which I much dislike, I shall hail with rapture. If dear Charlotte were with me, I should not so much care about these minutiæ, because I could then take a greater interest in them; but really chairs, tables, &c., and the choice that one has to make in matters most absolutely indifferent, give one greater trouble than I could have supposed possible. My dear mother is so delighted with our having fixed upon a residence near her, that I cannot but rejoice in our having obtained so comfortable a house in that neighbourhood. The dulness of the

spot [1] is to us rather a recommendation than otherwise, and it is very open and airy, though I cannot
agree with my landlord in considering that a pear-
tree in a dirty yard behind us affords, when in
blossom, the ' most beautiful prospect in the
world.' I should think the Bay of Naples superior
to it, but ought not perhaps to judge till I have
seen the effect.

To Mrs. Charles Stephens.

BIRTHDAY GREETINGS.—CONSCIOUSNESS OF SIN.—THE
MERITS AND DEFECTS OF THE EVANGELICALS.

Lincoln's Inn: November 29, 1833.

Many thanks, my dearest sister, for your kind
heartfelt wishes and congratulations which, be
assured, dearest Charlotte and myself do, with no
less affection and earnestness, now offer to yourself.[2]
Indeed it is most gratifying to me to receive such
kind and affectionate letters as reached me from
yourself and my dear mother and Maria this morning.
The love, I hope, I may continue ever to deserve,
as far as a return of attachment constitutes my
title to it. The many other kind things that you
say are very dear to me as being strong proofs of
regard, the stronger as proofs for being un-
merited; for surely it is only the eye of affection

---

[1] Dean's Yard, Westminster.

[2] My uncle's birthday was November 29, and my mother's
November 30.

that overlooks the numerous defects which a less
partial observer must be fully aware of, although
my bitterest enemy could not say half as much evil
of me as I myself, alas ! am conscious of.

. I find it most true, dearest sister, that the more
our eyes are opened to things spiritual, the more
do we perceive the inconceivable foulness and de-
formity of the human heart. And not only this ;
for we could soon, in our self-deceit, flatter ourselves then with the delusion that we are no worse
than others, whereas we are then only conscious
of our spiritual state when we see that we really
are individually most guilty—that we are conscious
of sins which we cannot know that others have
committed—sins against light and knowledge not
perhaps vouchsafed to others—sins of ingratitude
where unusual blessings have been bestowed.
One comfort, and a great one it is, of our increased knowledge of our sinfulness is the increased reliance on a Redeemer—the increased
love of One who could suffer such horrible torture
as the very descent into a world like this must
have been to an All Holy Being, solely out of love
and compassion to His bitterest enemies, for such
are all sinners.

To give all men their due, I think that until the
Evangelical Clergy, as they are called, preached the
peculiar doctrines of Christianity, we were fast

sinking into mere heathen morality. It was seldom recognised that 'there was none good, no, not one;' that 'the heart was desperately wicked ;' that, when all was done, we were 'unprofitable servants ;' that 'except we eat the flesh of the Son of Man and drink His blood, we have no life in us '—a doctrine which turned back many of His disciples (St. John vi. 66). Now all this is vitally important.

On the other hand, none can dislike more than I do the principle of separation (the very meaning of the word Pharisee) introduced by that party as a party. Their existence as a party is itself most dangerous, as opposed to the very spirit of Christianity, and generating the 'stand back, I am holier than thou,' of the Pharisee. I also much dislike their insisting on the observance of particular forms—as abstinence from playing at cards, and going to balls, &c. (theatres, as at present constituted here, are more questionable): this is like the 'paying tithe of cummin,' &c., and is essentially Judaising. Make the root good, make a man a firm believer in Christ, and we are told he will love Him and His commandments, and there will be no danger of his pursuing any amusement beyond the legitimate object of recreation. It is false in reasoning and dangerous in practice to make everything that may be abused unlawful; as I have heard some people object to a cigar as immoral because people smoke at public-houses. At least, no better reason could be found than this association.

To the Rev. W. F. Hook.[1]

BERKELEY'S PHILOSOPHY.

Lincoln's Inn : December 7, 1833.

. . . I am glad you are about to read Berkeley. There was never, I think, any man since Plato who was gifted with imagination and reasoning power in so high a degree ; and if he, like Plato, occasionally lets his imagination run wild, yet I question whether Plato ever, like Berkeley, practically acted on the views which were deemed visionary, and thus gave evidence of sincerity and singleness of heart. I am always in love with Berkeley when I think of his proffered resignation of the bishopric to ameliorate the condition of the unhappy Bermudians. . . . You will feel the great value of Berkeley as giving a sound resting-place for the mind amid the bewilderments of metaphysics. It is quite false to say that Hume has demonstrated that there is no such thing as spirit ; on the same principle Berkeley had shown that there was no such thing as matter. In the first place, Berkeley makes no such assertion, but simply that matter,

---

[1] This letter and the next have already appeared in the *Life of Dr. Hook*, pp. 170, 172, small edition.

considered independently of mind, is a nonentity. That all those sensations we daily experience from objects termed external are real, Berkeley, who is eminently an experimental or Baconian philosopher, was never absurd enough to deny. For ' external,' read 'independent of us, or our minds,' and you will have Berkeley's notion of matter as regards man ; but he boldly asserts that matter cannot be conceived of by us as independent of a mind. The Scotch metaphysicians, to a man, either wilfully or stupidly jumble *a* mind with *the* mind, meaning each individual's mind ; whilst by a mind Berkeley means *some* mind or other ; and admitting that the table at which I am now writing will exist when I do not think of it, the question is, Can it exist if there be no mind to limit out its nature, which is but an aggregate of sensations ? Berkeley says, No ; and experience, I think, demonstrates that that which can only be known as an object of sensation, owes its existence to a sentient power ; not mine or yours, because experience shows the sensations to exist independently of your will or mine, but to the eternal sentient power by whose will our minds perceive it as that which is created or willed by Him. This is always to me the most beautiful demonstration of a God, and most satisfactory refutation of the eternity of matter which is, according to Berkeley, an absurdity, matter being but the stage in which certain volitions of the

Supreme Mind are exhibited to man. The resurrection of the body becomes thus at once intelligible, because He who wills us to perceive the efforts of His will in a certain manner now, may cause us to perceive them in a similar manner at any future time, blessing us probably with additional pleasure by a more thorough perception of the beauty of His work. By ' us ' you will see I consider the mind alone, regarding the material about us as no other than a combination of God's impressed thoughts (if I may so say) which affects our minds with various impressions, such as pain and pleasure and their infinite varieties. . . .

I have not time to write to you about Miss Martineau's tales, of which, of course, you have heard, and we have read many. Some are, I think, excellent, and all are powerful where her imagination comes into play. Her reasoning is not, and does not pretend to be, original. It is taken verbatim from Malthus and M'Culloch—a bad school—and her sectarianism not unfrequently peeps out ; but I would recommend you strongly to read the ' Manchester Strike,' which might, I think, be useful to your poor people at Coventry hereafter, if the time should come when any such folly should be meditated.

To the same.

ADVANTAGES AND EVILS OF AN ESTABLISHED RELIGION.

Lincoln's Inn: February 1834.

. . . I think you have brought forward every argument in favour of an Establishment with the greatest force. You tell me you hope to convert me, and will, I dare say, think me an obstinate creature if not quite a convert. However, I will acknowledge that you have confirmed my perhaps hesitating opinion that where we find a Church established we ought not to lend any assistance towards unestablishing. I am not a lover of change at any time for the sake of change (though you may smile at this, looking to my Radicalism); I even consider change as a positive evil, for assuredly happiness consists in tranquillity, and He who is all wise and all happy is immutable; but there are cases, as all must admit, where the evils of abiding in your actual state and the advantage to be derived from a change, fully justify the effort and sacrifice required for alteration. Such, however, is not, I think, the case with regard to the Establishment. Amongst the evils, which I cannot but yet think incident to the compulsory support by the State of any religious doctrine, there are to be found unquestionably great and perhaps counterbalancing benefits, and I would not root up the tares, lest the wheat be rooted up also.

Of course I do not think an Establishment unscriptural—that is, forbidden by Scripture—or I should consider the question settled. ' Unscriptural ' is one of those convenient words for controversy which allow the opponents of the Church the widest possible field by keeping off any close attack. In one sense, unquestionably, the Establishment is unscriptural ; that is to say, the early Christian Church as delineated in Scripture rested, from the necessity of the case, upon no support from the State, and this the Dissenter falls back upon when pressed by argument. I think your argument as to the Jewish Church a very good one against the Establishment being unscriptural in any other sense ; but I do not think it equally good as a positive reason to urge us to an alliance of Church and State, for there was a direct temporal covenant between God and the Jewish nation. The Government remained in some sense a theocracy, even after St. Paul's conversion ; and where God was the temporal monarch, it was almost a necessary consequence that His ministers would be temporal governors also. My objections, or rather, I should say, my difficulties, as to Establishments are several ; first, political—the difficulty of choosing your Establishment, for I incline to think that the forcing of six millions in Ireland to pay for the maintenance of the religion of one million is almost unscriptural in the worst sense. In Scotland we have acted differently; whilst treating Ireland as a conquered country, that is, by the rule of force. I think an establishment of our Church in India, supported by forced contributions from the natives, would be monstrous. To this I know you will answer that the tithes are a gift by Christian possessors. This may, and, I think, does, apply to England ; but consider how the possessors acquired their property in Ireland —by nothing, in fact, but brutal violence done to the large majority of that nation, though a weak minority as compared with the overwhelming forces of England. My second objection to Establishments is, their effect on the clergy, but I will not enter into a long disquisition on this point ; and my third objection is, the effect on the laity, who become members of a Church because it is established, and make no further inquiry. I admit great force in the arguments you bring forward as to the indirect effect on families, and I admit also the difficulties entangling the whole question ; but I should ever wish, above all things, to see the questions kept separate, for there are not many who have our liberality in thinking one can belong to the Church of Christ without being over anxious as to the seats of bishops in Parliament, and the consequences of a union between Church and State ; and this species of bigotry is itself one of the evils of that union, for I fear many give the State at least equal consideration.

To the same.

THE DANGERS OF RELIGIOUS SENTIMENT.

Lincoln's Inn: July 24, 1834.

My dearest Friend,— . . . With one part of your last letter you may be sure I shall not agree. The truth is, I am a sad talker of Christianity, and I do really sometimes tremble at the thought of the additional guilt of my numerous commissions of sin, and omissions of duty, as compared with the same acts and defects in others, for this very reason. I think I have been blessed with a very keen and lively *sentiment* of religion, in itself unquestionably a gift, but still of a very dangerous kind, bringing those who rest upon it into the condemnation of ' him who knew his Lord's will and did it not.' This is an awful thought to me, my dear friend, and I am glad when I can reflect on it, to keep down a naturally buoyant and sanguine temperament, as well as a very vainglorious heart. You really can have no conception of the depths of my vanity, and the unaccountable folly with which even your extravagant, though sincerely intended, praise is treasured up by me, even whilst I feel that it is my condemnation. I endeavour to attribute the pleasure it affords me to the sense it conveys to me of your unalterable friendship, but that will not altogether satisfy my conscience.

Now, you know enough of me, my good, excellent friend, to be aware that all this is not said to be contradicted. Without appearing to return your praise, be assured that I regard your friendship as that which, next to my infant education, has been the most powerful instrument, under the guidance of God's good Spirit, in saving me from utter destruction. That I have much improved in the last few years I really hope, and this is a lasting source of consolation to me, for improvement is the only test of our being in a state of grace.

To the same.

LOVE, EARTHLY AND DIVINE.—HOLY BAPTISM.

Bealings: September 18, 1834.

[After referring to the illness of some relative.] . . . But as we advance in life we see every day more and more the uncertainty of every worldly enjoyment; and it is a beautiful dispensation of Providence that we should thus be gradually brought to wean ourselves from the habit of indulging in an unrestrained and thoughtless, too often, perhaps, unthankful, gratification of earthly affection. Tempered, indeed, with a Christian's thankfulness, affection cannot be too much indulged; for it is then also blessed with a Christian's hope, and we are enabled through faith to look forward to a time when we shall wonder that we can have really loved so little those whom we now appear to dote upon. For I imagine that the love which is perfected in heaven, centring in our blessed Saviour, will, through Him, flow in a pure and holy stream towards the utmost bounds of creation then known to us; and that every saint will feel towards those who are glorified with him an affection far surpassing the strongest that we can experience here. For it will be a powerful affection towards the immortal soul—one which, if properly and perfectly experienced here, would lead us to pray for those we love far more often and more earnestly than we do, to avoid ' offending ' them (I mean ' scandalising ' [1] them in the literal sense), by giving occasion to any weaknesses or infirmities, and would cause us to feel a far bitterer pang at the manifestation of a bad temper, or any of the other minor sins as we consider them, than we should at the appearance of any bodily distemper in those we love. These are thoughts on which I love to dwell, with a deeply humiliating feeling, however, of my own infirmities, and of the depth to which I fall below my own poor standard of holiness. What must we appear to an All Holy God ? This, indeed, if anything, must bring us to Him who alone can deliver us ' from the body of

---

[1] *i.e.* causing to stumble.

this death,' or 'this body of death.' And here I am reminded of your very interesting observations on infant baptism. The passage you mention I always thought was introduced by our Church for the very purpose of supporting the practice. That and the parallel case of circumcision are the two strongest arguments to my mind, and removed the doubts and difficulties I felt on the subject. The bringing of little children to Christ, and His blessing them, would have been a mere superstitious practice, had it not been accompanied by a spiritual blessing. The passage in St. Paul I have referred to, and all those metaphors in Scripture of dead bodies and a new birth, seem clearly to imply that without grace we are quite dead in our souls, *i.e.* have no power. We are driven about by our senses, our appetites, and the other apparatus of Satan, and cannot resist his efforts. The soul has to be born again as a living, active principle. This life or birth, like our carnal life or birth, is a direct gift of God, and, I apprehend, takes place at baptism. The soul thus born must, however, be kept alive, being first nourished with child's meat by the parent's instruction, till it can receive that spiritual food at the table of our Lord which renews our strength. And this, I think, is what you would rightly term 'renovation.' The metaphor fails entirely if regeneration be *perfection*, for childhood is not perfect.

To the same.

THE DESTRUCTION OF THE HOUSES OF PARLIAMENT
BY FIRE.

Lincoln's Inn: October 17, 1834.

. . . I do not know if you would have had
this letter so soon (as I am very busy), were I not
anxious to attempt giving you a faint description
of the terribly splendid scene we witnessed last
night, in the destruction of the two Houses of
Parliament by fire. It is one that cannot be forgotten in a lifetime ; and as such a calamity
awaited the nation I feel that I would not for
much have been absent from the spot.

We were sitting in the dining-room when
Charlotte saw the pinnacles of the Abbey gleaming
with unusual light, visible over the top of the
shutter, which, as you may remember, does not
fit the circular portion of the window. On opening the shutter there was such a blaze of light
that I thought the college was in flames. On
running to the upper rooms, however, we saw the
volumes of smoke and bursting flames towering
over the House of Lords, and bearing fearfully
towards the Hall. This was about seven o'clock,
and the fire had then been burning about a quarter
of an hour. I rushed out of the Yard, and there
the most awfully grand spectacle presented itself.
The hospital, St. Margaret's Church, and, above

all, the Abbey, were thrown out into bold relief against a lurid sky; whilst at times the moon shone through the dense volumes of smoke with a pure, tranquil light, that presented a strange contrast with the fiery redness of the flames. The beautiful north transept transmitted the blaze through its windows, and the whole was so magnificent that I went back for Charlotte, and took her with me to St. Margaret's Churchyard, and thence to Westminster Bridge, before the mob had collected. I then called on the Rickmans to offer any assistance, but found I was just forestalled; their house is at the west end of the Hall, and has escaped. I was much pleased with seeing Mr. R. coolly removing all public documents before his own furniture. I then attended a committee of our dispensary, and again went home; but at ten I returned to see the fire, both from Abingdon Street and the Hall, the only communication between which was through our Yard, as the police had blocked up the street. And now a scene presented itself which no tongue or pen can adequately describe.

The whole of Palace Yard, so far as a circle was not kept by the police, the whole of the wide space near Great George Street, and the whole of Westminster Bridge, were one dense mass of spectators. The buildings by the side of the Hall had taken fire. Engine after engine came thundering through the mob with terrific speed, and shouts of joy welcomed the arrival of each ; the different regiments of infantry came in detachments as rapidly as they could be formed, and, as their drums and fifes announced their approach, the mob again hailed them with cheers, as affording more men for the pumps.   In the midst of the din was heard the trumpet of the Horse Guards as a body of them galloped down to maintain order ; and then again there was a dead silence, whilst the thick, curling, black smoke announced that the roof of the corner buildings I have mentioned was about to fall.   Presently it fell with a hideous crash, and ten thousands of sparkling embers were thrown up, followed by a raging flame, when a kind of shriek arose at the imminent danger of the Hall.   Happily the wind shifted, and the Speaker's house suffered instead of the venerable fabric which excited such an interest as few would have expected in a mob like that by which I was surrounded.   On the whole, though there were several exceptions, I was much delighted with the conduct of the people, who manifested not only the usual good intention of most English mobs (however perverted), but a degree of sentiment I did not anticipate.

I have given you a feeble transcript of my own feelings, and a poor account of this sad catastrophe ; but I write in great haste.

To the same.

Lincoln's Inn: December 8, 1834.

. . . I do not know what you will think of me for not having yet read Bishop Jebb's Correspondence, which, however, I fully intend to do, and promise myself a very great treat from it.[1] I met a young Oxonian the other day who had been induced to read it from seeing the first letter prefixed to the 'Lives' published by the bishop which I remember you spoke to me of at the time. I mention this to show that the work is doing good, for it is of vital importance to young men to have an interest excited with regard to such characters. I know of nothing more stirring than personal anecdote; it brings every point so much more home to us; and for this reason, amongst others, I doubt not our blessed Lord has opened to us the wonderful mysteries of the Gospel first, as a personal history, before the Holy Spirit had prepared men's hearts to accept the systematic doctrine of the Epistles. I believe that missionaries are most successful when they begin with the Gospels alone. Indeed, our Church seems to entertain the same

[1] See *Life of Dr. Hook*, pp. 174 and 177, small edition.

view by the examination of the younger candidates for the ministry in the Gospels and Acts. I think that the personal love of our Saviour is the most beautiful preparation for the teaching of the Spirit ; otherwise, whilst imagining that we are searching into the deep things of God, we are in reality but too often indulging the fatal, unloving appetence of knowledge that generates pride and then disobedience.

Hannah More's Correspondence has been thrown in my way by our book club, which I am half-ashamed to confess, after my long negligence about Jebb, but I have in a fortnight read only one volume of the former. It is a kind of Boswell book, and would be very amusing light reading, I think, for you. It is wonderful to see the levity, frivolity, vanity, and self-conceit of that really excellent person in the early part of her career ; though it would have been more wonderful, perhaps, had a young girl who was made so much of by bishops, chancellors, &c., been wholly uninjured by the incense daily offered up to her. There is a very interesting account of Dr. Johnson's last hours, and it is delightful to think that the comfort so long withheld was at last vouchsafed to him. The more I hear of the doctrine of assurance (I mean prospective assurance), the less I think it warranted by Scripture, and the less I like it as tried by the test of reason. I have had much discussion lately upon it with a friend of Charlotte's, now staying with us, who, I fear, is rendered very unhappy by the opinion that such assurance may be arrived at, because she, one of the most humble-minded and delightful persons I ever met, cannot herself attain it.

To the same.

THE ADVANTAGES OF A CONVOCATION FOR THE CHURCH.[1]

Lincoln's Inn: March 3, 1835.

. . . I see a good deal of difficulty in your objection to a permanent convocation. Still, I cannot but wish that there should occasionally be a national council or synod, as well as frequent meetings of the provincial synods. I think you have often shown the besetting danger of Protestantism to be disunion. Such, I confess, appears to me the strongest argument of the Romish doctors against all who differ from themselves (for I waive the question of our being called Protestants). Now, assuredly, the English Church, *i.e.* the Church in England, presents to my eye rather a more patched surface than I could wish; and the intermixture of coarse and rotten threads is still more apparent when one narrowly inspects

[1] For a letter partly in reply to this, see *Life of Dr. Hook*, p. 177, small edition.

the whole fabric. It seems to me that much of this is owing to the political appointment of bishops, but yet more, perhaps, to the want of a fixed rallying point, such as might be established by the declaration of a decided majority in a national council. Besides, many of the clergy really err from ignorance; and their attention would be more strongly directed to the doctrines of the Church if a body existed by which it would be represented, and in which, perhaps, they might themselves be called to take a deliberative part. It seems that Peel promises something as to improved discipline, which I am very glad to hear. I do not know that I quite agree with you as to the non-residence of bishops. The case of the first Apostles was one of necessity; but Timothy and Titus were early established by St. Paul in their respective dioceses, and the custom of the Church in its purest days seems, as far as I am informed, to have sanctioned residence as desirable. The bishop ought, I think, to be personally known and respected by all his clergy, and by as many as possible of all those who consider him as their spiritual chief on earth.

I am much pleased at what is called the reaction in the country; for though I consider the alarm to have been excited for interested and party purposes and to be utterly groundless (in which, of course, our opinions differ), yet it is satisfactory to me to find that the large majority of the country is ready to rally round the Church.[1] But it will be with this as with the Reform Bill ; if a real, substantial reform be not effected, no alarmists will be able to keep in those who may oppose such reforms. You, I have no doubt, are satisfied that such a reform will be effected ; I am willing to hope it. I earnestly pray for it ; but of this, I say, the reaction has satisfied me—namely, that there would not have been, without a change of the ministry, any fear for the cause of true religion. It is all very well to refer to the French Revolution when you want to frighten others with your own views ; but the people of this country have never been what the French were in 1790 or are in 1835 ; and although we, as a nation, fall far short of what we ought to be, yet, thanks be to God, I know of no other country where there is a more solid substratum of spiritual truth for the support of the moral fabric. In spite of the flippancy of travellers, I consider the Americans to stand next to us in these all-important advantages, and why ? Because they are a portion of ourselves.

[1] For the condition of Church affairs here alluded to, see *Life of Dr. Hook*, pp. 105–110, small edition, or vol. i. p. 143, *seq.*

To the same.

SUNDAY SCHOOL TEACHING.—SPIRITUAL DESTITUTION OF
WESTMINSTER.

Lincoln's Inn: April 22, 1835.

. . . I stifle my mortification at not seeing
you at St. Margaret's[1] (of which there appeared, I
thought, once a faint chance) by reflecting on the
anxiety such a charge (twenty-six thousand souls)
might have entailed on you. The Bishop of Gloucester tells everybody you ought to have been the
man. . . . It would be an infinite blessing to have
a man at St. Margaret's who would co-operate
heart and hand with Jennings,[2] and that each
might try to do his best for the two parishes ; for
assuredly our poor neighbours, who were severed
from the wealthier parish in Queen Anne's time
only, have great need of assistance. . . . Charlotte and I each take a class in the school on
Sunday morning from a quarter to nine till half-
past ten, and like our employment much. As it is
the only day on which I can see anything of my
father, I do not undertake the afternoon. The
infant school (which will be all the week) is not
yet set on foot. Probably the St. Margaret's clergy

---

[1] Dr. Milman, afterwards Dean of St. Paul's, had just been appointed
Rector of St. Margaret's.

[2] The Rector of St. John's.

will attend more to that, for there seems to have
been some notion that the Sunday school was for
St. John's only. There are now three hundred
children in this school where Jennings found thirty-
five. . . . One thing I certainly do long to see—
the abolition of the only excuse for Methodism by
vigorous efforts to provide means for bringing the
Gospel home to the vast masses of population in
towns like London, Manchester, Liverpool, Bristol,
Coventry, &c. If one tenth of the adult population
of St. John's wished to attend the church they
would with difficulty find room, and there is no
chapel. St. Margaret's is little better, and the
pastoral care of fifty-two thousand in the two
parishes rests upon five clergymen ! Now, if expen-
sive chapels are thought indispensable, we shall
never get the better of this ; but why may not large
rooms be licensed, and why should there not be
junior deacons with little or no salary who, as a
probation for full orders, should aid the rector in
visiting, and officiate in these rooms, calling in his
superior, of course, for the administration of the
sacraments or on any other particular occasion ? I
have not well digested this or any scheme, but
something must be done if we would have God's
blessing rest upon our Church and nation. I verily
believe that there are at least ten thousand people
in our two parishes who never use God's name or
Christ's but to blaspheme. The Roman Catholic

and Methodist chapels would, if crammed, as well as the churches, leave at least this number wholly unprovided for.

To the same.

PREACHING, HOW FAR A MEANS OF GRACE.—POLEMICS.

London : November 27, 1835.

. . . Jennings confirms your statement as to the excitement of preaching, and says that you are always fatigued with your Sunday evening lectures. Now you must seriously reflect on this, and remember that to preserve your usefulness unimpaired is the great point to be attended to. Your own views as to preaching will render you less unwilling to abstain when your health renders it expedient for you so to do. I have not sufficiently considered the subject to make up my mind whether or no preaching be a means of grace. The only passage that occurs to me is that one in the tenth chapter of the Epistle to the Romans where St. Paul certainly seems to attribute belief to preaching as a means, and belief cannot come without grace. But I will look into the matter first in the Bible, and then I should like to see the tract you mention—which I will certainly get. I generally find it best, for my own satisfaction, to read the Bible on any disputed point, and then to see the interpretation which has been given to any particular passages, either by the Church or by its most eminent members. I quite agree with you as to the exaggerated estimate of sermons by one party, and value our liturgy (I need not say the sacraments) far more than the best sermon I ever heard or read. With regard, however, to all disputed points, I am beginning heartily to detest all polemical writing. It seems to me that it is so much easier to say 'do so and so,' than to say 'take care you do not this or that because the Romanists or the Calvinists do it; in short, to point out what you conscientiously believe to be right, without (otherwise than by necessary inference), attacking others as being wrong. Polemics generally improve the head at the expense of the heart, as the excitement of the brain is said to weaken the circulation and digestive powers.

To the same.

THE HAMPDEN CONTROVERSY.—EXCLUSION OF RELIGIOUS
BOOKS FROM MECHANICS' INSTITUTES, ETC.

Dean's Yard : March 2, 1836.

. . . The present controversy at Oxford fairly puzzles me. Can you tell me where the Socinian doctrines are broached? for if Hampden were appointed, as it is asserted, university preacher in 1833, and professor of moral philosophy in 1834, while the sermons were preached in 1832, it seems

to me a little odd. I saw this passage in the
' Chronicle ' from his ' Bampton Lectures ': ' The
Deity is revealed in Scripture as consisting of three
distinct persons, or " hypostases." ' Now that is flat
against Socinianism. I really wish to know the
truth. I never heard Dr. Hampden's name in my
life before.

I ought, before this, to have adverted to a very
interesting point in your last letter. I cannot
agree with you as to the necessity, or even propriety,
of abstaining from all societies where religious
books are excluded. Take the Royal Society, for
instance. They have funds raised from subscrip-
tions by persons of all religious opinions. Now,
knowing how sensitive all men are, and justly, on
this most interesting of all subjects, how could you
propose to introduce religious works into their
library (if it was a new proposal, I mean), without
a desire, on the part of the Jew or Mohammedan,
that there should be as many books on their side
of the question as yours? Yet is there any good
reason for saying you ought not to associate with
Jews or Mohammedans for the purposes of science?
You will say this is not a case in point, because
they have no such exclusive rule, and I have indeed seen religious books in their library. But
this arises from the good sense of the members ;
and if any committee were to purchase a considerable quantity of religious Christian books, I should

say a rule would become necessary to exclude all books relating to religion as being unessential to the objects of the institution. So it arose, I take it, originally with the mechanics' institute; and I should think, myself, it would be better for the members of the institute who wished for a religious library to found one, as a thing apart, rather than to establish a new society. It is not that the Saviour is excluded, but that it is thought better that the occasions on which the whole human race can be brought to act in unison with each other, for objects beneficial to mankind, should be multiplied rather than diminished, and the natural tendency to exclusiveness and consequent want of love, which is one of the chief curses of mankind, should thus be to a certain degree modified. Do not people of all religions subscribe to libraries and reading rooms, where much that is useful is taught (the Royal Institution, for instance)? and would it not be out of place to introduce religion at such institutions? and if it were introduced would not a rule excluding it be necessary? and would a Christian be less justified in subscribing then than he was before? St. Paul himself seems to think that a Christian may dine with a heathen (1 Cor. xi.). Would not Christian conversation be tacitly excluded there? I consider it right that the Church should have a real, not a pretended, unity of mind in the worshippers of Christ; but she

judges not 'those who are without;' and I think
that, looking to the narrow and exclusive views we
are prone to adopt, we should rather gladly avail
ourselves of all points of union with our fellow men,
unconnected with acts of worship.   At the same
time I entirely agree with you that those are in-
tolerant who interfere with you, when you take a
different view.   If you only secede, and do not
preach against others, they have no right to
complain.   Every man has an unquestionable
liberty to act according to his conscience.[1]

To the same.

A good Sermon.—A successful Speech in Court.

Dean's Yard: April 24, 1836.

. . . We had an excellent sermon this morning from the Speaker's chaplain on ' Stand in awe,
and sin not; commune with your own heart,' &c.
It seemed, I thought, specially intended for me,
who have had a most bustling time, especially
during this week, being up till two one morning,
and three another at work.   He spoke especially
of the necessity of meditation for the man of business.   . . . My vanity, which is superabundant,
and will have (I often really pray for it) some
severe check, has been perhaps over-gratified by
my having got well through a summing up of the

---

[1] For the letter to which this is a reply, see *Life of Dr. Hook*, p. 184,
small edition, and vol. i. p. 279.

Brighton Railway Case in the Committee of the Peers at a few hours' notice. Lord Strangford and the Duke of Portland, to neither of whom I had ever spoken, went out of their way to compliment me personally, and our chairman, the Duke of Richmond, ' puffed' me much to our solicitor. I am told I made two converts by the speech—a very unusual event, and, I may add, a very improbable one. It is to be printed ; so perhaps I shall treat you to a copy, which you need not read.

To the same.

CHRISTIANITY AND ETHICS.

Lincoln's Inn : February 10, 1837.

. . . It often occurs to me that none but a Christian can see ' good in everything.' I know not how the Deist (few, I believe, are in theory Atheists) can reconcile any evil with God's benevolence. They look upon the Deity as so benevolent that He will pardon sin, in the same manner as man pardons his fellow sinner, upon repentance ; forgetting the great distinction that it is because we feel our own infirmity and weakness, and liability to similar errors, that we are naturally led to forgive others ; whereas nothing of this kind exists in the Deity. The parable of the lord forgiving his servant ten thousand talents, whilst the same servant vindictively prosecuted his fellow servant for the hundred pence, is irresistible as an argument to every man, deriving, no doubt, additional force in the Christian's mind from his deeper sense of guilt towards God. Again, the Deist has a low notion of the purity of God. His Deity is, in fact, anthropomorphous, though he boasts that he alone worships in spirit and in truth. Hence his conception of the weak benevolence which requires no further atonement than repentance, the effect of which on the administration of the universe may be fairly estimated by comparing the result of a similar principle in the government of a nation. Repentance, even accompanied with restitution (which is not always possible), has never been deemed an adequate justification of the offender in any community. I use justification here as it appears to be used in Scripture—namely, as replacing the party in possession of all the privileges of an unoffending citizen. Now, to resume the point whence I digressed, I cannot see how the Deist can suppose that the same weak benevolence should permit any of those afflictions under which all, the best perhaps the most severely, must labour. He cannot look on them, and practically no Deist does look on the ordinary calamities of life, as judgments and partial punishments for sin, because they equally befall the moral and the wicked. I am at a loss, therefore, to conceive how he can support his afflictions, or maintain his confidence in God. And in truth we

may see examples not unfrequently of his inability
to do so. I have no doubt that Cicero was a Deist,
and a sincere and at times an enthusiastic one ;
but we see how his faith and his whole soul were
shaken by the death of his daughter. I have
known another fearful instance of a man of some
note in our own time, who, dying of a fearfully
painful disorder, several times exclaimed, ' What
can I have done to deserve this?' What a flood
of light breaks upon the Christian in such cases!
He sees the heinousness of sin requiring a no less
fearful expiation than the suffering of God's own
beloved Son; he knows his own weakness and the
strong bias of the natural man to fix his love on all
that is present and visible, though temporal, rather
than on that which is future and invisible, though
eternal. He looks, therefore, upon every trouble
as a messenger sent to call him more and more frequently from the absorbing thoughts of this life,
and these messengers become more frequent as his
pilgrimage draws towards its close. Each bereave-
ment at least fixes in his mind the transitory nature
of his present enjoyments, if it does not strengthen
his faith, and increase his love, by a conviction that
those who are removed from earth have been
translated to heaven ; so that the band of his earthly
friends and companions becomes more and more
numerous in his heavenly home, and his affections
conspire with his faith to make him regard the

earth as a place of exile, which before perhaps, and in their society, he was too apt to regard as at least a Zoar, without having energy to rise to any loftier height.

I intend to read the tract you mention. Happily, as you observe, the rationalistic philosophy is so ill adapted to our nature that men's affections are inconsistent with their theory, and it is, after all, ' with the heart that men believe unto righteousness,' or disbelieve to their condemnation.   This is indeed, I think, the leading point of Revelation. All heathen and all deistical philosophers apply themselves to the head in ethics, no less than in metaphysics, or mathematics.   Now, if it so happened that all mankind were born with an hereditary disease of the brain, so that they could not understand the fundamental axioms of mathematics, it is clear no mathematics could ever be taught ; if they all had a disease of the eye which made right lines appear crooked and the converse, it is clear that no correct notions could be arrived at in geometry ; and, if all were under the same delusions, there would be no standard by which the errors could be detected.   But suppose a miraculous birth by which some one individual is produced, —free, himself, from the disease of the brain or the eye, able to discover the mathematical truths which before could not be taught, and at the same time to find a remedy for the disease—it is clear that he would not attempt to teach the science, or correct the errors, until he had first cured the disease, else he would throw his pearls before swine, who would turn and rend him. Now this seems to me exactly the case with our hearts, by which we mean our affections as distinguished from mere reason, the movers to every action, the determining executive which may, or may not, accept the counsel of reason. Our hearts then are depraved, and are unable to determine us to that which is right and good, but are very powerfully disposed towards evil; and this disease must be cured before morals can be in the slightest degree understood. Thus selfishness, the worst part of our fallen nature, is assumed by some as the principle of moral conduct (Bentham). Sympathy, a better but a very erring guide (as our sympathies, too, are corrupt), is the rule proposed by another (Adam Smith). The general good or bad consequences of actions, if all men were to do the same, is the criterion proposed by a third (Paley), which assumes a foresight possessed by the Deity alone, and also a possibility of deciding on good and bad, which is the very point at issue. The Christian, on the other hand, says: ' I will first clear my vision by asking God to open my eyes that I may see the wondrous things of His law ; then I will ask for strength to walk in the way He has set before me ; and as there is no strength without life, and as He tells me that I have no life except I abide in His Son, and except I eat and drink His flesh and blood, I will avail myself of all these blessed means, and above all will seek the assistance of the Comforter.' With these supports the Christian moralist begins his course, and he soon sees that much which he thought innocent is impure in the sight of Him who ' charges His angels with folly.' He will be careful to avoid even the appearance of evil, as knowing it to be part of his duty to throw no stumbling block in the way of his weaker brethren : he will be no less sympathising than the moralist of any other school, but he will pray for guidance in his sympathy : he will be no less active and strenuous than if he were acting on the selfish principle, or rather far more so, since God's glory, which involves good will towards men, requires all his energy, and that energy, too, is now supernaturally quickened. He will also carefully study the general consequences of his actions, guided by Him who sees the end from the beginning.

I confess I do long to see a good sound work on Christian morals, drawn out with piety, and yet with vigour. I think many books, excellent in their way, are useful to those only who have made great proficiency in their Christian course. Many, also, are too declamatory, and I may add exclamatory. I think Knox or Jebb might have written just such a book as I mean. You would not have time for it.   It would require great leisure, because, to be thoroughly useful, it should bear in view, not controversially, but didactically, all the errors it has to confute, substituting truth for them, not directly attacking them—the only means, I think, by which those are to be reached who are unhappily imbued with error.   Pride revolts at a direct attack.

To the same.

QUALIFICATIONS FOR A DIFFICULT POSITION.—THE
LITURGY.—MORALITY IN POLITICS.

Lincoln's Inn: August 8, 1837.

I have been longing daily to answer or rather to acknowledge your very interesting letter received more than a fortnight back.   I had been wishing to know what you thought of your new territories,[1] when lo ! a letter quite in the old tone of our earliest friendship, which brought you and your flock before me more than a dozen descriptions by other persons could have done.   I quite see the nature of your task, and it will, no doubt, be uphill work at first.   It is never pleasant to find ourselves jarring in opinion with those amongst whom our daily intercourse is to be, but I know not of any one fitter than yourself in natural gifts for this position. . . .

[1] The parish of Leeds, to which Dr. Hook had just then been appointed.   For the letter here alluded to, see *Life of Dr. Hook*, p. 240, small edition, and vol. i. p. 404.

Your natural defect you have by God's grace been able greatly to overcome ; I mean your quick and irritable temper, which in boyhood caused you so much annoyance, and even misery.   I assure you it is often humiliating to me to look at your improvement and my own stationary position, to say the least of it (for to be stationary in religion is to retrograde), more especially as regards this point, for I think you have now decidedly the advantage of me in respect of temper. . . .

I shall be glad when you can set about your sermons on the Liturgy.   You will find, I am sure, so much interest in the subject, independently of the benefit to be derived by others from them. How much there often is in a small compass !   I am frequently struck with the prayer at the end of the Confession, ' that we may hereafter live a godly, righteous, and sober life, to the glory of Thy Holy Name,' thus summing up our duties to God, our neighbours, and ourselves, and directing us to the object of all holy living, namely, God's glory, not our own.   And, though in a more modern prayer, how beautifully are the passive and active blessings, the cause and effect, associated in the ' peace and happiness, truth and justice, religion and piety,' which we implore for our country !   It has been much in my mind during the late elections, for I have tried as far as possible to get rid of party violence and excitement, and to make the cause of my country a matter of serious and religious meditation. In fact we are all, I think, deficient here. We have a mass of crude opinion, the offspring of mere habit and prejudice, which we seldom bring to the test of honest religious reflection. Were it not so, we should not see men, otherwise good, indulging in the use of every coarse, vulgar implement that comes to their hand to annoy an adversary, nor scrupling at any lie that serves its temporary purpose, advocating, before the mob, principles they disclaim to the House of Commons, and all this on both sides. The mob have been pandered to on the Tory side as to the New Poor Law by men who have supported all its provisions in the House, as much as they were ever hounded on to outrage on the Corn Law and other questions by the Radical party. As we agree to differ on politics, I shall not discuss them with you. It may perhaps give you pleasure to hear that there certainly are many people turned into so-called Conservatives who were Reformers, and that I anticipate ten or twelve years of what I call misgovernment ; for I assure you, do what I can, and seeing all the faults (which are many) of our side, I cannot bring myself to think that a standstill system will be beneficial to us. Perhaps, however, it may be useful for a time ' stare super antiquas vias,' as Bacon is fond of quoting from Scripture ; but then he always adds, ' with a view to look forward for the better path.'

To the same.

Lincoln's Inn : November 29, 1837.

I have two very interesting letters to thank you for. Your last, though short, was not the least interesting. You may suppose we have all rejoiced, our neighbours included, in the great success of the subscription.[1] . . . I have often thought that Exodus xxxv. 21, or still more xxxvi. 5–7 (the chapters are little read), would afford excellent texts for stirring people up to such works. Luther's solifidianism has certainly much quenched charity in its fuller acceptation ; and though love to man be doubtless one of the best demonstrations of love to God, yet a little more warmth of affection towards both would, I think, make us delight in outward demonstration, just as we make presents to those we love, not because they want such testimonials, but because it is a pleasure to say in every possible way, 'I love you.' The ultra Protestants seem to have been zealous in knocking down churches and cathedrals, but they have erected few monuments of affection. They seem to have had little of David's ardent and affectionate devotion ; for the magnificence of modern dwellings contrasts strangely with the barnlike appearance of modern chapels. How St. Paul's ever was built is a marvel. It arose, I imagine, from

---

[1] For rebuilding the parish church at Leeds.

the iconoclasts being then out of fashion for a season.

I was delighted with your extract from Mr. Faber's letter, which I carry about with me and read, as well as I can (this I say in revenge for sundry impertinent observations [1]), to all those who are circulating lies about the Oxonians. It is marvellous with what activity these lies are spread, and assuredly they denote that the Oxford brethren are unpleasing to the father of lies, from his energy in opposing their works. The last lie was that they had canonised Bishop Ken ; who had acted as Pope I could not learn. At the same time the Tracts have not done so much good, I think, as they might have achieved had they been free from several blots which I cannot but consider of serious consequence. What, you will answer, is free from imperfection in human works ? This, alas ! is too true ; and, what is worse, we all have more of the spider than the bee in our composition, and like to suck out the poison rather than the honey. I have always liked Edward's [2] way of treating his boy when he has begun to criticise, as we are wont in youth especially to do, in order to show our nascent wisdom in the discovery of faults. He has always said, ' Look out for beauties and merits ; it requires far more talent to find them

[1] *i.e.* on his handwriting, which was remarkably bad.
[2] His brother-in-law, the Rev. F. Moor.

out. Any fool can see a blot, but only those who are well informed can discover the genius of an author, a painter, &c., or whatever the subject may be.' When we add to this that our Christian charity should be, above all things, active to edification, we ought certainly to feel ashamed of all the dirt we may have contributed to throw on many of the goodly stones that will hereafter shine forth in the glorious temple of the New Jerusalem. I have often deeply repented my share in this, when a young man, with regard to the so-called Evangelicals, many of whom, when I was little able to appreciate their excellence from my own lack of Christian faith and purity, I ventured to ridicule. It is surprising (though I ought, perhaps, hardly to use the word) what progress the real piety of the Oxonians has caused them to make. A very excellent and dear friend of Charlotte's, who was decidedly of the other school, has a sister now married and settled at Oxford, and both have become great admirers of Newman. I think the 'Churchification,' as you call it, of the 'Evans' would go further to make a perfect Christian than anything I know. It must be the work of the Spirit, and, as such, will of course be opposed by the enemy. . . .

I have been much interested lately by a letter I have received from Charlotte's cousin, Augustus Frazer. He is an excellent fellow, and is a most earnest seeker after truth, and part of the occasion of this letter is to ask your assistance and guidance in directing his course. He became a real Christian principally through the Evangelical party, and then became still less sound in Church views by seeing much of a clever and, I believe, pious man, Dr. Olinthus Gregory, who is a Baptist. We used to have frequent talks together, and one day, by chance as one calls it, I used your remark as to the Apostle cautioning us against those who walk ἀτάκτως.[1] It happened to strike me as applicable to him, particularly as a military man, and I argued on it in that way. Many months after this, just before I went abroad, he said he had thought much of our conversation, and he borrowed Newman's sermons and the Oxford Tracts, and your Oxford sermons of me. On our return we found he had left with his troop for Sheffield; and from Sheffield he wrote to me the other day saying he had been much struck with many new things in the Tracts, and altogether greatly interested in all the books I had lent him, but said he felt a little bewildered between his old and new ideas, and asked my assistance, the more so because my remark about walking ἀτάκτως had first set him thinking, and he was most anxious to get right. I have recommended him to read Hooker, especially the preface and the first book, and also Jebb's Correspondence; and now I want you to point out that which you

[1] *Anglice* 'disorderly.'

think would suit him. Wordsworth's book seems to me as if it might be very useful; but living converse is always wanting, and I wish much to know, before I write again, if you can recommend any one of the clergy of Sheffield with whom he should endeavour to become acquainted. . . . What you say of the Roman Catholic tactics is much borne out by an anecdote told me by an Italian who has become a Protestant, though not exactly a Churchman. When he in confession was ordered to pray to the saints, he said he could not. ' Well,' said the confessor, ' if you are bold enough to approach the Saviour without their intervention, you may, but do not mention it.' Now this was an Italian priest, so the scheme is widely laid. God grant it may issue in a reform from within of that unhappy Church !

To the same.

IGNORANCE OF CHURCHMANSHIP.—GRADUAL EXTENSION OF CHRISTIAN DUTIES.—A SCENE WITH A MADMAN.

Lincoln's Inn : February 6, 1838.

. . . I thought I had a good deal to say about your preface, but cannot now think of much beyond what I mentioned in my last. Both the work and the preface[1] will, I trust, be very service-able. Half the religious world (as it is fashionably

---

[1] The preface to Dr. J. M'Vicar's *Life of Bishop Hobart* was written by Dr. Hook. For notices of Bishop Hobart see *Life of Dr. Hook*, pp. 71–75, small edition, and vol. i. pp. 98–104.

called, instead of the Church) would be little able to appreciate such a character as Hobart's, from pure ignorance of what a Churchman is. It is singular to see how half the people you talk with stare if you speak of the Catholic Church with reference to any but Papists, as though they had never heard the Creed or Prayer for all Conditions of Men. This is unquestionably a sore evil; but I hope there are symptoms of a 'Churchifying,' as you have termed it, of the Evangelicals. Bishop Wilson [of Calcutta] is a remarkable instance of this process. I believe him to have been a conscientious man, and that, being placed in a new position, he for the first time began to inquire what a bishop was. Assuredly I prefer the appointment of such men to that of many others, some of dubious doctrine, others of still more dubious practice. . . .

I regret much that you should have had any family annoyance from the misjudging zeal of the party Christians; that subdivision into coteries, the substitution of some conventional language for the practical testimony of Christian fellowship, is one of the chief mischiefs of their mistaken course. It breaks up family ties, and leads not unfrequently to associations which are afterwards deplored. I think nothing is more essential to be impressed on us all, than a careful attention to the peculiar duties Providence has set before us. Thus our homes, our families, our parishes, our dioceses, form one widening circle for the exercise of religious sympathies, extending onwards to our own nation, and then to the universal Church. According to our proportion of talents it is evident that our zeal must be extended to one or more of these circles of duty. Some can only provide for their family ; they are guilty of a direct breach of the Divine law, and the Apostle tells us are worse than heathens, if they neglect this (say, for instance, to run after the establishment of some favourite Apollos in the parish pulpit); others can extend a portion of their time and influence to parochial affairs without injuring their family, but yet have neither fair time nor ability to be attending meetings at Exeter Hall for translating the Bible into Chinese, or sending missionaries to New Zealand, and so on. Τὰ ἑαυτοῦ πράττειν [1] is the definition of justice that Plato at last arrives at in his ' Republic,' and a very serviceable one it would be to many Christians likewise. . . .

Charlotte, I am happy to say, is quite well, notwithstanding a great fright she had last Friday from a poor madman insisting on coming to our house instead of going to Bedlam, whither I had departed to meet him. His wife went into violent hysterics till she was almost as mad as her husband, clasping Charlotte round the waist, and insisting that her husband had killed us both. Happily,

---

[1] ' To do one's own business.'

some of our kind neighbours managed to help
Charlotte out of her difficulty, and Jennings got
the man sent to the workhouse. Happily, too,
though the man has taken up a knife and threatened to kill his wife several times, he is very docile
both with Charlotte and me, so that she was not
so much alarmed as she otherwise would have been.

To the same.

THE NATURE OF HEAVENLY REST.—THE EVILS OF CONTROVERSY.

Lincoln's Inn: May 20, 1838.

. . . I shall much regret your losing a holiday ;
but, still, a change of occupation will be in some
respects a holiday to you. I can quite see by your
last two letters that you have been overworked,
and I fully enter into that craving for rest which
you express so feelingly. But I doubt not you
have also often felt that when your holidays have
been extended to any great length you begin to
feel uneasy. I am quite prepared for working
again at the end of any vacation I get. A something within us here is always whispering that man
is formed for labour, and confirms, if it needed
confirmation, the record of the primæval curse. I
have often, my dear friend, dwelt, as you now do,
in my heart upon the peace and rest of heaven,
which I apprehend will be principally felt as a

spiritual rest from sin, and from the assaults of the Tempter ; for no doubt the angels are continually and actively employed in God's service. A rest from the wickedness of others must bring unspeakable calm to the persecuted saint ; but oh ! how infinitely more overwhelming the joyfulness of heart of the wearied and trembling sinner when ' his warfare shall have been accomplished ' and ' his iniquities pardoned '! I dare not think often of these things, finding it not to be good for me. I am by nature much too sanguine ; too much inclined to dwell on God's mercy and the bliss of heaven, and to pass over my own horrible guilt and the awfulness of the sacrifice required for it.

I read yesterday Newman's sermon on the ' Religion of the Present Day,' in his first volume, and found it peculiarly applicable to myself ; yes, fearfully so. The world has run so smoothly with me ; I have always borne a good name, and have been, unconsciously on their part, so much flattered by many of those dear to me, that I seem at times as if I were in a dream of peace which will be hereafter frightfully dissipated. I greatly need your prayers, my oldest and best of friends, and not your praise ; for, if I know my own heart at all, I am devoured by a fearful vanity and regard for the world's good opinion which is a root of bitterness in me. . . .

I am sorry that you have been involved in a

paper war, and I particularly regret that your curate should have entered the lists—a proceeding of which you will bear the credit, or, rather, the discredit. It is always lamentable to see controversy in the Church; and, indeed, it seldom answers any Christian purpose when carried on with heretics. So difficult is it to argue for truth and not for victory! One expression which slipped from you in your letter betrayed the necessary irritation created by such contests. You say the pamphlet against —— should have been treated with 'sarcasm'—a most unchristian weapon, and the surest annihilation of love in the bosom of the combatants. In short, as I said before, it appears to me that controversy is most injurious to the cause of Christ. Sound exposition of true doctrine seems to me the surest and most faithful defence against the enemies of the truth, whether misguided or malignant.

To the same.

ON THE SERMON 'HEAR THE CHURCH.'

Dean's Yard : June 30, 1838.

I write in great haste to save the post. I have just had a long talk with Joshua Watson. I pointed out to him the passage that was omitted, and he thinks it a great improvement. But what I want to say is that the only thing he feels

annoyed about is the laxity of the composition.
This Archdeacon Bailey also felt, and, indeed, his
few lines of notice were these : ' This sermon was
never intended for publication, as may be seen by
the laxity of the composition ; but circumstances
having arisen which imperatively demand its publication, it is now printed, as it was preached, *verbatim et literatim.*' But, nevertheless, both he and
Joshua agree in thinking it ought to go to the
press. Joshua Watson, however, thinks as regards
the Archdeacon's notice (and I quite agree), that
you ought not to make any apology at all. People
will say, if you do, that you had no business to
write a sermon without taking pains, when you
knew you were going to preach before the Queen ;
and, after all, it is matter, not manner, which all
sensible people will appreciate. The sermon,
Joshua Watson thinks, will do much good, though
it will not do *you* any as a composition in respect
of style.

To the same.

Coach Travelling Forty-five Years Ago.

Lincoln : September 21, 1838.

. . . After leaving you and your dear wife and
children, we, happily perhaps on the whole, had our
sentiment entirely interrupted by a very unpleasant
scene in Briggate. The coach, it seems, carries six
inside ; and, just as we were congratulating ourselves

VOL. I. S

that we were only four, we found we had to take up two more. One of these was a very dirty-looking woman, who seemed to be very ill, poor thing, and was clad in almost rags. We asked what was the matter with her—for I really thought it might be some infectious disorder—when her companion said he was a constable, and that she was charged on a coroner's verdict with child murder, and was going to York Gaol. This I thought rather too much, there being another lady; in the coach besides Charlotte; and, as we should have to be very closely packed, I went to the 'Bull and Mouth,' the coachman and guard both saying it was too bad, and that, as the company had allowed her to be booked at Halifax, they ought now to make the best of it by sending her on in a chaise. The guard said this to a proprietor at the 'Bull and Mouth,' but he absolutely refused. I then said I should not go by the coach; upon which the said proprietor was very impertinent, and said one person's money was as good as another's, &c.; and amongst other things, when I stated that the county was bound to convey persons charged with felony by separate conveyances, he replied that 'his coach was half supported by felons,' which was complimentary to your Leeds gentry. I never met with more insolence. They threatened not to let me take my luggage off, though I had paid all the fare. I said, in that case, I must get a warrant against them for stealing my luggage, and then they let me take it down. When it was all off, they at last discovered that the poor woman could go outside. I did not much like this, but it was beautiful weather ; I offered my great-coat, but the coachman had two cloaks for her ; and so all the luggage was repacked, and at last at half-past ten we left, and got to York at a little after one o'clock.

To the same.

ALEXANDER KNOX, FABER, AND NEWMAN ON JUSTIFI-
CATION.—SECESSION OF A FRIEND TO ROME.

Lincoln's Inn : October 29, 1838.

By the time you receive this it will be six weeks since we left Leeds, and I am really longing much for a line from you. I want to hear what you are about in the parish. We arrived in town on Thursday last, and are very thankful for the retrospect of our late travels, for all the kindness we have experienced, and for the happiness of seeing so many who are dear to us, in health, and, what is better, actively and beneficially employed in their Christian course, and for all the opportunities thus afforded us to advance in holiness. Yesterday we received the Holy Communion in our own church, and I feel much awakened to a sense of all my own deficiencies. At such times we feel, notwithstanding our own unworthiness, a great interest for

S 2

others who are dear to us, and the great blessing of
being permitted to pray for them, and to feel
assured that their prayers also are assisting us. . . .

The Suffolk clergy are, many of them, young
men, with perpetual curacies of only 50*l.* or 60*l.* a
year. Their zeal may be partly estimated from this
fact, and I am convinced they only want a little
information to be set right. In one, for instance, I
have witnessed a very considerable change. When
I last met him he was strongly opposed to baptismal regeneration and tradition. Faber seems to
have brought him round on both these points, but
now he is equally vehement against the Oxford
school on the score of their doctrine of justification.
He has read Newman, and thinks his views the
same as those of the Romanists, and he pressed
'Faber on Justification' upon me, which I read ; but,
on the other hand, I have begged him to read the
Oxford Tracts and your sermon (the visitation one)
which has just reached us.[1] I have read Faber
carefully. Alexander Knox is tremendously injudicious, to say the least of it, in one paragraph,
where he talks of the time coming when we shall
cease to rest on any foundation but a moral one ;
but this error is in unguardedness of expression,
for it is quite clear to me that Faber has mistaken

---

[1] 'A Call to Union on the Principles of the English Reformation,'
printed in vol. i. of the *Church and its Ordinances.* See *Life of
Dr. Hook,* p. 254, small edition, and vol. i. p. 431.

Knox throughout. The passage quoted from Knox in Faber's preface speaks of justification as 'presupposing a moral change.' Now look at Hooker's sermon on Justification, § 21 ; you find he defines the righteousness of sanctification as twofold—the one habitual (a ἕξις), *i.e.* a character of soul, part of its substance as it were ; the other as evinced by works, the result of the habit, ἕξις ; and he says that justification is preceded by this habit, so that, though first in dignity, it is last in order. Now this, as it strikes me, is the very meaning of Knox, not only in the passage I have last referred to, but also in the more objectionable one above. He does not say that this habit procures our justification, but that it is a necessary part of it, just as Hooker also says that justification and sanctification all come at once, and metaphysically the substance of righteousness is implanted, as preceding our being held or declared righteous ; this substance being in Newman's opinion no less than Christ Himself dwelling in us, and not merely externally by His merits procuring our justification. But, to speak candidly, I much regret all this metaphysical disquisition. As I told the clergyman in question, I do not find myself one whit the better for reading Newman or Faber, save and except the splendid passages in ' Newman on Holiness ' independently of his metaphysics.

Now if these worthy men would only just ask

themselves where they agree instead of where they differ, the case would, I think, stand thus : Romanists, Knox, Newman, Faber all agree—

(I.) That Christ's death is the only meritorious cause of our receiving justification or any other good gift.

(II.) That justification and sanctification are so inseparable that no one can receive the one without the other.

(III.) That one who produces no good works, time being allowed (to avoid the question of the penitent thief, who, I think, did a good work in trying to convert his brother malefactor), is not in a justified state. Knox, Newman, and Faber further agree—

(IV.) That our good works after justification can never exceed what is required of us ; that we are, after all, unprofitable servants in doing at least no more than we ought to do; and here comes in the broad distinction between Knox and the Romanists which Mr. Faber says he cannot see, but which just brings forward all the horrible notions of indulgences, transfer of works, &c. &c., and which is intimately connected with the worshipping of saints and of the Virgin, though, perhaps, in order of time the worshipping of saints led to the other error of supererogation.

Well, now, if these four points are fairly looked at, why should such men as Faber and Knox or

Faber and Newman be thought to differ funda-
mentally? Perhaps the latter think (I am not
quite clear of this) that perfection may be attained
in this life; still they do not say that more than
enough can be done; and with regard to the main
stress of Faber's argument as to external and inherent righteousness, I am sure he himself will not
say a man can be saved without sanctification,
which is admitted on all hands to be inherent, nor
will the others say a man can be saved without
Christ's merits. Then the difference seems to me
principally metaphysical, partly also arising from
the natural leaning of man to a one-sided view,
to a half truth, to a system, in short, whereas the
New Testament has beautifully avoided all system.
Perhaps Newman's school dwells too much on
inherent holiness, as Faber's would on external
holiness; but observe, the words inherent and external are scholastic and not scriptural. There are
striking texts on both points. Careless men, sensual
men, worldly-minded men, require the strong texts
as to intrinsic holiness; while weak and timid con-
sciences and men of desponding temperament require the texts as to Christ's merits being all-
sufficient. . . .

I have received a beautiful letter from old
Minchin[1] in answer to that I sent from Leeds.   He

---

[1] An old schoolfellow, one of the Shakspearian Club. His lapse
to Rome was predicted by Dr. Hook. See *Life of Dr. Hook*, p. 185.

is full of kindness and affection, but the most interesting point is his announcement that he has been received into the Roman Catholic Church. He appears to have failed in distinguishing between oral and written tradition, and between uniform tradition and modern invention, and he asks how we can define the period of the antiquity to which we refer, and whether that must not rest on human authority. He asks, as to our unity, whether any two of our parish priests agree as to justification or election. I think I can observe, as to this, that we agree quite as much as the Jansenists and Jesuits; and, indeed, here I would refer to your sermon on Unity which I will try to get to him. Now what think you of my entering into any controversy with him, which he evidently solicits? I doubt its propriety a little; and if he but firmly hold the foundation, as Hooker calls it, I should be loth to unsettle him. If you think best, I would rather recommend him books than argue, which, in fact, I am incompetent to do. Help me in this matter. You would be delighted with the affectionate tone of his letter, which shows more than anything his real conversion or renewal to Christianity.

To the same.

THE BLESSEDNESS OF SUNDAY.—THE NATURAL AND
THE SPIRITUAL MAN.

Dean's Yard: April 28, 1839.

You are the only person to whom I ever write
on a Sunday, nor do I often, even with you, break
in on any portion of this blessed day of rest. Few
can feel its value more than I have done of late,
for I have been so hard worked and so immersed
in worldly matters these last few weeks that, were
it not for the calmness of this day, I should become
a mere machine; the sport of all the events in
which I find myself as it were irresistibly engaged,
and should scarcely be conscious of a soul within me. The ψυχικὸς ἄνθρωπος[1] has certainly
much the most of me during the week. In writing
a few lines to you now that Charlotte has gone to
bed, I feel that I am enjoying some refreshment of
spirit which harmonises with the day. . . . I am
becoming more and more sensible of its being a
besetting sin with me to pine after the enjoyment
of ease, tranquillity, and freedom from pain.
These are the things craved after by the natural
man, as I have just been reading in a beautiful
sermon of Barrow's on the gift of the Holy Ghost.
The spiritual man knows that suffering and labour

[1] 'The natural man.'

are his portion in this life, and that, though he may have the same longings after happiness, he will not look for it on earth, though he may thankfully receive what is permitted him. Long-continued mercies have, I fear, rendered me wilful in this respect, and I know not how I should bear severe trial. I remember two of Keble's lines—

> Lovest thou praise? the Cross is shame;
> Or ease? the Cross is bitter grief;

and I often think both may be required to bring me to God.

To the same.

REMINISCENCES OF BOYHOOD.

Bealings: October 7, 1839.

. . . I cannot tell you how interested we both were in all your description of the early scenes of your boyhood at Ilfracombe.[1] They are, indeed, vividly imprinted upon your memory, for your description could not be more accurate, had you been there with us on this last tour. The Summer House at Linton still exists. We sat in it; and what a touching as well as magnificent prospect it commands! It would, no doubt, have been more interesting to us had we known all that you had then felt in the poetic dreams of childhood—the poetic age; for assuredly our imagina-

---

[1] See letter in *Life of Dr. Hook*, p. 209, small edition; vol. ii. p. 401.

tion is then all-powerful. Our reason is then
weak; our active, buoyant spirits allow little reflection on the past; the senses are in their fullest
activity and vigour ; the impressions made on them
are novel, and therefore vivid ; and the joyous
anticipations of the soul, unchecked by experience
and its consequent disappointments, form a thousand
varied pictures of imaginary beauty and happiness.
Dull, indeed, must he be whose childhood has been
unimaginative.

With regard to yourself, my dearest friend,
how much did your letter recall to my mind your
early habits of thought, and somewhat wayward
reserve of character ! How often, too, have I again
lived over those early days in the few hours which
I and Charlotte spent at Winchester ! She and I
walked our favourite walk in meads where, when
I became a prefect, we used to enjoy the facility
given to our solitary rambles. We saw the old
tree where you read me your tragedy of ' James
II. ; ' and I read some stuff of mine, which I remember I always felt to be wonderfully inferior to
your really poetic turn of mind. There, too, you
used to read to me any new play that came out.
We strolled to the end of meads and then turned
up past sundry places, called Dalmatia, &c., to
Tunbridge. There we saw the old chalk-pit where
at Evening Hills you used to sit with me, and we
each had our Shakspeare, and read in dialogue

with each other; and then we wended our way by the river-side, passing Newbridge and along Goddard's Walk, home. How deep is every impression of these old haunts! It seemed to me but yesterday that we were there together. I can well recollect, in Goddard's Walk, even the very spot where you got angry with me for interrupting you in the middle of a story; and many little, trifling matters like this, which seem so mysteriously to entwine themselves around particular places. But I am thankful that I had better and deeper thoughts, too, to feed upon. We were at Winchester by twelve o'clock on Tuesday, and we went at once over the college. How solemn did the chapel seem to me! Last night only we were reading here a sermon of Newman's, called ' Christ in remembrance ' (I think), in his last volume, in which he says that we do not feel the greatest blessings at the time, but afterwards. He illustrates this from Scripture, as Jacob not being conscious of the great Angel's presence whilst wrestling with him, but on His departure, and so of the same mysterious Being's appearance to Gideon and Manoah ; and then he says how many things we can look back upon in life, and see God with us. Amongst others he instances the school we were sent to as children ; the occasion of our falling in with those persons who have most benefited us. This almost made my voice falter, when I thought of Winchester and the inestimable blessing of your friendship. In that chapel I received my first Communion. It seems as though it had been an anchor to my soul when tossed by more storms than even you can tell. I look back with amazement to the interval between my first admission to such a wonderful privilege, and the time when religion really seemed to take some hold upon me. I do not know whether I have ever had the same strength of faith and love that I then had; but assuredly for many, many sad years of a sinful and comparatively godless life I had not. It was not without deep emotion, therefore, that I looked upon that place, that very altar, where, as it seemed, God plucked me as a brand from the burning! Would that I had never looked back from that hour! I was quite upset by excitement during that Winchester visit, but I hope it may be profitable to me.

From the chapel we went to the cloisters, where we saw Mrs. Wordsworth's grave. We had seen her as a beautiful girl, just emerging into womanhood, shortly before her marriage. What a lesson for us not to fix our affections here!

We then went to the school; you had told me of our seat being removed. I am sincerely sorry for it. As we wished to attend the cathedral service we did not go over commoners on the Tuesday, but I just walked as far as the bishop's palace and into the garden, almost as coolly as we used to do when we took possession of his parlour as our House of Commons.

To the same.

'PRESBYTERIAN RIGHTS ASSERTED.'[1]

Lincoln's Inn: November 25, 1839.

You have spoiled a joke of mine by your letter of to-day. I only got 'Presbyterian Rights' on Friday evening, and meant to have written on Saturday a furious critique upon it, but in term time I have hardly a moment to myself; and to-day, when I was going to scribble a few lines for the same purpose, I got your letter, and I can therefore no longer assume ignorance of the authorship.

Hall sent me the pamphlet as a present from himself, but I had not read five lines without finding out the author. I think you would find it difficult to take me in, and especially if you *will* put in old jokes about 'an examining master, plus a proctor,' and eulogise Palmer.[2] Not that I mean to say Palmer can find no one else to eulogise him. Dr. Pusey[3] has done so in his admirable letter, with the whole of which I cordially sympathise, except, perhaps, the parts as to the invoca-

---

[1] Title of an anonymous pamphlet by Dr. Hook. For an account of it, see his *Life*, pp. 267–272, small edition, and vol. i. pp. 461–470.

[2] W. Palmer, author of *Origines Liturgicæ*.

[3] A letter to the Bishop of Oxford on 'Tendencies to Romanism.'

tion of saints and prayers for the dead ; but the spirit of the whole is beautiful. This is, however, a parenthesis. Seriously, I much like your vindication of the priesthood, which has, no doubt, been rendered more necessary by the Oxford writers having somewhat too highly exalted the episcopate. There is much material for thought, too, in your point as to the domestic Church. The view you take is, I think, the only sound one against priestcraft on the one hand, and fanatic assumption of the priestly office by laymen on the other. To speak candidly, I have thought the tendency of the Oxford school somewhat too strong to the former error. Compulsory confession has led to an entire invasion of the rights of the paterfamilias by the Roman priest.

Could I have seen your little work, however, before its publication, I should have liked to recommend the omission of one or two matters, and the softening of others; for instance, even your joke about the ' examining master, plus a proctor,' is tacked on to an offensive epithet of a ' high Establishment prelate,' and, being told as of a living person, that person will be justly annoyed at the epithet thus affixed to him. The portion, too, as to the Bible Society meeting, evidently alludes to some threatened annoyance you have anticipated on the part of your own bishop, and assumes somewhat of a personal character of complaint. Now, in exact proportion as any part of your argument can be represented as personal, it will lose the weight attached to calm and well-considered observations and reflections. The work will do good, however. What most disturbs me is that it may do you harm; and, as it may tend to shake the apparent good feeling between you and your bishop, it will, to that extent, be injurious to your public usefulness.

To the same.

LUKEWARMNESS IN RELIGION.—THE LIFE AND CHARACTER
OF LUTHER.

Tenby: October 9, 1840.

. . . It strikes me fearfully in our towns that we see very few of the lowest poor in our churches. In this little place, for instance, I do not think I have seen one fisherman, though there are hundreds, I suppose, in the town. And, on the other hand, it strikes me no less fearfully that, judging by the deadness of the responses, so few amongst the higher classes appear to have been instructed as they ought to be, or to be aware of the blessings and privileges they possess. The non-attendance at the Lord's Table is, of course, a yet more awful proof of this. To the rising generation we must look; and, thank God, our National and Sunday schools will, I believe, by His blessing be a means of preparing the poor and shaming the rich till they awake from their deadly torpor. It is a fearful state to be 'neither hot nor cold,' which is, I apprehend, the state of the large mass of the middle-aged population of our country. On this account one feels the stirring of the waters by the Oxford men to be most healthy, though I am not inclined to call them individually 'Rabbi.' I long to read Sewell's book, and hope to do so when I get home. I will get Poole's also. We have been reading here a very ill-written 'History of the Reformation' by D'Aubigné, a Genevese pastor, but valuable from its full details, from original sources, of Luther's history. In fact, it may be called a life of Luther, and it is, of course, a panegyric ; but, at the same time, his faults are not the less apparent because the writer happens to take them for virtues. I must say, however, that, on the whole, I rise with a deep impression of the piety and fervent love of God and of our blessed Saviour which alone can have upheld Luther in his arduous struggle. His celebrated answer at the Diet of Worms when called on for the third time to retract, and brought before the greatest of earthly potentates, Charles V., and all the pomp of the Roman nuncio, and of the mitred as well as lay sovereigns of the German States, is one of the finest events in history : 'I stand here and can give no other answer, God help me ! Amen.' This too when he well knew that, only a

few years before, John Huss had been delivered up
to the stake, notwithstanding the Emperor's safe-
conduct. Luther struggled long also not to break
with the Church. Every step he took was, as it
were, forced on him. His journey in early life to
Rome taught him that the cardinals were infidels,
and he shrank with a child's simplicity and horror
(he was but twenty-four or twenty-five years old)
from their impious conversation. One tract which
he prepared, but never published, owing to the
scandal it would create, related to some of their
most dreadful deeds of darkness. One cannot
wonder that he saw Antichrist on the Roman
throne. No doubt Luther has many and grave
offences to answer for ; but who can read of him
without feeling that he himself is liable to the same
sins, and falls far below his exalted virtues ?

To the same.

LACK OF LEISURE.—THE PRINCIPLE WHICH SHOULD
GUIDE ELECTORS.

Lincoln's Inn: November 14, 1840.

. . . I have, as you desired me, bought
Poole's book ('Cyprian'). When I shall read it, is
quite another matter. Jennings, too, has promised
to lend me the 'British Magazine' containing the
articles on the Poor. I do not take in any
periodicals, for I should be sorely tempted to read

them, and yet I know that I have no right so to enjoy myself. When I look sometimes even on my own small library I feel that it is a daily self-denial that one exercises in devoting so much time to the labours of life, and I trust I do not deceive myself when I conclude that a sense of duty, and not a love of money, impels me to my work. There is, unhappily, no medium in our profession. You cannot say, ' I will give up so much time to my profession, and so much to other pursuits.' It requires unqualified submission to its demands on your time, and you would not merely lose money but break faith with those who entrust their interests to your charge if you hesitated to bestow your undivided energies on their protection.

In the midst of my work, however, I managed to get to Cambridge on Wednesday last.[1] The Vice-Chancellor rose for the day to facilitate the departure of the Bar; he himself and the majority of our fraternity going for Lord Lyndhurst. I was, as you may suppose, in the minority. I confess, after your letter as to the High Church portion of the clergy, and after hearing that Baptist Noel and Cunningham had also taken up the contest as one of principle, I did not expect quite so sound a thrashing; and I question the wisdom of Lord Lyttelton's committee in going to the poll, though I do not personally regret that nearly five hundred

[1] To vote for the election of Chancellor of the University.

votes, together with my own, were recorded against the flagrant sin of exalting a man for the sake of party. I think, if I know anything of myself, I should not have voted for Lord Lyndhurst had he been a Whig, the post being merely one of honour. The case of a member of Parliament is different: he is the instrument by which alone as an elector you can ensure the advancement of your political views; and you have to balance whether A., personally good, but supporting (as you think) most mischievous public measures, is to be preferred to B., personally bad, but supporting the most beneficial course for your country. You are not doing evil that good may ensue, but are compelled to an unpleasant choice between two evils. Now, nothing of this sort is applicable to our late contest.

To the same.

TRACT 90 AND THE TRACTARIANS.

Dean's Yard: March 18, 1841.

. . . I have been much vexed at this Tract 90 business. I have not yet read it, and do not, of course, judge by extracts; but the censure it has called forth from authority is at all events a proof to me of its being injudicious, to say the least of it, and I shall have great difficulty in believing it (from its subject) to be necessary, though I doubt not Newman thinks so. I have read his letter, beautifully expressed, as is everything which he writes, and one is unwilling to suppose so holy a man to be in error, and it perhaps argues a want of humility in me to judge of him at all. But my fear about the Oxford men is, and has been, that, shut up in a limited society, they will have a tendency to fanaticism which more intercourse with our fellow-creatures softens.

The more I see of these matters, the more I am convinced that society is the proper sphere of man, and that all recluse habits are mischievous. I was amused to see you denounced, in a letter in the 'Morning Chronicle,' as the 'real author of Puseyism.' What a pity it was not called ' Hookism,' and what a decided ' Hookite' I should have been, whereas I am but a half-and-half Puseyite ! Seriously, I am much vexed at the tendency to schism in all ultra proceedings, and such, I think, many of the Oxford party to be pushing on.

A late number of the ' British Critic' lamented that our prayers were not in Latin. Such, at least, was its tendency ; nor can I at all follow the doctrine about reserve.[1] I find none in St. Peter's sermon on the day of Pentecost, nor even in St. Paul's sermons before heathen governors and heathen people. He told them the great but startling truth of the Resurrection of Christ and of

---

[1] On ' Reserve in communicating Religious Truth,' by the Rev. Isaac Williams, one of the 'Tracts for the Times.'

His being our judge, nor is there any reason to suppose that he kept back the Atonement because he does not mention it in his first-recorded address. He makes a boast to the elders of Ephesus that he had kept back nothing from them, and seems to direct them to deal with their flocks in the same way.

To the same.

AFTER THE CONSECRATION OF LEEDS PARISH CHURCH.

Reading: September 16, 1841.

How can I express all the mingled feelings of the past week in which, assuredly, great thankfulness to God should be predominant! Such a day as Thursday I have never known. I do believe that of the immense multitude which was then assembled in God's presence there were few whose hearts could be insensible to the blessing vouchsafed them, and I think that the setting forth of His honour and glory was the first aspiration of all our hearts. At the subsequent meeting I own I felt a more earthly satisfaction in the well-deserved homage paid to my oldest and dearest friend, not unmingled, perhaps, with something beyond complacency that he was my friend; but, if in any undue excess, assuredly my pride was sufficiently humbled by the comparison of my own uselessness with the work that you have been permitted to do in our Master's service in building up not only the material fabric, but the spiritual edifice of the Church. May God's blessing rest, my dearest friend, upon these and all your labours! I should much have liked to remain over the Friday, but it was as well, perhaps, that I did not. I was very nearly knocked up when I reached the railway on Thursday evening. What must you and your dear wife be! but special strength seems given for special occasions. I am sure I shall never forget her quiet, cheerful reception of all of us, her somewhat troublesome guests.

To the same.

TRACT 90.

Lincoln's Inn: November 26, 1841.

. . . . The more I think of Tract 90—and I have lately thought of it much—the less I like it. It requires one almost to know Newman personally not to feel great indignation at the sophistical explanation of subscription to the Articles, which may really mean anything if they mean what he says. I am, however, content and thankful to believe that the author of the most heart-stirring and deep-searching sermons I ever read is a single-hearted man; but I think that the Tract has done infinite mischief, which, however, was begun by the publication of Froude's 'Remains.' With all his extravagant faults, I believe that Luther was single-hearted, and it was this alone that gave him such power; and though I by no means regard sincerity as an excuse for error, yet I think straightforwardness in error far less mischievous than casuistry. I believe Newman's Tract to have been meant for others, rather than as expressing that he himself holds all the doctrines which he says *may* be held consistently with the Articles. I suspect that he saw much to dread in the hotheaded young men who have only just had their eyes opened to the evils of ultra Protestantism, and are inclined to be blind to the deformities of Popery, if not to rush headlong into it. Young men are usually honest, and he was afraid of their following out some of the principles of Froude, and that, finding the Articles to be framed by those whom Froude so abundantly vilifies, they would think it inconsistent to subscribe to them.

I confess I do not much like the expostulations in the ' Lyra Apostolica ' with the Church of Rome ; their tone is too deprecatory. All this, my dearest friend, I say to you, though I have too much of your own feeling, as to turning round with the popular tide, to admit so much to others. I feel daily more and more thankful that as a Catholic I, with God's blessing, am determined to follow no man—no one man, I mean. The Bible and Prayer Book seem to me the real guides for an unlearned Christian, and amongst such I must, alas ! reckon myself, such being the state of education in our Christian country. I think it would be well if the study of the Fathers were made a part of our education. Even supposing (which, however, we will not admit) that the Greek of Chrysostom, or the Latin of Augustine or Cyprian, would corrupt our classical taste, yet what is that in comparison with the corruption of our hearts by the false notions of true glory and true happiness instilled into us by the pages of heathen authors, unsanctified and uncorrected by any holier studies?

To the same.

FROUDE'S 'REMAINS.'

Lincoln's Inn: January 22, 1842.

. . . One of my main reasons for writing is to say how truly delighted I am with your letter to the bishop.[1] It is most gratifying to me to find that we do not disagree on such all-important subjects, but, as my instruction came first from you, it is not, perhaps, very likely that we should. Still, I confess your enthusiasm which led you to stick to Newman after No. 90, though I thought it but chivalrous feeling, seeing that he was unjustly abused, and not explicit assent to all the notions in said 90 contained, had somewhat alarmed me. I have, since the publication of Froude's 'Remains,' been on my guard against Newman. I mean not

---

[1] Letter to the Bishop of Ripon 'On the State of Parties in the Church of England.' See *Life of Dr. Hook*, vol. i. p. 74, and 323, small edition.

as to his honesty, but as to his judgment. Froude, an intemperate young man, led fearfully astray in early youth, by God's grace wonderfully reclaimed, and no doubt a saint in heaven, chooses to scribble a number of crude notions about the Reformation, amongst other things, and leave them unpublished, and then Newman must needs fire off all these combustibles. The startling notion, the reserve notion, and several others I confess I object to. People are not to be set raving for fear they should go to sleep, nor to be starved for fear they should take poison. There was a slight want of humility, I think, in all this, and I question also whether anonymous tracts on such important subjects should be issued by sober-minded men at all. I think your letter will do very great good, though the zealots on both sides will abuse it. It is to myself personally a great comfort. Alas! the Church is indeed in a sad state; but the storm may be necessary for the purifying of the waters, and is, I admit, better than the dull, and slimy, and deathlike stagnation that preceded it.

To the same.

Sudden Conversion less trustworthy than gradual.

Hatherley: August 28, 1843.

. . . I do not know that I should have written so soon but for your interesting account of

Mr. Aitken. It seems but the other day that I saw his name placarded all over Westminster as about to preach in some Methodist chapel. I am truly glad that he has now received a commission for the edification of the Church, but I candidly confess that I am not sanguine of those who in a week have been brought to pour out their hearts to him in confession. Neither, until I know the circumstances, can I judge whether the young man you mention ought to have given up his 300l. a year. Any scheme which you on deliberation approve, you know it will be a privilege to me to be permitted to aid in; but I hope you will not think me cold-hearted if I cannot at once feel confidence in those who have lately undergone a considerable change of opinion, nor should I have chosen such a one for my confessor. Greatly, indeed, do I rejoice in his zeal, and in God's mercy and grace in directing it aright, and I quite feel, with you, that a little 'ultraism' is desirable in this Laodicean age; but one never feels sure where the change is sudden, and not the result of progressive conviction, strengthened by progressive perseverance of action. At the same time there is, I believe, more discipline and regularity and restraint in Methodism than in the other lawless sects, so that probably the change is not so violent as it must be from any other class of Dissenters. I would rather have seen Mr. Aitken your curate for a while. In the meantime it is a great mercy for such a place as Leeds to be stirred up to *think*; and if the little ones are brought to the font, and some stop put to the inroads which Satan is making amidst the heathen population, the unbaptised youth of our large towns, much may yet be hoped for. I should have doubted whether his congregation were yet prepared for daily Communion. Has the demand come from them? I by no means concur in the absurd notion of some of our commercial legislators that the demand should precede the supply in spiritual things; but I do think that, where the means of grace are supplied and used in weekly or monthly Communion, the fitness of the congregation for more extended privileges would be best evinced by their desiring it themselves.

To the same.

'THE EFFECTUAL FERVENT PRAYER OF A RIGHTEOUS MAN AVAILETH MUCH.'

Bealings: August 30, 1843.

. . . We have, as you may suppose, been watching in the papers with some anxiety the proceedings in the manufacturing districts, and truly thankful have we been to see that you have hitherto escaped the incursions of the misguided mobs that are parading the country all around you. I do not apprehend any serious injury to you or yours personally, but any interruption of the labour of your population must bring with it many disastrous consequences, and add tenfold to the calamities which poverty entails on so many of your parishioners. They seem to have evinced hitherto much patient forbearance at Leeds, and I trust that your efforts have, by God's blessing, been of great service in promoting good order directly; but far more efficacy I attribute to the indirect consequences of the prayers and faithfulness of real Christians. To nothing else is it owing, in my firm belief, that we are spared as a nation, and permitted to prosper, in spite of grievous sins in all shapes, amounting to almost national offence. Thankfully ought we to remember that Sodom would have been spared for the sake of ten righteous men.

To the same.

THOUGHTS RETROSPECTIVE AND INTROSPECTIVE.

Bealings: September 11, 1844.

. . . I grieve to say that my poor, dear uncle is in a state which makes me very anxious; for though he rides a little and walks about, yet still there is evidently disease of an alarming character about the brain; but God's will be done. I learn, I hope, daily to say this entirely from the heart, and to look for any rest where alone it can be found. I well recollect that (as in all spiritual things), you not only greatly helped, but first gave me the right impulse in this matter. It seemed to you, I dare say, a small thing, and you forget it; but ' a word in season, how good is it!' Some years ago, ten or twelve perhaps, I was talking of my working hard and hoping some day to retire as my greatest ambition. You said: ' You are looking for a time to rest, and when that comes it will be time for you to be taken away.' I felt it to be very true, and more especially for one who had so horribly wasted his youth as I had; and indeed I daily more and more learnt, and have still to learn, how fearfully I sought my own ends, my own comfort and indulgence, in everything; and I do really believe now that I have almost got over my wish to retire, or wishing indeed anything, which is a most foolish and morbid exercise of the mind. I now rather expect than otherwise that each day will bring fresh trials, and pray earnestly I may be directed and guided in them to do my Master's work aright, and to seek His glory in all my doings, and most chiefly to set it forth by love to my fellow creatures. In truth, I can hardly tell you what a self-loathing my selfishness gives me, when I think of it in all its past activity, and when I see it breaking out in almost all my first impulses still. I should be ashamed to tell you, or any human being, one tenth part of the first thoughts that occur to me daily on the passing circumstances of the day—so utterly selfish are they—and most truly may I know that it is only by God's unspeakable grace that any good thing is in me !

I can well imagine what passes in your mind in these affecting confidences which are reposed in you ; but the sense of the comfort which, by your sympathy and experience, you are able to give, must be a great consolation. I often feel that I would give worlds to be of any use extensively to my fellow sinners ; but am quite aware of my incompetency, and, yet more, of my unworthiness for the task, and am not at all depressed, as I used to be, by the sense of my unprofitableness, knowing how merciful the check is to my own most inveterate love of praise, and being confident that He who has so wonderfully spared me hitherto will not forsake me, nor suffer me to perish, if I but trust in Him and not in my own strength.

To the same.

EXPECTED SECESSION OF J. H. NEWMAN.

Lincoln's Inn : November 23, 1844.

. . . What a terrible business this is about Newman ! for none seem to doubt that it may be very near the truth. The comfort of Catholic doctrine, when well understood, is that it is the Church, and no individual of the Church, that we rely on as our guide ; but those who know nothing of this as yet, and whom one would wish to perceive it, are just the people who will be kept off from the right track by such an alarm. However, God orders all as seemeth Him good, and deeply humbled ought one to be when one so every way above us is permitted to fall into error.

To the same.

DR. ARNOLD.

Bealings: December 26, 1844.

. . . I have read bits of the 'Life of Arnold,' which have interested me much. His one great fault seems to have been self-confidence. How difficult it is to steer between that rock and the shoals and shallows of adopting the opinions of all whom we associate with! The Church alone seems to afford a resting point between the two extremes, or rather, to continue the metaphor, the 'Via Media.' He felt the necessity of a Church; but, whilst he would 'lengthen the cords,' he forgot the necessity of 'strengthening the stakes.' Nor can I conceive how, if pushed upon the point, he would have drawn his line which excluded the Unitarians from his ideal of a Christian Church. Nevertheless, it is impossible not to love the man, though one rejects with repugnance his theories; and, as the first to Christianise our public schools, the future generations will owe him a deep debt of gratitude.

To the same.

QUIETNESS THE STRENGTH OF THE CHURCH.

12 Great George Street: January 26, 1845.

. . . I endeavour to think only in prayer of the sad divisions in the Church! I am determined to read fewer books than ever on disputed points, and the Bible more. I have not read Ward's book, therefore; indeed, its length would render it impossible to do so. I think they are wrong at Oxford in endeavouring to fix bad faith on him in their censure, whether they be right or not in censuring him.[1] I read Gladstone's review in the ' Quarterly,' which seemed to me admirably done, as far as one who had not read the book could judge. A little quiet parish work, each man in his own parish, would be better, I think, just now than all the volumes of pamphlets. Our strength is to sit still.

To the same.

PRAYER.—BAPTISMAL GRACE.—ILLNESS OF SIR W. FOLLETT.

Lincoln's Inn: June 27, 1845.

. . . What an awful thought it is that prayer is so often (apparently) unavailing with reference to the spiritual condition of others! The undervaluing of baptismal privileges has, I fear, done

[1] See *Life of Dr. Hook*, vol. i. pp. 185–189, and 391–394 small edition.

much towards the hardening of men's hearts against the consequences of wilful sin after baptism. The anti-baptismal (rather than anabaptismal) heresy has been very deadly, and the denying of regeneration can be deemed little less. When any worldly evils attend a fall from holiness, all can sympathise, as in the case of a lost woman ; but the first presumptuous sin of any kind is no less fearful, and yet in a few weeks, sometimes hours, is forgotten ; and those who have often lied, acted selfishly, or otherwise polluted their baptismal robe, it is supposed, may at once be restored not even by an act, but by a *feeling* of faith. Those fearful instances of the result of single acts of disobedience in our first parents, in Esau, in Reuben, in Saul, and others, nay even in God's saints, as in the case of Moses, are rarely brought before men's minds. But I do not know how I came to ramble on upon this topic, except that it is Friday, when I feel that my own sins are ' more in number than the hairs of my head,' and they sometimes ' take such hold upon me that I am not able to look up.' I much need all your prayers for a heart of flesh and not of stone. . . .

Follett[1] is, I fear, rapidly sinking. I cannot say what interest I have felt in his case. In every qualification of intellect and grace of manner

---

[1] Sir William Webb Follett, Attorney-General, died soon after the date of this letter.

he was as perfect as man can be, and at an unusually early age had the highest post in his professional career apparently within his grasp. Since his first attack, more than a year ago, I have not ceased to pray daily for him. His wife, too, is so very interesting a person, in her quiet earnest supplications, which one must feel sure were constantly offered; and I know no fellowship so close as that of communion of prayer, though she will probably never dream that we have been thinking of her or of her husband.

To the same.

EFFECTS OF ROMANISM ON THE CHARACTER.

Lincoln's Inn: October 25, 1845.

. . . I cannot compare Newman to Athanasius. I think his case much more like John Wesley's—I mean so far as it is presented to our judgment, for I dare not, of course, say anything of his internal guidance.

I cannot but fear that others are imbued with the deadly taint of Romanism. I mean that poison which perverts the uprightness and candour of the mind, and allows people to think themselves honest when they are speaking only half their real thoughts, and that in such a way as to mislead those who are not aware of the concealed purpose. The Italian character pervades the English Romanists. If they went to Germany, or perhaps even to

U 2

France, for their education, it would be far better, for the German character is frank, like that of the English.

No. 90 shook my confidence in the party to the foundation.

To the same.

NEWSPAPER WARFARE.—THE CHURCH AND SCHISMATICS.

Lincoln's Inn: November 11, 1845.

. . . I have been surprised that Pusey should write letters in the papers ; ——'s doing so did not surprise me, for his conceit is such that he would be very sensitive to the world's opinion. Even as an individual I should never notice newspaper abuse ; but, as representing a body of Churchmen, a man should be very careful not to recognise the newspaper jurisdiction.

I always loved that text ' Their strength is to sit still,' and I am sure there never was a time when it was more necessary to bear this in mind. No abuse can make truth less truth ; but it may make us more humble, and this will be the better for us. To confuse Churchmen with the Romish schismatics will, of course, be Satan's principal device just now ; but we know our weapons, which are ' not carnal ' (newspapers, reviews, or pamphlets), ' but spiritual,' namely mortification and prayer, and these will yet be ' mighty to the pulling down of strongholds.' The most humbling circumstance to my mind is the wandering of such a man as Newman. . . . Perhaps it is intended to show us the fearful extent of the 'Paul and Apollos' system. Ward scrupled not to avow that he followed Newman. The great beauty of the Church system is that you follow principles worked out by holy men at the time they were under the direct guidance of the Holy Spirit, Whom we must believe to guide the Church, and all its authorised branches, in their solemn deliberations; whilst those who have joined the foreign schismatics have mostly followed an individual who is, of course, subject to all the weaknesses of our nature, and may, for aught we can tell, have taken the first decisive step in a moment of weakness.

To Mrs. Charles Stephens.

ADVICE TO A UNITARIAN IN SEARCH OF RELIGIOUS TRUTH.

12 Great George Street : Sunday, December 14, 1845.

My dearest Sister,— . . . I sit down to talk with you a little on paper as I should do if you were present. Nor is the day unsuited to the subject of your last letter, which greatly interested me.

After the enjoyment of the infinite blessings provided for us by the Church in her services, I do, indeed, from the bottom of my heart, sympa-

thise with those yearnings of your afflicted friend
after something positive. She will not, I feel
assured, discover it in the wild schemes of Rouge,
or the other Polish leader of the German movement, whose name I forget. They have, like John
Wesley and so many others, and like those who
tore the Church to pieces of old—such as Arius,
Donatus, and other leading schismatics—separated
from the Church Catholic, instead of endeavouring
to reform and purify her from within. This
naturally places them in antagonism to her. They
will begin by professing, probably sincerely, a
hatred only of the impurities and follies which they
witness in that portion of the Church to which they
belong ; they will also profess, and probably at first
exhibit, great moral personal purity, and personal
piety,—no leaders of a schism ever succeeded without doing so ; but presently it will be assumed that
the Church is radically and hopelessly corrupt ; that
they, the new apostles, are eminently the reverse ;
personal vanity will make sad inroads on their
personal piety ; and, as their followers increase, they,
too, will become, as the Church whence they proceeded, a mixed body of good and bad ; but having
no principle of union, and being, indeed, founded
on a principle of separation, they will never have
any power of reforming themselves, but will sub-
divide into innumerable lesser sects and schisms.
The fundamental error is that which I at first

mentioned—the not seeing that it is our plain duty not to rend Christ's garment. They really seem as if, in their horror of the mockery of the Holy Tunic exhibited at Trèves (which occasioned the whole movement), they had imbibed an equal horror of the beautiful type of the garment without seam.

If I had the misfortune of being born under a tyrannical government I should not endeavour to destroy it by rebellion, but to remove the evil by every lawful means that was left. Still more in the Church which Christ plainly meant to be a visible one (the parable of the net of good and bad fishes, of the tares and wheat, which were to grow together till the harvest, are proofs of this), our plain duty is, with an humble spirit, to endeavour to reform the existing evil on a principle of union, and not of separation. The unexampled mercy to our English Church has been, that she, a branch of the Church Catholic, did so reform herself, neither did she ever separate herself from the rest of the Church Catholic. She rejected the usurpations of Papal dominion ; and the Pope, therefore, refused to communicate with her, and influenced those under his sway in doing so ; but our clergy have still been received, and have actually officiated, in the Eastern branches of the Church Catholic. You cannot point to any Church in England from which we separated ; for down to the tenth of Elizabeth all Churchmen frequented the Reformed worship. It

was one whole body, as it had ever been ; but about
that time the Pope sent, not Englishmen, but
foreign priests and foreign bishops who did not
even dare (and do not to this day) to take the title
of English Sees (for they were full), but who
preached and taught schismatically the doctrines
of the synod of Trent, and founded not a Church,
but the Papal schism in our country. Then came
the Puritans, who broke off, like Rouge, in pretence
of the impurities of the English Church—and see
the consequence ; they became Presbyterians, the
Presbyterians split into Independents, then into
Arian and Socinian congregations, whilst, the principle of union being lost sight of, up sprung
innumerable sects of Anabaptists, Quakers, Moravians, Brownists, &c.

As Mrs. —— feels, all these rely on something
negative. They are small fragments, becoming
daily smaller and smaller, for want of any principle
of cohesion ; while amidst all her trials the Church
of England holds to Catholic truth, and is largely
spread over America and our colonies, and seems to
be gathering new strength ; for the blessing of God
on His Apostles, ' Lo, I am with you till the end of
the world,' is with her as a part of the Divine in-
corporation. They then represent the Church of all
ages ; our creeds are those of the Church Catholic ;
our prayers are those which have been offered for
at least fifteen hundred years, the greater part of

them by the Church Catholic; and also all our
Communion service, whereby we become, as the
Apostle strongly expresses it, of 'His flesh and of
His bones,' is an identical service with that of the
Eastern Churches from the earliest ages. I never
can join in it without feeling that our Church
militant is one with that which is triumphant, with
those innumerable saints who have offered the
same praise, joined in the same prayers, had the
same faith, the same hope, the same means of grace ;
in short, have had ' one Lord, one faith, one baptism,
one God and Father of all.'

I do not see so much to fear as many do in this
step of Newman and others. I deeply lament it
for their sakes, not for the Church, which can never
depend on individuals, but rests on Christ's promises
to the whole body. There are strong rumours of
the Pope's intention to give way in some points ;
the marriage of the clergy and restoration of the
cup to laity are spoken of. I think that earnest
men like Newman and others may facilitate this,
though nothing can justify their leaving their own
Church ; but I should be most happy, and rejoice
to see the Roman branch of the Church Catholic
(for a branch, though foul and sadly blighted, she is)
purifying itself, or rather imploring the Heavenly
Husbandman to purge her, that she may bring forth
much fruit. This would be life from the dead ; but
Rouge's movement is the galvanising of a dead

body. I think one leading mistake in all persons who run into schism is the forgetting the parable of the good and bad fishes, the corn and the tares, which are to be in the ' Kingdom of God '—for that is the subject of comparison—till the day of judgment. To find, therefore, bad men and bad practices in a Church is no sign of its not being the true Church, but exactly the reverse ; for it would not answer the prophetic description of the Kingdom of God were it otherwise constituted. The Holy Tunic of Trèves and all its mummery was a very bad practice, but no matter of principle of the Roman Church as such. I hope yet to see some Pope or zealous Romanist arise to wash away by lawful authority within their Church the cobwebs that so much obscure the real beauty of it; for, after all, it is a wonderful thing, that branch of the Church Catholic which has had its successors at Rome from the time of the Apostles. In the meantime we should be most grateful that we have, by lawful authority of the Church itself, removed these impurities. It has never been doubted that each national branch of the Church Catholic has full power over everything but articles of faith ; and not one article of faith has our Church altered, as determined by the General Councils before the separation of the Eastern and Western Churches from communion with each other, since which time no General Council has been or could be held.

As regards your excellent friend, I trust it may please God under her circumstances to turn her thoughts more to her own personal state than the outward distinctions around her. She took a right course in following the views of her parents, who are our lawful instructors till we are of age to judge for ourselves. Such is the evident order of God's providence. She was placed in difficulty, no doubt, by this system ; not only cold in its negative views, but so singularly irreconcilable with Scripture that when Priestley was pressed with the numerous assertions of Christ's Divinity in St. John's Gospel, he said 'he would rather believe the old Apostle was dozing than that he meant so and so ;' but our blessed Lord, who is all compassion, well knows and estimates her difficulties ; and if she, with the simplicity of a little child, will grasp firmly the great leading truths of His death for us, showing His unbounded love, and His resurrection, showing His equally unbounded power, and will pray earnestly for His assistance by the Holy Spirit to enable her to do this, she will, I am sure, experience more solid comfort than she can ever do by inquiring after systems of doctrine. ' He who doeth my Father's will shall know of the doctrine ' is always to my mind a strong discouragement of speculative, and encouragement to practical, Christianity. Now, part of that will was ' that all men should honour the Son even as they honour

the Father.' Only let her try to do this, and she will
find it a better mode of clearing difficulties than
reading any author—nay, even than reading the
Book itself. It is wonderful what peace my uncle
found in simply expressing his love and trust in
Christ as redeeming him on the Cross, and rising
again, as evidence of His power.

Alas! I am most unfit to teach any or to pray
for any; but your friend will ever be in my thoughts
and prayers; and may we all, my dearest sister, be
gathered together within His fold Who, knowing us
sinners as we are, can yet love us with a love passing all understanding! I feel deeply all you say
about society, and my own fearful danger and
weakness is constantly present to me; but it is a
plain duty to associate with those of our own
station in life, and we have a right, therefore, to
expect His blessing and protection whilst exposed
to the danger.

To Mrs. C. Stephens.

ATTITUDE OF THE CHURCH TOWARDS 'THOSE THAT ARE
WITHOUT.'

Lincoln's Inn: January 29, 1846.

. . . I wish to say one word (which I have
not had time to do before) on Mrs. ——'s letter,
which I thought very interesting. It is clear, I
hope, that she is earnest; and, if so, she must be

directed by God's Spirit, and, praying fervently, I have no doubt she will be guided to the truth, enabling her to cast herself on the Saviour only, which is the fundamental point. But I hope she quite understood my letter as *judging* nobody. It is not the province even of Church authority, much less of individuals, to judge those who are out of the Church. The Church only decides who do, and who do not, belong to her own body. She believes that those who are in her body possess great privileges, which she does not believe to be distinctly promised to any out of her body ; but she presumes not for a moment to say what the Almighty will decide with reference to those who are in that position. 'Who art thou that judgest another man's servant ? ' should be always present to the mind of every member of the Church. . . . When I see others not enjoying my advantages, I deeply regret it, for their sakes, and often, as I do in your friend's case, think with shame, how much better use they would make of them than I have done. Her notion that you cannot stop short at our Church, but must go to Rome, is a common one with those who, like herself, are ignorant of the subject from want of early instruction in it, practically as well as theoretically.

To the Rev. W. F. Hook.

OBLIGATIONS TO BISHOP BERKELEY'S PHILOSOPHY.

Matson: April 4, 1846.

. . . I read Bishop Berkeley, of course, in the April number of the ' Ecclesiastical Biography.'[1] I feel how much I owe to that truly wise man, or rather should say, do not feel half of what I really owe to him. Cambridge was a dangerous place for a young, inquiring mind, and the philosophy ' falsely so called' would have been singularly dangerous to me had I not from a boy been imbued with Berkeley's spiritual views. It is often supposed that his notions are pure theory: to me they were singularly practical; and I cannot say how fixedly, in its worst state of sinfulness, my mind clung to the reality and eternity of spiritual things as being the ' ὄντως ὄντα ; ' the only realities. The miracles also which in youth (not childhood, which is all believing) are a severe test of faith, were always made so plain and easy to me on Berkeley's views, who resolves all phenomena into the direct will of God, that I was saved from the influence of works like Hume's. I have much to answer for in not having been saved from other sins, with all the helps I have received, but shall ever feel deeply grateful to Berkeley for the assist-

---

[1] *Dictionary of Ecclesiastical Biography,* edited by Dr. Hook. It originally came out in numbers. My uncle wrote the article on Bishop Berkeley or it.

ance he has afforded me. Such men are like the
pious Eastern sovereigns who dig wells and build
cisterns for the wayfaring traveller.

To the same.

DR. HOOK'S PAMPHLET ON NATIONAL EDUCATION.

12 Great George Street: July 21, 1846.

. . . You may suppose I have been thinking
much of the pamphlet.[1] It is, I hear, in the third
edition. The 'Morning Chronicle' of course
puffed it largely. The 'Athenæum' of last Saturday has an article and copious extracts. The
'John Bull,' I am told (by Joshua Watson), is very
fierce against you. I hope the pamphlet will do
good with the Whigs by its tone ; but I still remain
sceptical, as do many who do not abuse it, as to
the possibility of finding a religious master who
will consent to play the part you assign him in a
Government school. Cotton, who spoke very fairly
of it, said he could not conceive how history could
be taught on your plan ; as, for instance, what
answer would the master give to a boy who, in a
mixed school of papists and others, should ask
whether it was right to burn Cranmer? But a
much more serious difficulty, to my mind, is the
tone of the school generally.

[1] Dr. Hook's 'Letter to the Bishop of St. Davids, How to render
more efficient the education of the people. See *Life*, p. 403 seq.,
small edition, and vol. i. pp. 205–211.

You will rejoice in last night's division as to the Welsh bishoprics, and still more at the tone of Lords Lansdowne and Grey, as compared with Lord Stanley.

To the same.

CASUISTRY.—AN EX-GENERAL OF THE FRANCISCAN ORDER.

Bealings: January 4, 1847.

. . . It is difficult to determine whether —— be honest or not. If he be once entangled in the Italian sophistry, he will not himself know. I have just been reading a very curious book lent me by an Italian—an account by the ex-General of the Franciscans (P. Capestieri) ; of his trial by the Inquisition at Rome, by whom he was condemned for fraudulently assisting an abbess in pretensions to sanctity. I think it would be a very useful thing to have extracts translated in some review, as his narrative shows much of the horrible perversion of truth common amongst Romanists.

Amongst other things, the ex-General has a lie pointed out in the examination of the alleged saint, and is asked how he can explain that consistently with her sanctity. His answer (which he evidently thinks triumphant) is, that they have not shown him the whole examination, to enable him to judge of her intention in telling the lie ; perhaps it was only an equivocation, &c., &c. In another passage an intimate friend of his, a cardinal, one of the Inquisitors, had denied receiving a letter from him, on which he says : ' Pardon me, your Eminence, your golden sincerity has been some- what clouded by the duties of your office. Your Eminence does not lie any more than a confessor who denies all knowledge of what he has learned by confession only.' And then he proceeds to prove that the letter was put into his Eminence's hands and repeatedly referred to by him. It is altogether a very curious book, and but few copies are extant. . . .

Whilst reading your lecture on the ' Three Reformations,' I found the same view of the Tri- dentine Reformations in Ranke's ' History of the Reformation '—a most interesting work. He says (vol. i. p. 268), after speaking of the malpractices at the time of Luther's rise : ' We must not con- found the tendencies of the period now before us with those evinced in the doctrines and practices established at the Council of Trent. At that time even the party which adhered to Catholicism had felt the influence of the epoch of the Reformation, and had begun to reform itself; the current was already arrested.' Then in a note he remarks : ' I hold it to be the fundamental error of Möhler's " Symbolik " that he considers the dogma of the Council of Trent as the doctrine from which the

Protestants seceded, whilst it is much nearer the truth to say that itself produced Protestantism by a reaction.' I have not the original, but Mrs. Austin's translation—which makes the last words awkward. I think he means that the dogma of the Council of Trent was itself a protest, to a certain extent, against the existing corruptions.

I think we now want a concise book, to be called ' Rome, her Corruptions in Doctrine, Morals, and Practice,' or some such title. In the first would be put the objectionable parts of the creeds of Pope Pius, the offensive litany to the Virgin, and the like ; the extravagant views as to merits and indulgences, and so on ; in the second, many extracts might be made from Jesuit works approved of at Rome, as is done by Pascal in his ' Provincial Letters ; ' and in the third, the approbation of the Massacre of Saint Bartholomew, the Marian perse-cution, the connexion of Jesuits with the Gun-powder Plot, the deification of very questionable saints, and the like.

To the same.

CECIL'S ' REMAINS.'—THE CANON OF HOLY SCRIPTURE.

Brighton : April 10, 1847.

. . . On my way hither I read your ' Eccle-siastical Biography.' I am very glad to find you do justice to Cecil. I think I told you of my having found his ' Life and Remains ' in my rooms at Cambridge, among my books. I never knew how it came there, and it did me infinite good at a time when I sadly needed it. I have a great love and reverence for him.

I was thinking, the other day, that it is a very special Providence that amidst all the errors and schisms of Protestantism, one most important Catholic tradition has been held (except by Unitarians) in the canon of Scripture. It seems the only truth held in common, and the addition of the Apocrypha was a sadly schismatical act of the Tridentine Synod.

END OF THE FIRST VOLUME.

S.

LONDON : PRINTED BY
SPOTTISWOODE AND CO., NEW-STREET SQUARE
AND PARLIAMENT STREET